HOSTILE TAKEOVER
BLACKWOOD BILLIONS BOOK ONE

CHRISTINA C JONES

ONE
NALANI

SOMETHING WAS... *off*.

I felt it permeating the air as soon as I breezed through the doors of the office suite that kept *Nectar* running smoothly.

Sweet potato latte in one hand, a green smoothie in the other. My cell phone and laptop were both tucked securely in the bag anchored on my shoulder, but the tense vibe I walked into had me wishing I had a hand free to answer my steadily buzzing phone.

Maybe it *couldn't* wait until I was at my desk like I thought.

Unwilling to risk one of my drinks—*or* the thick white cashmere sweater dress I'd chosen for today's wardrobe—I put as much speed in my stride as I could in heeled boots, making it to my personal office just as the phone rang again. Once my hands were free, I pulled the device from my bag, trying to catch the call before it ended as *missed*.

Daddy flashed across the screen, causing my breath to catch in my throat.

Him ringing my line at barely eight in the morning, when he usually wasn't even in the office yet until ten, was a major clue.

Something was wrong.

"Hey, Daddy," I answered brightly, some part of me hoping my cheery tone would bleed into whatever unappealing news he was about to deliver.

"Hey Nala," he replied with a somber undercurrent that made me hold my breath for whatever was coming next. "You on your way to the office yet?"

"I just walked in," I answered, eyeing the drinks on my desk, knowing one of them was about to go to waste. "Why, what's going on?"

"We need you in the big office."

The big office.

Meaning, *his* office.

"Why?"

"Does it matter?" he countered, and I pushed out a sigh.

No, it didn't.

"I'll be there in just a moment," I said, not bothering to formally end the call since *the big office* was just down the hall from mine. Glancing between my options on the desk, common sense told me to pick the coffee.

I had a feeling I was about to need it.

―――

NECTAR HAD what some would call *limited* office space, but it was really all we needed. The store, or market as I liked to call it, took up most of the room. Our footprint was only five thousand square feet, but we'd multiplied that by expanding upward, with four open floors of organic grocery space, and one floor, the top floor, of *"Personnel"*. Just over half of the floor was dedicated to employee spaces—a well-appointed breakroom, restrooms, showers, and a small daycare I liked to peek in the windows of whenever I passed.

The offices were tucked off to the back, with a separate, keycard-access only entrance. In the hall that led to the different offices, one side of the floor was glassed, giving a perfect view of the open spaces below.

As a kid, it terrified me, but I loved it now, so much that it was a bit of a source of calm as I navigated my way down to *the big office,* emotional support coffee in hand. I'd already burned my tongue downing half of it, but I refused to let it grow tepid on my desk like the smoothie would, while I listened to why father *needed* me in the office.

There was no way it was *good*.

That suspicion was confirmed as soon as I walked in. Our accountant, or rather, CFO, was seated at the large conference table that took up a good part of the office, looking grim as usual. He wasn't my favorite person in the world; I hated being told no, and he employed the word way too often when I was presenting ideas that would help *Nectar's* growth. His favorite thing to say was *we can't afford that*, but I suspected that had more to do with him and my father being old school. I got enough of what I wanted to keep me cool.

For now.

"Good morning, Alan," I greeted him, before looking at the head of the table for my father. "Let me guess, the market is down again?"

We weren't publicly traded and never would be as long as I had anything to do with it. All growth wasn't good, but like any business of our size, we had investments that made us vulnerable to the ebb and flow of the stock market.

Much more vulnerable than I liked, but the store's finances weren't my lane.

The look my father exchanged with Alan said a *lot* while saying nothing, which was exactly what I planned to do as well. More than once, I'd warned about the dangers of leveraging too much, but it was always brushed off like I knew nothing, despite my flourishing personal portfolio.

Again—old school patriarchal bullshit.

"The difficulties of the market aren't the problem right now. The rent is," an unfamiliar voice spoke. I still hadn't sat down, and quickly realized the high backs of the rotary chairs surrounding the table had obscured someone else in this meeting. I watched, frowning, as a chair near my father turned, revealing a handsome face that was only vaguely familiar, but *supremely* annoying, because — "Who the fuck are you?" I asked, the question spilling out before I could catch myself to deliver it in a more... personable manner.

The stranger's full lips spread into a smirk as my father admonished my language choices.

"Sorry," I said to my father, *not* the man who looked a bit too self-satisfied for my liking. "Who is this and why is he here?"

"I'm your landlord, nice to meet you," he said as he unfolded a much taller, sturdier body than expected from the chair and extended a hand in my direction. "Orion Sterling, CEO of Wholesome Foods, which... you have a background in corporate retail, right? So... I'm sure you're familiar with Stellar Foods, the parent company."

Who wasn't?

Stellar Foods was an enormous company, with stores spread all around the country. They had more brands than I could count on one hand, at varying price points—big box stores, wholesale warehouses, and maybe most notably, organic supermarkets.

Which made them a direct competitor.

I looked at his hand, but made no attempt to return his niceties. "Uhh… good for you, but um… my family has owned this building and the land it's on since before Blackwood was Blackwood, so… landlord?" I looked at my father. "What is he talking about?"

"I'm talking about—"

"*Please* shut up!" I said, holding up my hand. I had to look up to properly glare at him, but I wasn't backing down. He seemed shocked by my audacity, his head rearing back a little in response. "I don't mean to be rude, but I'm talking to my father, *not you*."

"Nala, baby girl, please treat our guest with some respect," my father warned, making it *my* turn for disbelief at *his* audacity. He was the very reason I'd been declared "slick at the mouth" as a preteen, buoyed by his encouragement to always speak up for myself, to not be afraid of getting loud.

Now he was giving off this energy that was damn near *deferential* to some overgrown motherfucker who had to be my age or not much older. Certainly not someone we owed meekness to.

"Nala," Orion said in a deep rumble as he took a step closer to loom over me. "What a nice nickname. I'll have to keep it mind."

"The hell you will," I countered, eyebrows drawn together, unmoved by my father's plea for manners. "Again," I said to my father, completely turning my back to the man to make sure he understood *no* respect was coming from me. "What is he talking about?"

He opened his mouth to speak, but it was like the words

escaped him, and speechless was *not* this man's default by any stretch of reality.

"Your mother was sick," Alan spoke up, since my father couldn't seem to bring himself to. "The family's personal accounts were drained, and the store was failing. *Fast.* We needed cash. We needed a Hail Mary, so…"

"No." I held up a hand and shook my head. "No. Absolutely not," I declared, looking back and forth between him and my father, knowing *damn well* neither of them was about to confirm my worst first thoughts about what those words could mean. "You wouldn't do that… *please* tell me you didn't—"

"There was no other choice, everything else was drained," my father finally spoke, his shoulders drooped distinctly low.

"*Not* everything!" I hissed. "You never asked me, and I know you haven't asked Soren, because he would've talked to me. We both have money—"

"Not *that* kind of money," he countered, sounding—and *looking*—more defeated than I'd ever seen since the gravity of my mother's illness really hit us.

William Stark didn't *lose*, except back then, he had. We all had.

"How much?" I asked, nostrils flared, my chest feeling hollow as I spoke. "What number was so big we couldn't get out of it?"

"Ten million dollars," Alan answered. "Between the medical bills and trying to save—"

"*Ten*?!" I shrieked. "*Ten?!* That's it?! We could've come up with ten! We could've asked the family, could've borrowed from friends, emptied the trust funds, and—"

"I didn't want to drain my damn *kids*!" my father insisted, slamming a fist on the table. "What kind of man would that have made me?"

"Better than one who sold off my mama's legacy—my *birthright*—to our goddamn *competitor* to what? Lease back from them?! Is that what's been going on?!" I replied through gritted teeth. "Is this why you didn't want me in the books?! Or better question, *did she know you did this*?!"

Whatever anger my tone may have incited was pushed to the back burner to make way for some other regrettable emotion on his face. "Of course not. I… couldn't bring myself to tell her and she… never recovered enough to ask."

"*Of course not,*" I repeated, shaking my head as I turned to Orion, mouth open, ready to lash into *him* too.

Before I could speak though, my father had a few more words. "And I didn't sell it to *them*."

My eyes narrowed at Orion, who was standing entirely too close to me, looking incredibly amused. "Then how did you get it?"

"It was a pretty neat trick." He chuckled. "He just didn't *know* it was us. I bought it through a shell company, and for a *steal* at that, with the change in my cupholder."

Immediately, I blinked back tears of confusion, hurt, and most of all, *rage*.

Of course ten million dollars was seat-cushion findings to him. *Stellar Foods* was a multi-billion dollar company, who swallowed little places like ours wherever they went.

That was why he'd looked familiar.

As Chief Operating Officer of Nectar, I didn't deal with those details—which I now understood exactly why—but I remembered the hullaballoo a few years ago around a buyout offer from *Stellar*.

Of course, the offer had been rejected.

Nectar was a community-focused business, had always been that way. My mother's people's people had owned the land we stood on, fighting to keep it from becoming a casualty of the race riots and other hostile takeovers since before this building stood.

It would *always* be in the family.

Or at least… it would've been.

It was *supposed to be.*

I swallowed the desire to scratch the man's eyes out, knowing an emotional display wouldn't get me very far.

"So… what is this?" I asked, lacing my fingers together in front of me and fixing him with a glare. "You here to try bankrupt us? What's the offer? What is it going to cost to buy this land back so you don't… what, kick us out, bulldoze the building?"

"Oh, it's not for sale. A space like this, in *Blackwood*? One of a kind." He grinned, stepping close enough that the linen and vetiver of his cologne tickled my nose. "As I said in my opening volley… the *rent* is the problem here, not the markets."

"Why would the rent be a problem?" I asked. "I'm sure the lease—"

"Expired," he interrupted. "The lease you had… *expired.* So… there's a new lease you'll need to review and agree to… or immediately vacate the premises."

I crossed my arms. "How much?"

Orion's eyes stayed on my cleavage for a moment before they lifted to meet mine, pure evil glinting in them before he delivered a number that damn near made my eyes bug out of my head.

"You're insane," I snapped. "That's damn near a *quarter* of revenue! You can't do that."

"I do whatever I want, Nala." He grinned. "So… do we have a deal, or are you leaving? I hope you're leaving. The *Wholesome Foods* logo is going to look so good over that big open front entryway."

"We're not going *anywhere*," I sneered, shaking my head as I turned to Alan and my father. "Where is our legal team? There has to be some way out of this… *bullshit*."

"Oh, everything about this is ironclad," Orion spoke up. "But, in case you want to try it… *Stellar Foods*' legal team *loves* litigation, and we will *bury you* under years of it."

Fuck.

He was probably right.

"Whatever," I shrugged. "We're still not going anywhere. Even if we have to just—"

"Just *what,* Nala?" he asked, stepping even closer. "Just… pay it?" That evil ass grin spread even wider as he looked to my father. "William… Alan… aren't you going to tell her?"

My head whipped around to them. "Tell me what?"

Instead of answering, the two men looked at each other, then began careful inspections of the damn ground.

"I'll tell you, Nala," Orion spoke in a singsong that made it much harder to keep my hands to myself. "You can't afford it. *Nectar* hasn't operated in the black in… *years*."

"*What*?!" The word came out in a whisper that defied the intensity of what I felt. "How is that possible? We get more new customers every day, we've been having record sales numbers. We have investments, we should have *savings*—"

"Not with your Daddy's gambling problem."

My hand was out before I could stop myself.

The entire room went quiet and still, reacting to the fact that I'd just smacked Orion Sterling dead across his fucking mouth.

He put a hand to his lip, checking for blood before he gave me a brief nod. "That's your *one* time." Looking past me, he pinned a glare at my father. "It's time to wrap this up."

"What is that supposed to mean?" I asked.

"It means *pack your shit*. The old lease has a ninety-day grace period. Figure it the fuck out."

Immediately, my mind started racing.

I didn't *want* to go that route, but I could pay a few months of rent on the store until we figured things out. But beyond that… what was going to happen?

"What about our charities that run through this store? Our employees, their kids? It's fucking… it's *Christmas* time, you —*mmmm*," I grunted, buttoning my lips to keep myself from saying something that might cross a line while still trying to appeal to *some* humanity in this man. "Why are you doing this? You have a *billion* dollars and more market share than we could ever dream up. Why *us*? Why now?"

"Oh, don't get emotional on me, Nala, I was just starting to respect you," he said, taking a step back before he tossed his hands up. "It's not… personal. It's business. This space is already prepared for grocery sales, one of a kind in an area like this. Do you know how hard it is to get this much commercial space in the city? Nearly impossible, unless it's being practically given away in under-the-table deals," he added, with a nasty smirk at my father. "If we got our hands on any other space, we'd have to do major renovations, wait for permits, this and that. It would take years and I'm not a patient man. Like I said, this store is already here, and it was ripe for picking. You even already have such a *loyal* customer base, community support—"

"These people will *never* support you," I quipped. "They've loved this family, this store, for *decades*. And when they hear the *underhanded* way you pushed us out, and I promise, I will make it my life's work to make sure *everyone* knows, they will go literally anywhere else to avoid shopping at your knock-off Whole Foods."

Instead of that putting even a tendril of fear in him like I'd hoped... he smiled.

"You're right," he said, coming back into my personal space to tower over me again. "Which is why... I have another possibility for you."

TWO
NALANI

THERE WAS no possibility I was going to like the *possibility*.

I knew that as soon as the words crossed his lips.

And yet, with the most obvious path being painfully clear, there was nothing I could do but cross my arms and glare, waiting for him to keep spewing bullshit.

"You might want to take a seat," Orion suggested, but I didn't move.

I stayed right where I was, *on my feet*.

I wasn't about to have him towering over me any more than he already was.

A little smirk spread over his lips. He was amused by my obstinance, but it wasn't for his benefit, or some damn show. He wouldn't get my legacy without dragging me, clawing and screaming and biting, *every* step of the way.

"Is this better?" he asked, taking his seat first. Once he'd given up his height-implied dominance, there was no reason for me to remain standing either. Unless, of course, he was about to say something that necessitated a quick escape, which I somehow doubted.

Reluctantly, I sank into a seat several chairs away, waiting to hear about this *possibility*.

"Nala… you and I have a lot in common," he started, prompting an immediate raised eyebrow of skepticism from me. "There's the obvious of the shared industry, of course, but outside of that, we're both well-educated, well-groomed, attractive, and enmeshed in… a certain social stratum," he said.

"We don't run in the same circles," I commented, shaking my head. "I'm quite sure your family bank accounts have several zeroes mine will never see."

"That's one of the pros of this situation, of my proposal," he clarified.

"Which is what?" I sat forward in my chair. "Let's cut through the bullshit, because I don't give a fuck about whatever little spiel you're building up. What is the other option besides you destroying my family's business?"

Orion met my gaze, no hesitation, unwavering. "You become my wife and I make sure Nectar *never* dies."

The silence was deafening.

For a long moment, I couldn't do anything but stare at Orion, lips parted, *stunned* by the suggestion that had just left his mouth. Then, my head whipped to my father and Alan, neither of whom had reacted as if they'd heard the same outlandish idea I had.

In fact… it kinda looked like they were… *thinking about it.*

That brought me out of my speechless state *real fast.*

"Have you lost your goddamn mind?!" I asked Orion. "Have you *all* lost your minds?" That time, the question was for everybody. "This is not... it's not... I'm not a fucking consolation prize or some damn trading card to pass around!"

"Oh, but you are," Orion argued. "A prize, that is. And no, not the participation trophy either."

My face wrinkled into a frown. "What the hell are you talking about?"

"I'm talking about the fact that you are, like I said, educated, well-raised, incredibly attractive, reasonably successful, *and* Black," he answered, in a tone that clearly indicated he was complimenting me, thought it somehow didn't feel like it. "You were on the cover of Sugar & Spice last year, with word going around that you were *the* most sought after woman in the city. Did you think it was a lie?"

I raised an eyebrow. "I would think someone in your tax bracket would do their choosing from women of a similar… pedigree. Or perhaps among the aspiring kept women of the world?"

"No, that's exactly what I *don't* want," Orion argued. "A bit too typical. I'd prefer a woman who *wasn't* groomed into this shit. One who is thoroughly uninspired by my perceived wealth."

"Perceived?"

He grinned. "I think you understand very well what I'm saying."

"My comprehension isn't the problem here," I snapped. "If you understand that I'm at no loss for eligible potential partners and your wealth doesn't move me… why the *fuck* would I marry you?"

He sat forward. "Because I've got you by the balls, Nala. Remember?"

Shit.

I'd been so caught off guard by his proposition that I *had* lost sight of where this started.

He did, indeed, have me by the proverbial balls, and I knew better than to think he was bluffing about it. He could bury *Nectar* today and there wouldn't be shit I could do about it, not when the account balances I'd been so proud of before now were chump change to him.

"What do you get out of this?" I asked as soon as it occurred to me to wonder. "You have the advantage already, why is this *insane* suggestion of marriage even an option?"

He shrugged. "What can I say? I like a *deal*," he preened. "And this is the best thing I've lucked up in the last five years. It satisfies two things. I need to settle down and I need a foothold in the heart of Blackwood. And I want *both… right now*."

"What if *I'm* not for sale?"

"Everything is for sale," he countered, pushing away from the table to stand up. "I can see you need a chance to think it over, so—"

"I don't need to think about *shit*, I'm not some virgin on auction to pay my family debts," I snapped, standing too. "Everything *else* might be available to you because you're a Sterling, but I personally could not care less. *Fuck you*."

Orion shrugged and turned for the door. "Fine by me, I'll choose someone else." He stopped, snapping his fingers as he turned to speak as if something had just occurred to him. "And I can give her *Nectar* as a wedding gift or maybe a push gift," he mused, then shrugged. "Either way, she'll love it, I'm sure."

"*Wait!*" I called out, against my better judgement when he was halfway through the door.

He turned again, waiting, but I couldn't seem to form any words.

"Think it over." He smirked. "I'll be in touch for your answer tomorrow."

And then he was gone.

As if he hadn't just dropped a pipe bomb on my life.

"Okay," my father spoke, after being firmly on mute for that whole… *thing*. "There's a few ways—"

"What the fuck is wrong with you?" I interrupted, turning to glare between him and Alan.

"Nalani Stark, watch your damn—"

"I won't watch *shit*!" I screeched, desperately wishing there was something in here for me to flip over. "Our family land, this business, this *building*, it's been…. This was *ours* and you *sold it*! For what, exactly? Please explain this to me."

"I told you; your mother was sick—"

"So there were medical bills, *so fucking what*?!" I cried. "Get a payment plan, let them default, sell the cars, sell the houses, your goddamn boat, or, here's a thought, *ask for help!*"

"Our reputation would have been ruined!"

"*And what do you call this*?!" I asked, waving my arms around at… nothing, I guess, to illustrate what we *currently* had. "Do you think *this* is going to be good for the family name, flushing the legacy down the toilet? Huh? Does our reputation feel intact *right now*?!"

"Let's all just calm down," Alan attempted, and I was quick to turn my glare on him alone.

"I most certainly *will not*. You helped him flush my mother's heritage down a toilet to protect his fucking pride and I'm supposed to *calm down*?"

"All isn't lost!" my father said, stepping around the table.

"You heard the man. He's offering an option that could save this family, assuming you might be—"

"If I do anything, it will be to preserve the *Joyce* family claim," I told him, unmoved by the obvious blow in my words. "And will make sure neither of you *ever* get your hands on it again."

"Now you hold on, young lady. All he has is the land and the building, this *company* —"

"Is fort-nine percent yours – the other fifty-one percent is me and my brother, and if you think for a *moment* that Soren won't be on my side when he finds this out, you are incredibly mistaken as to where his loyalty lies."

His lips parted in surprise. "So you'd turn against your own father? Is that what I'm hearing?"

"What you're hearing is that you have shit your last pair of britches where *Nectar* is concerned," I snapped. "Between me and Soren having the controlling interest, and what I am *sure* will be a very unhappy board, you can consider yourself relieved of duty," I told him, grabbing my wasted coffee and heading for the door.

"Little girl, you *cannot* do this!"

"Watch me."

Just before I stepped out the door, he tossed one last jab in my direction. "You're going to need my help when Orion Sterling kicks your ass out of this building!"

I turned to smirk. "I fail to see how that's your concern anymore."

―――

"He's a BILLIONAIRE, Nala. Yes, you're going to have to fuck him."

I pushed out a sigh, balancing my overfilled wine glass as I dropped to a seat on the couch in Demetria's office. She wasn't the one who'd offered that insight though. That was her twin sister, Desiree, consulting via video call from her Vegas office.

My *first* stop after leaving the *Nectar* offices in a hot mess of rage was to the one person I knew for *sure* would have my best interests at heart.

My lawyer.

I paid her entirely too well not to.

Once I'd bullied my way past her receptionist into an impromptu emergency meeting to explain the crisis at hand, she'd immediately called her sister.

This was an all-hands situation.

"This is… *insane*," I mused, taking a deep gulp from the wine.

It was entirely too early, but when Demetria offered, I didn't have the fortitude to turn it down.

Across from me, she shrugged. "It's actually… not that extraordinary. When you have that kind of money, things move a little different."

"A *lot* different," Des chimed in from the laptop on the coffee table between us. "And honestly… Orion Sterling wouldn't be the worst thing that could happen to you."

"Neither would a refrigerator landing on my big toe, but I don't want *that* shit either."

Demetria laughed. "I understand where you're coming from, Nala, but Des is right. He's got *real* money, he's fine as shit, and I've never heard any um… *stories* about him. If you know what I mean."

"I don't," I insisted. "And with all this shit, I don't have the brain power for inference. Just tell it to me straight."

"She means he's not an abuser or a freak, in the bad way," Des clarified. "People always act shocked when these rich men get their business put on blast in the media, but the *truth* is that... certain people know these... open secrets. Orion doesn't have anything like that. He's probably just your run-of-the-mill womanizer, which... again, at that tax bracket...?"

"Got it. So I won't get my ass kicked or get fucked with a bat, but I should expect cheating? Where do I sign?" I grumbled, rolling my eyes.

"You don't have to accept anything," Demetria said. "You can write it into your end of the contract that if he cheats, the whole thing is null and void, and you get... whatever he agrees to. Or, maybe you don't care what he does, as long as it's kept on the low. Side bitch runs to the blogs? Deal is off. If that's what you want. *Everything* can be negotiated."

"But if you tell him he can't fuck anybody else, you *definitely* have to fuck him." Des giggled. "You can't have it both ways. You can even pick a frequency, once a week, once a month, only on federal holidays—"

"Fine. I'll fuck him once a year, on his birthday. With somebody else's pussy."

"I do *not* think it works like that." Demetria laughed.

"*Ugh*," I groaned. "When can I get divorced?"

"That's probably going to depend on if and when he wants kids, and I can almost guarantee you, he's going to want kids," Des said and I sucked my teeth.

"Why is everything you say *awful?*" I asked her.

"Because I know very well how all this stuff works. That's why y'all called me, remember?"

I pushed out a deep sigh, dropping back against the couch cushions for another long sip. "I remember."

"Good. Now, I'm just telling you what I know from a lot

of experience dealing with men like Orion, from his kind of family. I'd bet good money that he's on some sort of timeline, and that's why he's doing this. He'll be forty in another two years. He's probably crossing off criteria for another level of his trust fund."

"Oooh," Demetria mused. "That's a great point. He probably needs a wife and an heir to get it. Those might even be prerequisites for a higher job role that he wants within *Stellar Foods*."

"This is the worst thing I've ever heard in my life. It's like a shitty romance novel," I whined.

"Truth is much stranger than fiction, my dear," Demetria said. "Now... come on, sit up, we've got to get serious about this if we're supposed to be giving him an answer by tomorrow."

I huffed. "I don't think I can *get* more serious."

"Let's try," Des said. "We want this to favor you as much as possible, unfairly, even, because he's going to pushback. So ask for more than you even want."

"All I *want* is my damn building back."

"So *ask* for it," Demetria countered. "Didn't you say he made some smart remark about *Nectar* being a great wedding gift? *Ask for it*," she insisted. "He may not give it to you outright, maybe just partial ownership, or it reverts to you after a certain number of years, something like that. But a closed mouth will not get fed. And if you've gotta eat shit... I'm assuming it's much better with some sweet extras on the side."

I shook my head, not *wanting* to accept anything she was saying, but knowing it was futile. Just to be sure though, I asked, "And there's *nothing* we can do to get around this?"

"Unfortunately not," Demetria confirmed. "It shouldn't be

an issue to get *Nectar*. If the board doesn't put you at the head, you've got enough capital to simply buy your father out. *If* it comes to that. The issue with the land and the building is a whole other thing, and everything is on the up and up with that. Now, I can talk to Clayton Reed, and get him on looking for a new building if—"

"No," I cut her off. "That's not… I don't want that."

"Which we understand, completely," Des spoke up. "But… you don't have a lot of options."

"I don't have *any* options," I countered, but Demetria shook her head.

"Don't think about it like that. Look, you can marry a billionaire and keep your mother's store, or you start fresh somewhere else. Honestly, I think you'll be perfectly fine either way."

"Of course you find a positive spin for it," I chuckled, then took the last hefty swallow of my wine. "But… I think we all know what the only *real* option is here."

Instead of speaking up, the sisters waited for me to do it, neither of them speaking until it was clear I was still hesitant to put the decision somewhere other than my mind.

"What's it gonna be, Nala?" Demetria asked, nudging my knee with her hand. "What's the verdict?"

I closed my eyes, pushing out a slow breath before I finally met her gaze. "I guess… I'm going to have to go dress shopping."

THREE
ORION

"So, I know the answer to this already, but I have to ask. Are you sure this is a good idea?"

I looked up from my computer to smirk at Shiloh at the doorway of my office. She was right, she *did* already know the answer.

I sat back in my chair, saying nothing, just waiting for her to expand on what she was thinking.

"You don't think it's presumptuous to set up your '*fiancée's*' accounts?" she asked, eyebrow raised.

"Is it presumptuous or confident?" I countered.

She rolled her eyes. "*Arrogant* is the word I'd use, if we're being completely frank."

"Which you can always be, so I'm not sure why you tried to come in with a soft touch anyway. Your ass is mean about everything else."

"I'm not *mean*," she argued, fully stepping into my office now. "It's called being straightforward."

"So keep that energy now, and make your point, Shi." I

shifted my gaze back to the figures clouding my screen. "Otherwise, I've got shit to do."

"Fine. I don't think it's wise to move as if Nalani Stark is *for sure* going to say yes to this… *arrangement* of yours," she explained. "You're treating this as if she has no options, when she *does*."

"She has multiple options, yes, but only one *smart* one," I argued. "She'd be stupid *not* to take my offer and you know what she *isn't?*"

"Stupid," Shiloh answered, and I nodded.

She absolutely was *not*.

As clear as it was that I hadn't been on her radar, she'd certainly been on mine and I was far from alone. At this tax bracket, yes, there was an abundance of available women who checked certain boxes and everybody had their own winning combinations among the crowd.

Fine was easy.

Smart and fine?

A little harder.

Wealthy, smart, and fine?

A gem.

Wealthy, smart, fine, and ambitious?

Quite a rare find.

Wealthy, smart, fine, ambitious, slick at the mouth, thighs bigger than my head and an ass to match?

A fucking *unicorn*.

"You don't think she'll turn you down purely out of spite?" Shiloh asked, breaking through my thoughts with a possibility I'd definitely considered, but chosen not to entertain, because —

"She will not let spite overrule preserving her mother's legacy." I shook my head.

Shiloh shrugged. "Maybe not. But she definitely might make you regret forcing her into a choice."

I grinned. "I'm absolutely hoping she tries. Why do you think I have you setting up accounts for her? Most likely, she'll try to shop her way onto my nerves."

"I was thinking more like... stab you in your sleep?" Shiloh said, then breezed out of my office, presumably back to her own to finish the task at hand.

She didn't give me a chance to argue against the idea that Nalani might get violent, which was honestly a consideration not to be taken lightly. I'd backed her into a corner before she even knew a predator had her scent. And unless I was sorely mistaken, she wasn't one to simply cower.

Even if she "surrendered" now, it would *only* be for the opportunity at a better position for when she flexed her claws.

The idea of which was a turn-on for me.

I loved a tussle.

Which was precisely why instead of being annoyed when Shiloh showed up at my door again an hour later to let me know I had an email from Demetria Byers, I smiled.

"So she put her lawyer on it," I mused, sitting forward.

"Like you said, smart woman," Shiloh replied. "She has a contract. A premarital agreement with expectations, not to be confused with a prenup, which she wants as well."

"I expected no less." I was already navigating to my email when I asked, "So what does it look like? What is she asking for?"

"What makes you think I read it?"

"Besides the fact that this email arrived thirty minutes ago and you're just now letting me know?"

"I could've been busy."

"If you were busy, you would've pinged me. Instead, you

came to the door. So it must be juicy. Come on, spit it out," I jeered as I double-clicked the summary attachment for myself.

"Scheduled sex," Shiloh answered, clearly amused by the idea of it. "She fucking hates you."

"It's better that way," I chuckled, skimming the document for myself, a high-level breakdown of the things Nalani wanted in the deal.

"Do you *really* believe that?"

"Believe what?" I asked, pulling my attention to where Shiloh was standing in front of my desk, arms crossed.

"That the sex will be better because she hates you?"

I smirked. "I do and I'm going to fuck her into hating me even more—" I looked back to the screen, "At least once every two weeks, but no more frequently than once a week, with consideration for her menstrual cycle."

"Are you saying your dick is wack?"

"The opposite, Shi, keep up." I chuckled. "She's gonna hate that she wants it."

Shiloh's face curled into a frown. "Ew. If you say so," she mused. "Just make sure you wrap it up. You see she says no babies for at least two years?"

"That's a nonstarter." I shook my head. "That will need to be the first ball to get rolling."

Her eyes went wide. "She'll never agree to that."

"She will if she wants me not to redline her request about ownership of the *Nectar* property. Which, she can hang up this hyphenated fantasy," I said. "Sterlings don't do that."

"She is *definitely* going to stab you."

"Wouldn't be me first rodeo with knife play." I shrugged. "When is Ms. Byers sending over the *actual* contracts, so my lawyers can dissect this shit?"

Shiloh grinned. "Oh. You didn't read the actual *message*,

did you? They're insisting on an in-person meeting to hammer out details. In their building, on their terms."

"*Oh.*" I chuckled. "Audacity in abundance. I like it," I said, already pushing back from my desk. "Clear the next two hours on my schedule," I told her, moving to the coat rack by my door to grab appropriate outerwear for the frigid Blackwood weather.

"Do I even need to ask why?" she asked, rolling her eyes.

I shook my head as I pulled open the door. "Nope. You already know." I stopped halfway through to grin. "Did I see a minimum carat requirement for the future Mrs. Sterling's engagement ring?"

She nodded. "That was the other thing I loved about that summary."

"Of course you enjoyed that." I laughed. "Find my future wife's ring by this afternoon, please."

"I will get right on it," she agreed. "Any stipulations?"

"Whatever the requirement was, double it."

Shiloh frowned. "Ri, that would be obnoxious."

"Yeah. That's the point."

―――

NECTAR WAS the kind of business—*especially* in the grocery industry—that sparked admiration and envy in anyone with enough savvy to know what they were looking at.

No thanks to William Stark.

Even before his fine-ass daughter caught my attention, Nectar had been a topic of conversation for Stellar Foods. They had the market placement we sorely wanted, but hadn't quite been able to master.

The community support I wasn't sure we ever could achieve. At least, not without a time machine.

It might be considered a bit "blasphemous" in the family for me to criticize the way my ancestors had built the business, but the internal attitude for a long time had been *growth over everything*. There hadn't *truly* been any type of focus on supporting and sowing into our community until probably my grandparents' generation, even though the business itself went back further. And it was my parents who really leaned into the "Black-owned" designation when I was a kid, in the nineties.

Nectar had been about it since the beginning, which made it easy to see *why* it was so well-loved and supported in the community. They could've leaned on that, doing the bare minimum like so many others, but walking into the building, the re-investment was clear. The historic architecture was intact, and impeccably maintained, with just the right amount of modernized touches—screens, sleek surfaces and neutral tones, current music piped throughout the building—to keep it relevant to millennial customers and younger, without scaring the older generations away.

It was something to be proud of.

Which was exactly what made it a perfect bargaining chip.

I took my time sauntering around the first floor, taking in the eclectic mix of pure retail and third-party vendors that made *Nectar* such an attractive destination. I nodded to myself as I passed a small Urban Grind café. They had a full-blown storefront that was always crowded barely a block away, and yet, the café was bustling with people as well, dropping in for a quick pick-me-up before they continued their shopping.

It was a *brilliant* use of space.

They would've been fine with all-*Nectar* everything, but

bringing in these small footprints from various small businesses in the surrounding areas only deepened their roots.

Besides whatever commissions or rental fees they were making.

I was practically itching for a look at their books, into the fine-grained details that weren't available to the public, for no other reason than satisfying my selfish curiosity.

An interest that would, unfortunately, have to wait.

"What the hell are you doing here?"

With a grin on my face, I turned to the sound of Nalani's voice to find her standing behind me, arms crossed.

Not even a *little* amused.

"A man can't visit his fiancée?"

"That paperwork has *not* been signed," she countered, shaking her head.

"*Yet.*"

Her eyes narrowed for a moment before she rolled them, pushing out a sigh. "Again, Orion, *what are you doing here?*"

"I thought we should talk," I told her, stepping in to close some of the distance between us. Before, the heels she wore had balanced our heights a bit more. Now, she had to tip her head back a bit to look up at me.

Which meant I got to stare down at her pretty chocolate ass.

"There is *nothing* for us to discuss before our lawyers have completed contracts," she insisted.

"I disagree, you want shit I'm *never* agreeing to."

Her neatly-arched brows furrowed. "Such as?"

"Two years before a baby, not happening."

She sucked her teeth. "If you think I'm letting you in me raw before then, you're delusional," she snapped and turned to walk away.

And at first... I let her.

Because in the slim-fitting pants she wore, *walking away* was quite a sight, and I damn sure wanted to see.

After a moment, though, I went after her.

"Not even if it means immediate transference of the land and building?" I called after her.

She stopped, arms still crossed, as she halfway turned to face me. "Immediate?"

"*Immediate*," I agreed. "To your married name, obviously. Nalani *Sterling*."

Sick, I know, but the immediate return of annoyance on her face—the tongue running over her teeth, eyes to the ceiling—made me a little giddy.

"I want it in writing," she gritted through her teeth. "And *recent* STD testing. Meaning, take your ass to the clinic *today*."

I smirked. "Clinic? Nalani, come on. The doctor comes to the crib for us, you should know that, baby."

"Absolutely *not*."

My smirk dropped. "Absolutely not *what*?" I asked.

"You calling me *baby*."

"Get used to it, *baby*," I told her, closing that distance again. This time planting a hand at the small of her back. Before she could snatch away, I'd grabbed her under the chin and leaned in to speak in her face. "Just because this marriage might be *convenient,* you need to understand something right now; it ain't *fake*. I'm gonna parade you in public, fuck you in private, and otherwise ignore you, just like most wealthy marriages."

"If you *really* believe that? That's the saddest thing I've ever heard," she declared, not backing away. "Is that why you're like this? Mommy and Daddy hated each other, and took it out on poor Ri-Ri?"

In an instant, my grip under her chin had shifted to her neck, pulling her even closer. "You don't know *shit* about my parents, or *me*," I warned, locking in on her gaze.

"You sure this is how you want to start this marriage? Domestic violence in a public place… *baby*?" she asked, her tone all but *daring* me not to let her go.

So I didn't.

I gripped her tighter, eyes not wavering as I told her. "Nothing violent about it… *baby*."

She didn't seem surprised when I pressed my lips to hers. She pressed back, giving me clear aggression.

I had painfully fewer qualms than she did, though.

It was *nothing* to me to push my tongue into her mouth and drop my free hand to her ass for an overflowing handful, all in the *public place* she was so worried about. She realized, quick as fuck, that challenging me on something like public decency was a mistake.

I had too much money to *care*.

This time, I let her off easy. When she gently pushed at me, trying to put an end to it without making a scene, I granted her that, ending the kiss with a quick peck on her lips before I stepped back, beyond amused at her obvious blushing.

She ran her tongue over her ruined lipstick and just stared at me, chest heaving, clearly too stunned to have anything to say.

"I'll see you at our meeting later?" I asked, and she quickly shook her head.

"No. Just the lawyers," she answered, looking away.

"Fine. I'll make sure our agreement from today is relayed."

"Okay." She nodded, still not looking at me.

I smirked, not even bothering to wipe her lipstick from my mouth as I walked away.

This was going to be *fun*.

FOUR
NALANI

Shit.

Frantically, I pushed the covers off my legs, in desperate need of cooling off. The feel of Orion's hands—lingering remnants of the dream I'd just woken up from, still erotically vivid in my mind—made me glance around my room, making *sure* I was as alone as I'd been when I retired for the night.

Once my eyes confirmed my solitude, I scrubbed both hands over my face, torn between laughing and crying.

Both felt appropriate, honestly.

This situation I'd found myself in was *so* ridiculous, *so* far from anything I could've imagined that it was… heartbreaking.

And fucking hilarious.

Only me, I mused as I climbed from the bed, with a disdainful glance at the empty carafe on the bedside table. I grabbed the robe that matched my nightgown, slipping it over my clammy skin as a bit of protection from the chill in the air before I started the short journey to my kitchen in search of water.

The things Orion had done to me before I pulled myself awake had me feeling a little... *parched.*

Glass in hand, I made my way to the big picture window in my living room area. I could see the roof of *Nectar* from there. It was one of the biggest reasons I'd chosen this building in the first place. I wasn't working in the family business then, climbing the corporate retail ladder had me by the throat. I was committed to reaching the highest possible level, and really... it had been right at my fingertips.

Then my father called and said he needed help.

How could I say no?

It was a demotion in title, and a major drop in pay, but my brother and I both had been raised with a *family first* attitude. So even though the move to *Nectar* would decimate my resume and force me to tighten the belt on my finances a bit, there was nothing I *truly* wanted more.

If my mother was still alive, it's where I would've been in the first place.

... if my mother was still alive, I wouldn't be in the situation I was in.

I was trying, *mightily,* to understand my father's actions, wracking my mind for the logic that would justify the selling of the *Nectar* property.

I couldn't.

Every time I tried, my brain practically screamed at me, that selling the property was too risky to be anything except an absolute last resort. I would much rather have been informed that the business was in a mountain of debt, or on the verge of bankruptcy, *anything* except... a fucking predatory lease, on land that was *supposed* to be ours.

Not his.

Mine, and Soren's.

The more I thought about it, the more I wondered if the timing around my mother's death was purely convenient; less to do with paying bills, more to do with the way the wills and trusts were structured. I was in grad school, Soren in the late years of high school. Neither of us twenty-five yet, which would've been the age certain things kicked into place.

When *more* money unlocked.

Money that would've made his supposed concerns obsolete.

It maybe would've hurt, but if we'd split the costs, Soren and I could've handled what *Nectar* was facing. We were far from a billion dollar business like *Stellar Foods*, where the stakes were much higher.

But instead of simply waiting, my father had taken a risk with the potential to ruin us.

Which... I might believe was the whole point, if William Stark wasn't too fucking arrogant to believe he'd ever lose.

Hell, he hadn't even "lost" now, because *Nectar* was too important to me to let *it* fail. And as much as this thought made my ass itch... I was, in the most twisted of manners, *somewhat...* grateful.

To Orion.

Because really, he could've just snatched our legacy from us and walking off laughing, and what would we have been able to do about it?

Not a damn thing.

Could Nectar rebuild and move and regrow and all that?

Yes and no.

All the reasons Orion and *Stellar Foods* wanted that building, in that location, would apply to us as well. Where would we get another prime location like this in Blackwood? Nobody who understood what they had was selling, *besides* the fact that huge spaces like what we'd need were few and far-between.

Even if we did luck up on something big enough, the renovations would suck our coffers dry, during a time when there wasn't any revenue coming in.

And *building?*

From scratch?!

We may as well just hang it up.

Nothing else would make sense.

Which made this situation all the more frustrating. There was precious little I hated more than feeling like my damn hands were tied.

On the way back to my room, my phone started ringing, prompting me to put a little pep in my unhurried steps, trying to catch it before the call ended. A quick glance at the screen told me it was my good friend Morgan, who I was supposed to be meeting for a breakfast date a bit later in the morning.

I halfway hoped it was to cancel.

I had so much on my mind that I'd rather have a smoothie in my office while I pored over *Nectar's* books.

Finalized the holiday events happening over the next few weeks.

Tried my best not to have a mental breakdown.

You know, the usual.

"This is your reminder call," were the first words out of her mouth once I'd answered. The amusement in her tone made me grin as I took a seat on the side of the bed. "Since you're a busybody these days and so damn hard to pin down."

"The busybody has gotten even busier," I replied. An answer that earned a deep sigh from the other end of the line.

"*But*... I will still show up to *Honeybee* for my chicken and waffles."

"Bitch you'd *better*." She laughed. "Do you have any idea how hard it was to get you and Alexis to agree to the same time?"

"So it's my fault that empires don't just build themselves?" I teased.

As much heat as they could give me for being busy, I could send it all right back. Morgan was imperative in her family's business too, and Alexis was one of the most influential women in Blackwood's finance industry.

All of our schedules were hell.

"Maybe?" Morgan quipped back. "I want to hear all about what has you so busy over these mimosas though."

"Of course," I agreed, knowing that there were *no* mimosas in my future.

Not on a weekday.

Okay... maybe *one*.

Honestly, I could use a drink after the way I'd woken up.

The damn papers weren't even signed yet and Orion Sterling had already disintegrated my nerves.

───

"THAT WHOLE FAMILY is the fucking *worst*," Morgan declared, pausing to take a sip before adding, "Why are they always trying to take over something?!"

My eyes went wide over her response to my revelation of this whole thing with Orion, which I hadn't shared with friends until now. "Wait a minute, you've dealt with them before?"

She nodded. "Unfortunately. Well... kinda. They wanted

my parents to cut a deal, only supplying to them. Which could've been great, right? Except they lowballed the fuck out of us, half market rate for *everything. And* they wanted to use *our* east coast connections for crab, oysters, all that stuff. When we wouldn't do it, they tried to get us blackballed. Luckily our suppliers weren't really on that, but can you believe the audacity?!" she fussed.

Rightfully.

"I'm not remotely surprised." I shook my head. "With the way Orion came into *Nectar* with *such* disrespect, that apple couldn't have fallen very far from the tree."

"It's a shame," Alexis said, her first time speaking up at all. "I hate that your experience has been so negative."

Morgan and I looked at each other, eyebrows raised, then both turned to Alexis, brows furrowed.

"What an odd statement," I said, leaning toward her. "Very... *measured*."

She cringed a little, then tried to pick up her fork, no doubt intending to stuff enough food in her mouth to stall the conversation.

Morgan was quick though, snatching her plate to move it out of reach. "Uh-uh," she said. "*Talk*."

"I can't say much!" Alexis insisted. "It could be considered... a conflict of interests..."

My eyes narrowed even further. "*How?*"

"I... *fuck*," she huffed. "Orion has brothers, you know?"

I nodded. "Yeah, Ares and Titan. I looked the family up so I'd at least know what I was marrying into. *Why* do you bring them up?"

"Well... I kinda... manage some of the family's portfolio? All of Titan's, actually."

"*Traitor!*" I gasped, planting a hand to my chest as

Morgan unceremoniously returned Lex's plate. "How could you work with the enemy?!"

"I didn't know he—well, his *brother*—was going to 'become the enemy'," she huffed, crossing her arms. "Or that the whole family was *already* yours," she said to Morgan, who rolled her eyes.

"They're awful people. Why would you want to work with them anyway?"

Alexis frowned. "Bitch they're *billionaires,* and wealth is my trade." She laughed. "Why wouldn't I? Besides…" She flipped a handful of blonde-streaked layers over her shoulder. "Titan is… cool people. He introduced me to Dale."

I'd been taking a sip from the watered-down mimosa I'd nursed for the whole meal, trying to get the sour taste of this news out of my mouth and choked when she said that. "He introduced you to your fiancé?" I whisper-yelled. "You told us you met him through a friend. Is *Titan fucking Sterling…* your *friend?!*"

Instead of answering, Alexis poked at the remains of her poached egg, which was *plenty* of answer. "Oh my *God*," I groaned.

Across the table, Morgan sucked her teeth. "I should've known my life was going a little *too* good. Do I have to come to the wedding?" she asked.

"Do *not* fucking play with me!" I said, motioning at her with a pointed fork. "You're my maid of honor!"

Alexis gasped. "I thought *I* was going to be your maid of honor!"

"*Before* I knew you were besties with these people!"

"Okay, y'all are officially dragging it," Alexis huffed. "Titan is the baby of the family, and everybody knows the baby of the family isn't like the rest of them. He's practically the black sheep."

"Because he's a damn hoodlum, or used to be," Morgan mumbled, bringing our attention to her.

"And how do you know *that*?" Alexis asked. "Because of the supply deal gone wrong?"

Morgan sighed. "No. That's… not my only connection to that family. *Unfortunately*."

"Oh God," I grunted. "What else could there be?"

"I don't want to talk about it," she *attempted*, but — "I don't fucking think so." Alexis was the one to speak. "If *I'm* gonna be in the hot seat, girl you can bring your ass too. What are you not telling?"

Looking *truly* defeated, Morgan flagged down a server to request another round of mimosas, making us wait for them to be delivered before she answered.

"I… may or may not have been… high school sweethearts with Ares Sterling."

My mouth dropped. "*Say sike!*"

"You don't know how bad I wish I could," she groaned. "I wasn't good enough for his family though. His mother called me *the fish market girl*."

"To your *face*?!" Alexis asked.

Morgan shook her head. "I overheard it. But Ares must've agreed because he never talked to me again after that summer. And then I went off to BSU, and… blah blah blah. Y'all know the rest."

"So *he's* the boy that broke your heart and had you hoeing all over the yard?!" I asked, completely serious.

For a moment, there was complete silence at the table, the three of us just looking at each other before we broke into laughter.

"*Wow*," Alexis gasped, the first to somewhat regain her composure. "So all this time... *Ares Sterling* was *he who must not be named*?"

Dabbing away tears of laughter with her cloth napkin, Morgan nodded. "Yup."

"So what the hell are we going to do?" I asked, giving up my previously established limit to take a deep gulp from the fresh mimosa. "I'm supposed to marry this man while one of my best friends has a secret blood feud with the family and the other is their fucking accountant? No shade, Lexi."

"No shade my ass." Alexis laughed. "This *accountant* could've kept you out of this position in the first place. Y'all should talked to me!"

"Trust me, if I'd known, I would've! Alan's ass should've *never* let my father sell the building. Zero debate there. But again... what do I do now?"

"You make the best of a fucked-up situation," Morgan spoke up, reaching across the table to grab my hand. "Marry him and destroy the whole family from the inside."

"*Mo*, please." I giggled. "You know damn well that wouldn't work in my favor."

"A girl can dream though, right?" She laughed. "But no, in seriousness... you know you have my support, right? The thing with Ares was damn near twenty years ago at this point and more than a decade since *Stellar Foods* tried to pull their bullshit. I'm sure I can tolerate them for the length of a wedding."

"I wish that was the only amount of time I had to tolerate my soon-to-be-husband," I muttered, draining the rest of my glass.

Across from me, Lexi's eyes went wide and so did Morgan's.

"Speak of the damn devil," she whispered.

I glanced behind me to follow her gaze, and indeed… there the damn devil was.

It was *beyond* irritating that the sight of Orion's handsome face instantly took me back to the dream that had pulled me awake this morning. He locked eyes with me immediately and the visual of his head between my thighs was hard to shake as he sauntered towards our table wearing a confident smirk.

And turning heads.

To the untrained eye, he was dressed "simply"—nice pants, nice shoes, nice sweater.

I knew better. The way the fabrics were cut, the way they hugged his thick frame, everything was designer, down to the chain around his neck, the glasses on his face, and probably that fucking nose ring.

Inappropriate probably, for a man his age, but he was a billionaire.

He could get away with what he wanted.

Instead of giving Orion the satisfaction of being watched—at least by me—the whole way, I turned back to my plate.

"Good morning, ladies," he greeted the table. "I hope it won't be considered too much of an imposition that I covered your bill."

I rolled my eyes, but Morgan and Alexis *both* just grinned at him.

"No, not at all," Morgan said, her expression morphing into mischief right in front of me. "We've been celebrating the happy news…"

I almost choked on the mouthful of biscuit I was using as a reason to not say anything, tossing a glare in her direction as Orion planted a hand on my shoulder.

"That's good to hear," he said, giving me a gentle squeeze.

"And in that case, I'm sure you ladies won't mind if I borrow my lovely fiancée for a moment."

Before I could offer how *I* might feel about being "borrowed", Orion had already grabbed my hand. Knowing I couldn't make a scene in this restaurant, I accepted his help in leaving my seat, sending another glower at my "friends" before being led away from the table.

"What the fuck do you want?" I hissed when he finally stopped, in a somewhat private area. We were still visible for plenty of patrons, but far enough away that the contents of the conversation could remain between us.

"Why so hostile so early?" he asked, wetting his lips with his tongue.

Shit.

I couldn't look at his mouth.

"Make your point before I walk away," I demanded, faltering a bit when he stepped even closer into my personal space.

This was dangerous, considering how our last "conversation" ended.

"Our lawyers have finished up our agreement," he said, speaking into my ear.

I took a step back. "This could've been an email. Instead of you hunting me down at breakfast."

"This is entirely coincidental, *my love*." He grinned. "I enjoy breakfast too, believe it or not."

I scoffed. "And here I was thinking the blood, sweat, and tears of the people your family destroys would be sustenance enough."

Orion tossed his head back, laughing. "That's funny. I like laughing. Keep it up."

"Fuck you."

"Soon enough, sweetheart," he said, stepping in again. "Sign your papers today."

I rolled my eyes. "Why the rush? The sooner we do, the sooner we have to start playing pretend."

Orion hooked a couple fingers under my chin. Suddenly, I was incredibly conscious of the spot he'd chosen for this conversation. More than a few people were staring right in our direction.

He smirked at me, still holding me as he leaned in to press a soft kiss to the side of my head.

"In case you haven't noticed, Nala, the show has already begun."

FIVE
ORION

Five new stores?

I scribbled that line in the margins of the printed document I'd been staring at all morning. It was one thing to see the vision for the next five years at *Wholesome Foods* up on a screen, a whole other to have it right in front of me.

I scowled at the line. It was supposed to replace where I'd crossed out *twenty new stores*. That was a stretch for a period as short as five years, even for me. Risky endeavors didn't scare me, but putting a plan for four new stores a year for the next five years—*doubling* the current number of stores—was practically breakneck speed.

It was too much.

Just five though?

One new store a year was safe, and perfectly manageable, which… was what made it so unattractive. *No guts, no glory* was the first thing that came to mind when I wondered what my father's advice would be, if he was still here.

Wholesome Foods was his brainchild, after all.

When he left it in my hands, it had been with the understanding that I wouldn't let it grow stagnant, that we would innovate and expand, prove *his* father wrong about Black folks wanting bougie groceries.

His words.

I refused to be reckless with his legacy, but pussyfooting around our growth wasn't going to cut it either.

I scratched out the previous line, replacing it with *ten new stores*.

No question mark.

We would open ten new stores over the next five years.

That was a prospect to be excited about.

Instead of moving on to the next part of the vision statement, I woke my computer up, navigating to the folder our market research team had already put together. Even though I knew the list of possible expansion cities like the back of my hand, I still wanted it in front of me to reference as I thought through exactly where those ten new stores might land.

"*Mr. Sterling.*"

I frowned at the formality of Shiloh's greeting over the intercom, not to mention this time was *always* uninterrupted. It was built into my schedule.

Brows furrowed, I hit the button that would allow her to hear my response. "What's going on, Shi?"

"William Stark is at the security desk downstairs, insisting on seeing you. He says it's urgent. Should I let him up or inform him on how to make an appointment?"

From the inflection in her tone, it was clear what *she* preferred. She didn't play the pop-up visitor shit and knew it wasn't my preferred method of engagement either. It went without saying that the only reason she was even entertaining him was his place as Nalani's father.

The same reason I told her to allow him up.

Showing up here was a bold ass move, and I was curious to hear what was on his mind.

Some bullshit, no doubt.

William Stark was exactly the kind of man I endeavored *not* to be—weak-willed, selfish, reckless, just to name a few. His mistakes in business aside, when I showed up in the *Nectar* offices, I'd hoped to find *something* I could respect about him, anything that made me view him in a somewhat positive light.

So far, the only thing working for him was that he hadn't *completely* run *Nectar* in the ground, and if I had to make a wager, my money would be on foolish luck.

It was a *wonder* that he'd raised a woman like Nalani. Her mother had surely borne the brunt of the work there. Even her barely-out-of-college brother, who research told me was more interested in innovative tech than any sort of corporate shit, would've been an improvement over William.

Nalani and Soren just needed their eyes opened.

Moments later, my door opened, and a clearly irritated Shiloh appeared.

"William Stark to see you," she said, in a professional tone that contrasted the restrained annoyance in her eyes.

"Thank you, Shi. Go have a nice lunch, on me," I told her, offering a smile she met with narrowed eyes.

"I was about to do that anyway."

I suppressed a grin over her response as she moved out of the door, making way for my surprise visitor. He was escorted in by Henry, one of my security officers, who remained in the office after closing the door behind them.

William raked a hand over his hair—seemingly even more gray than it had been the last time I saw him—glancing between me and Henry. "I was hoping to have a private conversation," he said.

Ignoring that, I gestured at the chairs across from my desk. "Have a seat, Mr. Stark."

"But—" he attempted, and I shook my head.

"This is as private as it gets. Henry is very well paid for his discretion. The only two people who might carry our conversation beyond these walls would be me or you," I assured, not bothering to entertain other possibilities.

I didn't negotiate with weak men.

"I—"

"Have a seat," I spoke over him, before he could get out whatever rebuttal he was still trying to push. "Or you can vacate my office so I can get back to important things."

From the way his eyes narrowed, I could tell he picked up on my clear implication, *this isn't important.* But he apparently had a point to make. He walked up to the desk, taking one of the seats I'd pointed out.

"Speak your mind," I urged, lounging backward in my chair, arms crossed.

"I have an offer to make," he said, sitting forward. "Everybody walks away a winner."

I smirked. "That's doubtful… but I'm listening."

"I can sell you *Nectar*."

Bullshit.

I kept my face impassive, but my mind went to work immediately, picking apart the possibility of that.

"I know what you're thinking. I don't have the shares in the company to do that. But what I *do* have is control of the executive board," he prattled, trying to get as many words as possible out.

"Not for long," I countered. "That's why you're here. You know you're getting voted out at the top of the year, right?"

On my part, it was purely conjecture, but if I were Nalani, *that* would be my first move.

Getting rid of the incompetent CEO.

"Even more reason to take the offer now," he pitched, and I shook my head.

"What benefit would that hold for me, hmm?" I asked, running my fingers through the coils of my beard. "You try to sell this company—from under your own children, at that—and I accept, the *first* thing coming my way is a lawsuit."

"One you'll win."

He was confident; he'd thought it through.

"I don't like lawsuits, Mr. Stark. They're time consuming, annoying, and expensive. So when I can, I avoid them," I said. "So you tell me why on *earth* I would take this new offer, when I already have a perfectly good deal already in place?"

"If you take *my* deal, I can stay in place as CEO, work for you—"

William's words trailed off, overshadowed by the volume of my laughter.

"You're shittin' me, right?" I asked once I'd regained my composure enough to speak. "You don't believe I'd allow you on my payroll, do you?"

"*Nectar* has been a staple of the Blackwood community—"

"No thanks to *you*," I cut in. "Let's be absolutely serious here, *Mr. Stark...* your *wife* and her family are the reason *Nectar* is what it is. Your executive board operates out of love and respect for *her* memory. *She* was one the community adored and put up plaques for, not you."

"You're going to sit there and disrespect me in my face?"

"You disrespected *yourself* by showing up here unannounced," I explained. "Because you clearly don't have anything better to do. You know... I thought *maybe* this was about protecting Nalani. Now that, I could've respected. I wouldn't have moved, but I could understand you coming here to plead for me not to corrupt your daughter. Man to man, that would've showed me there was some molecule, just a *modicum* of dignity about you. But... no." I shook my head. "You're here to beg for a fucking *job*?"

"Nalani is a grown woman; she can make her own decisions."

"Can she?" I scoffed. "'Cause I could swear she's navigating *your* idiotic judgement, trying to right a sinking ship you *never* should've been at the helm of."

"You keep speaking as if you know me, *young man*."

I grinned. "Oh, are you... putting me in my place?" I chuckled.

"Someone needs to."

"It *won't* be you. It won't *ever* be you," I informed, sitting forward to prop my clasped hands on the desk. "See... I'm speaking as if I know you, because I *do*... or do you think my father never told me about his coward ass 'friend' who married into the competition's family because it was the only avenue he had to claw his way into making a name for himself?"

I fought the urge to smirk as William's light brown skin flushed. He *didn't* think my father had talked about it.

"Did it hurt when you realized the Joyce family wasn't even interested in becoming some mega corporation?" I asked. "Did you even *love* Larena Joyce or was she just a means to an end for you?"

"That's rich, considering the offer you made Nalani."

"The difference is that she knows exactly what she's getting into," I countered. "She signed a contract detailing *exactly* what this is and isn't because I don't have to trick her."

"You bought the building!"

"I've bought a *hundred* buildings in the last decade, Mr. Stark. And need I remind you; I didn't have to seek you out, you practically put it in my lap. Because you are a fucking imbecile." I chuckled, shaking my head. "And the worst part is, you don't even see it, do you?!"

"You smug little motherfucker!" he barked, lunging out of his seat.

Behind him, Henry stepped forward, but I held up a hand, urging him to stay where he was as I met William's gaze, eyes brimming with rage.

I stayed exactly where I was.

"Is there something you need to get off your chest, Mr. Stark?" I asked. "If so, please feel free to speak up about it."

Chest heaving, William glanced over his shoulder at Henry, but I shook my head.

"Henry understands this is a conversation between me and you. Man to man," I said.

"Man to *little boy*," he snapped. "If your damn daddy was alive, you'd be somewhere doing grunt work."

"But he isn't." I shrugged. "So here the fuck we are, now what?"

"You think you're so smart. I'm not surprised, your daddy had the same malfunction; thought he was five steps ahead of everybody."

"Not everybody, *William*," I said, dropping any pretext of respect. "Just you. Is that what all this is about? You're mad that even in death, he is *still* ahead of you? He had more money, a better business, a wife who actually wanted him, so there's no *question* about the lineage of *his* son."

William's eyebrows shot up in clear surprise and I grinned.

"Don't tell me you *never* wondered about Soren… I mean, I've seen the pictures, Nalani looks just like her mother, nothing strange there. But your *son*… who does he look like, Billy?"

Chuckling, I stepped back, easily dodging William's grasp as he *did* dive over the desk that time. I didn't have to do any more than that. Henry had him hemmed up before he could make another move, unperturbed by the older man's cursing and squirming.

"Get him out of here," I said, taking my seat again. "In case I don't see you before then, Merry Christmas, father-in-law!"

That set him off even worse, but I didn't hear much more of it.

The commotion had drawn Shiloh's attention, and she was at the door, holding it open for Henry to drag William Stark from my office.

Her face was curled in contempt as she watched them leave, then turned to where I'd already picked up my mission statement again.

"You think that was a good idea?" she asked. "Riling him up like that? It's begging for trouble."

"Fuck him," I countered, shaking my head. "He's an old man, trying to cling to anything he can. I'm not worried about him."

"Maybe you should be though. You're marrying his daughter."

I sighed. "You might have a point, but... I don't get the feeling he's on her good side right now anyway."

"Wouldn't be if I was her."

"Exactly. Now, no more interruptions. I need to get this done."

Shiloh's mouth opened, probably to tell me *she* wasn't the one who facilitated the interruption anyway, but... she didn't say it.

"Yes, your majesty," she chose instead, rolling her eyes. "Anything else before I go?"

I laughed. "Yes, *please*," I added, which softened her expression. "Find out where Nalani is planning to spend Christmas."

SIX
NALANI

"Now WHO TOLD you to come in here looking this cute this morning?!"

An expansive grin spread over my lips at the sound of my Aunt Lucinda's voice. Every year, Blackwood Community Center hosted a Christmas morning "breakfast." Tons of hot, delicious food, yes, but also dinner boxes and plates people could take home, blankets, toiletries, and wrapped presents for the kids, categorized by interest. It was all free of charge for the community, powered by donations from Black businesses near and far.

Every year, *just* like my mother had, I made sure *Nectar* gave a financial contribution. *I* made a financial contribution, and I showed up to serve in whatever capacity the organizers needed.

It was something my mother and I used to do together.

Even as a kid, I loved spending Christmas mornings like this. Sure, presents were waiting for Soren and I at home, but they'd always be there. This kept us firmly grounded in reality we wouldn't have otherwise seen from our private schools and tutors and exclusive neighborhoods.

My father *hated* it.

But we showed up anyway.

"Hey, Auntie," I greeted, gladly submitting to the tight hug and air kiss she sent my way. She'd never risk messing up her flawless lipstick for a real one. "You doing alright this morning?"

"Blessed as always, baby. You wanna come help me with these hand pies?"

"Lead the way," I insisted, then followed to the crowded kitchen, where other volunteers were already hard at work. She led me to her workstation, already set with a neat assembly line for the little mini pies we'd be rolling out, filling, deep frying, and then packing into parchment paper pouches.

"Am I cutting, filling, frying…?" I asked, moving to the prep sink to wash my hands and grab a clean apron.

"I'll cut, you fill. We're making the afternoon batch for the next shift," she explained, already back in position.

By the time my clothes were protected, and my hands were clean and dry, she already had a stack of perfectly floured circles of the Joyce family signature pie crust ready for me to fill.

Nectar wasn't the only business that had been passed down. *Sweet Ambrosia* was an expansive, full-service bakery that had been operating since… basically forever. My mom and her sister loved to tell the story of flipping a coin to see who was going to take which business.

They both—lovingly—claimed the other sister had won.

"You haven't been coming by for your pecan croissant in the mornings, what's going on?" Aunt Lucy asked as we worked side by side, with her adding new circles of dough faster than I could spoon a perfect serving of sweet potato filling inside, fold it all over, and crimp the edges.

I shrugged. "I've just been grabbing it at the shop inside the store," I explained, unsurprised that my answer got a little derisive grunt in response.

"That ain't the same thing and you know it."

"Are you saying the pop-up *Sweets* is phoning it in over there? You better talk to the manager…"

"Don't play with me lil' girl." She chuckled. "You know what I mean."

Yeah.

I did.

She was talking about how I'd been avoiding my usual routine of popping into the flagship store a couple times a week to see her face. I could have always grabbed my favorite pastry there at the store, but I went out of my way to see my aunt and for her to see me.

It was important.

There was a few years of age between them, but they'd been close as long as I could remember, and they looked just alike. Even their kids had been a mirror. My cousin Sheila was born the same year as me, Preston was born the same year as Soren, and we'd all been thick as thieves.

Now though, it was just me, Aunt Lucy, and Soren.

We'd lost the others.

Gut punch after gut punch after gut punch.

Losing *Nectar* would just be another, except I could *do something* about that one.

"What are you trying avoid telling me, lil' Rena?"

Even though her tone was stern, I smiled. She always called me that, my mother's mini me, when I was on the cusp of getting fussed out.

"Nothing I can say with this many ears around," I admitted, still moving through my job, while she'd stopped. "Let's do dinner or something though, before New Year's."

"Mmmhmm," she muttered, accepting being put off. There were a few minutes of quiet, steady work, and then she spoke again. "You know that damn *EJ* is running around here today?"

I sighed. "Yeah. I didn't see him, but I saw his… people."

His people being a bunch of all-black clad men with visible guns at their waists.

Every year, they showed up making people nervous.

Every year, the organizers let it slide.

With good reason, if I was honest about it, despite the way it irked me.

Law enforcement volunteers creating a security team aside, it was the presence of EJ and his "people" that kept the people who didn't give a fuck about the cops on their best behavior. For the most part, Blackwood was safe, but criminals existed everywhere.

EJ was, in fact, a fucking criminal.

The kind that other criminals knew about all too well, so they gave him a wide berth.

Which was why he was allowed to stay.

He wasn't into the kind of petty, individual crime that might need prevention today.

"You gonna go speak?" Aunt Lucy asked — pried, really — but that wasn't unexpected.

I shook my head. "I'm sure he'll find me, doesn't he always?"

Sure enough, I'd just left the kitchen after crimping the last pie and was hunting down an audience with one of the event organizers wearing bright green *Blackwood Community Center* crewneck when EJ himself sidled in front of me, looking and smelling criminally good, as always.

"*Lani Stark*, I knew I'd see your big pretty ass today," he crooned, opening his arms for a hug.

I raised an eyebrow. "Is that a compliment, Eric?"

Immediately, his eyes darkened, arms dropped. "You know I don't like being called that shit," he said in a low growl.

"And *you* know the accepted short version of my name is Nala, yet you insist on being different," I countered.

"You ain't mind that shit when I was tossing you around."

Heat rushed to my face, but I kept my expression neutral. "Yeah, but times change."

"We could always circle back," he suggested with a smirk, stepping in to crowd my space. "You know you always have an open position with me, right?"

"I think I'll pass on the slot in your harem."

"The *head* slot," he argued, and against my better judgement, I laughed; a reaction he used as a reason to move even closer to me. "I see that smile, girl. You know how I used to have you twisted up. These little corny corporate boys ain't doing it for you, and you *know* it."

"You don't know my business, EJ."

"You don't know *what* I know, baby girl," he said. "Tell me, what other nigga has what I have, to do you like I did?"

"*This one.*"

Holy shit.

My heart leaped into my throat at the sound of Orion's voice, way too close to *not* have heard the conversation. Before I could get my body to respond to anything my brain was signaling, Orion had a hand on EJ's chest, pushing him back.

"I need some space between you and my lady," Orion said. Pleasant enough wording, but there was an edge to his tone I'd personally never heard.

EJ looked at him, then at Orion's hand that was still touching him, keeping him back. Then he looked at me, eyes wide, incredulous. "Who the fuck you think you talking to?"

"Whatever the fuck your name is," Orion immediately countered, with the most disrespectful shrug I'd ever seen.

I… didn't even know a shrug could *be* disrespectful.

But that one?

Was.

EJ took a step back, chuckling, but… fully unamused.

Shit.

Shit.

Shit.

"Please tell me you're a comedian or something? The entertainment for the kids? Wait. What do you call it when the actors get a little too invested in the role?" EJ directed that question at me and all I could in my frozen state was blink once, twice, and then give an answer.

"Um… a method actor?" I stammered, not knowing what else to do.

"*A method actor*," EJ parroted, with a nod. "That's gotta be it. You picked the wrong the motherfucker for your little improv, funny man."

Orion smiled. "The only thing amusing here is that you're still in my face, spouting out bullshit—for what, I don't know.

Maybe you're angry, embarrassed, whatever, I truly don't give a fuck," he said. "But I would suggest you move on, you and your friends go play with your guns, anything other than speaking crudely to my lady."

"So... you *do* know who I am?" EJ asked, doing the exact opposite of Orion's encouragement to back off.

"I'm vaguely aware."

"So you've got a death wish then?"

"I'm quite certain you're speaking for yourself, my man." Orion looked him right in the eyes. "We can see who gets touched first. I'm very confident. How confident are you?"

I... felt like I should be warning someone.

All around us, people were milling about, going on with their business, eating, laughing, having a joyous time as if there weren't two short-fused bombs smack in our midst.

"Nalani."

My head snapped back to them at the sound of my name. EJ had spoken it. Barely constrained rage hid behind his eyes as he posed a question.

A serious one, this time.

"This really your nigga?" he asked.

Immediately, I looked at Orion.

Outwardly, he was cool, *frustratingly* so.

He looked downright *bored.*

Meanwhile, he was wearing the same scarcely controlled wrath as EJ, simmering just beneath the surface.

I wasn't sure if it would help or hinder the peace, but I told the unfortunate, contractual truth.

"Yes."

I could practically *feel* the furious heat coming off EJ.

"Out of the respect I have for you and your Pops... I'ma walk away. *Only* because of that," EJ said.

A snort of laughter broke from Orion. "Whatever you gotta tell yourself to feel good about it."

"Orion, *please*," I snapped, quickly stepping into the minimal space between him and EJ, even as EJ stepped back.

"Orion?" EJ repeated, giving me a quizzical look.

"Yes?" Orion trilled, so damn obnoxious that I tossed a glare behind me.

"Nothing," EJ grunted, turning around to walk away without another word. Surprising, but relieving. When I turned back to Orion, he was wearing that frustrating smirk again.

"I think he might be regretting his tone," he said, and I shook my head.

"What the hell is wrong with you?!" I whisper-yelled. "EJ is fucking dangerous, are you crazy?"

"You think I should be scared of him?"

"I think he's not somebody to get under the skin of."

"Why do you think that?" Orion asked, frowning. "Oh, it seems you're quite familiar with his… *skin*, and vice versa."

"I'm *not* talking about that."

"Let's talk about him being all over you in front of all these people though."

I let out a huff. "So this is about your ego then?"

"*Yes*," he admitted, with a deep sigh as if he were relieved I finally "got it." "Everything about me is prominent. Get used to it, *wifey*."

"Don't call me that," I countered. "I'm not wearing your ring yet."

He smiled.

Letting me know I'd messed up.

I just didn't know how bad until he grabbed my hand to

pull me to the front of the common room and then dropped to one knee of front me.

"That whole… *not wearing my ring yet* thing?" he said, pulling a black velvet box from his pocket to lift before me. "Let's fix that."

SEVEN
NALANI

It would go down in people's memories as "romantic."

A Christmas day proposal, in the middle of doing community service?

Orion was… calculated.

I'd certainly give him that.

He was also incredibly obnoxious to me and so was the ring he'd put on my finger—probably five or six carats worth of undoubtedly flawless diamonds. One big one in the middle and a halo of smaller diamonds around it, set into a platinum, diamond pave band.

It was beautiful.

Right on the line between classy and gaudy.

Fitting for the future wife of a billionaire.

It *really* hadn't struck me until then. I'd been thinking about this whole thing solely in abstract terms. Yes, I'd weighed out my options on paper and all that, I'd thought through future implications, considered contingencies.

But the actual factual reality was that I was about to become this man's *wife?*

I'd been—somewhat purposely—avoiding that.

And now I couldn't.

The rest of the event passed in a blur of congratulations and admiration; both of the ring, and of Orion, who'd turned the charm up to full blast. I barely even reacted to his announcement of a new charity—pledging a cool million in housing assistance and grocery vouchers for families in need, because of course he was doing that.

I just applauded and smiled, like a good little wife.

And then my aunt pulled me aside.

Away from prying eyes and nosy ears, and she didn't even say anything. She just *looked* at me, until I tossed up my hands.

"It was the only way to keep Daddy from losing the store," I admitted, voice cracking. "He fucked us over, while Mama was… *dying*," I said, shaking my head. "And then *he* showed up." I waved my hand in the general vicinity of where most people were gathered, referring to Orion. "With this… fucked-up lifeline. And I had to take it."

Aunt Lucy sighed, lacing her fingers through mine to squeeze. "Are you sure? Is it about money? Because—"

"Daddy deprived us of the chance for it to be *just* about money, and… I'm having a hard time believing it wasn't on purpose," I said, putting my thoughts into actual words for the first time. "He could have asked me, or Soren, or *you*. He could've taken loans, anything except what he did."

Her eyes narrowed. "Which was?"

I blew out a harsh sigh, not even wanting to say the shit out loud. Not to *her*. But I couldn't keep avoiding the truth. "He sold the land and the building."

"No he didn't."

A wry smile spread over my lips. "Yeah, Auntie. He did. But don't worry," I assured, squeezing her hands like she'd done to mine. "I'm getting it back. It's in the contract Orion and I signed; ownership comes back to *me* and we're getting Daddy off the board. Soren and I agree, he's not the best choice to make decisions anymore."

"He *never* was," she huffed, shaking her head. "I did my best to warn Rena he didn't have her best interests in mind, but she was so damn stubborn."

I raised an eyebrow. "What made you feel that way about him back then?"

"It was just too… *fast*," she said. "Like he was rushing her along, so much urgency about it. Our daddy hadn't passed yet, so it wasn't as if the store was hers, but I always felt like it was one of the reasons he was so '*in love*'. I don't know." She shrugged. "I just never really trusted him."

Interesting.

It was no real secret that Aunt Lucy wasn't my father's biggest fan, but I'd always just assumed their personalities didn't quite mesh. I was rarely around them at the same time, which became them *never* being in a room together after my mother was gone.

It all made so much more sense now.

"Listen to me, Nalani," she said, pulling my attention back to her. "You won't be the first or last woman to marry a man for reasons other than love. As women, we do what we have to do all the time, but the only way you're going to make it through that is to *never* forget why you're there, you hear me?"

I scoffed. "Trust me, that won't be a problem."

"Don't be arrogant; you heed my words," she warned.

"That man is handsome, rich, and intelligent. Those qualities make it easy to go blind. *Especially* if he starts slinging dick the right way."

"*Auntie!*" I gasped, and she sucked her teeth.

"Don't you *auntie* me, I'm telling you what I know, what I'd tell my own daughter if she was here, and the same kind of warning I give the young ladies around the bakery all the time. A man like that will have you all twisted in knots before you realized you're being tied."

"Trust me," I assured. "I have my eyes *all the way* open."

I was confident.

Super confident.

And yet, her warning stayed on my mind.

All the way from the center back to my apartment, her words played in my mind for me to turn over and dissect.

I refused to bury them.

Naivete could cost more than I was willing to lose.

Even being immersed in the jumble of my thoughts, I'd noticed I was being watched a bit harder than usual. From the time I climbed into my car to the time I unlocked my front door and hurried inside, it felt as if there were eyes on me.

I wished I could call myself surprised.

Such a public outing as Orion's apparent wife-to-be would bring increased scrutiny, and frankly, the perceived value of the damn ring would turn me into a target.

Annoyances I couldn't imagine Orion had considered when he jumped the gun with his proposal, which wasn't *really* supposed to happen for another month.

There was a cadence written into the contract—a period of public courtship to establish a dating story, give an opportunity for us to be photographed together, stuff like that.

And yet, because he was himself, it was nothing to him to

jump over all that, just to make some silly point in front of an ex Orion didn't even know *was* an ex.

Or... did he?

Something about the way EJ backed off when he realized who Orion was—or rather, the family he was from — it was a little unnerving. EJ and I went back to when he was just Eric, a kid from the neighborhood up the block my parents really didn't want me around, but I was young and reckless and stupid, so *of course* I thought I was in love anyway.

Even then, he was fearless.

Not that *fear* was exactly what I picked up, maybe more that a problem with Orion was something he'd rather avoid. Thinking about it made me feel like there was something I didn't know about the Sterlings; something deeper than freaking... *groceries*.

Demetria and Des had looked into things for me, sure, but... did I *really* know what I was getting into?

It was yet another thing to have on my already overcrowded mind, and instead of dwelling on it too deeply, the idea of clearing my head with a hot bath was much more appealing.

I grabbed a bottle of wine too, to *really* help clear the bullshit away.

While the bath was running, I checked my phone. I'd already talked to the most important people, but there were still random *Merry Christmas* texts to field.

Once I'd cleared them all, I tossed the phone down, trying not to give in to the disappointment of one number that hadn't appeared in my notifications at all.

Asshole.

For a week now, my father had been ignoring my calls, not responding to emails, pretending he didn't see texts, all in what I could only assume was some immature effort to not be removed from his position. As if his lack of communication would put a damper on the process.

As angry as I'd been—and still was—I was missing a key level of understanding that was the difference between my father being simply incompetent or outright malicious.

I *hated* that I couldn't be certain without speaking to him which of those it was.

And now, today, *Christmas* of all times, he'd decided the silent treatment was his highest card. Today, I was reversing it back at him. I would *not* send a text; I would *not* press the button to make a call.

I would *not* be the "bigger person" when it came to my damn *father*.

It wasn't my responsibility, and I refused to take it on.

I was doing enough already.

I cracked the wine open before the bath was ready and was already on my second glass by the time I slipped into the hot, soapy tub. To treat myself a bit, I even turned my music on and threw in a sachet of bath tea I'd gotten from a newly minted shop at *Nectar*, honey&hibiscus. It was filled with herbs and oils and flowers and all kinds of stuff that made the water look milky, but was supposed to make it more relaxing.

Exactly what I needed.

In the tub, I tried to clear my mind, but instead, my gaze fell on my left hand.

The ring.

Still obnoxious, yes, but incredibly beautiful.

And... it *did* look good on my hand.

If this was just the engagement ring, I could only imagine that the wedding band was going to be—*seriously, bitch?*

Was I... *really* giving life to this line of thought?

I shook my head, shifting brain power to what needed to happen with *Nectar*. If I couldn't clear my mind, I could at least think about something useful.

Except... my brain wasn't *that* useful anymore by the third glass of wine.

Finally, I started feeling loose and whatever was in that sachet must've really kicked in. When the urge to close my eyes hit, I didn't try to fight it. I just gave in and let them stay that way.

For a while.

Orion was seated at the end of the bathtub when I opened them again.

"What the *fuck* is wrong with you?!" I gasped, glancing down to make sure I was fully covered by the now tepid water. "You broke into my house?!"

"Better me than someone else, right?" he asked, completely casual, as if this shit was... *normal*.

"How about *nobody* should be in here uninvited?!" I snapped. "Why the hell are you here, anyway?"

He frowned. "I just put a ring worth more than a lot of people's annual salary on your finger and you're not answering phone calls, baby. I had to make sure you were alright."

"*Oh*," I mused, sarcastic. "You mean you had to make sure no one had responded to the fucking *target* you put on my back?"

"Call it what you will. It was way too easy to get in here without raising any sort of alarm."

"I *have* an alarm on my door and I know for a fact it was set."

"It was child's play for my guy." Orion shrugged. "We've gotta get you somewhere more secure. I can't have my wife so easily accessible. We'll move you to the house."

"The house?"

"*My* house," he clarified. "It makes the most sense."

"I don't care how much sense you think it makes. I'm not living with you before we get married."

"The wedding is next week, anyway, so does it really make a difference?"

"*Next week*?!" I shrieked, sitting up. His gaze dropped, and I quickly put an arm over my breasts to cover up. "Orion, we just got engaged *today,* which I haven't even had a chance to curse you out about. What the fuck happened to the agenda we agreed on?"

"Things changed," he said. "Why does it matter? It means you'll have your family property back in your name before the board meeting to get rid of your father. It will help your claim, so I don't get why you're complaining."

My eyes narrowed. "Because I know better than to believe you're doing this for me. What's in it for you?"

"That's none of your concern."

"We're getting *married,*" I huffed. "How is any part of it not my concern?"

"Because I said so."

I scoffed. "Well, I hope you find some *said so* about planning a wedding in a week, because I'm not doing it. I've got better things to do."

"It's already being handled." He smirked. "The only appointment I'm putting on your calendar is choosing a wedding dress."

"Oh, you haven't decided what you want me in?" I asked, letting every bit of snark in the question drip out.

"I definitely have ideas, so—"

"*No!*" I interrupted, surprising myself with how emphatically it came out. "I got it. Just... send me the damn details, budget, whatever."

"Budget?" he chuckled, moving from his seated position to one on his knees, next to the tub. "You think that's something that exists for you now?"

"You're insane if you think I'm spending your money," I told him. "I won't be put in a position to owe you more than I already do."

He shook his head, rolling up his sleeve to past his elbow. "You've got me all wrong, Nalani. I'm generous with mine. Which... you *do* realize that's what you are now, right?"

"I prefer to believe I belong to myself."

He smiled. "I'll let you have that delusion. For now."

"You're horrible."

"You're beautiful," he countered, slipping a hand into the semi-opaque water, where it disappeared.

"What are you doing?" I asked when I felt the pads of his finger on my thigh, but didn't move away, for reasons unknown.

Instead of answering my question, he posed one of his own. "Do you want me to stop?"

Curiosity wouldn't let me say yes.

Or maybe it was the wine.

Either way, when his hand slipped from the outside of my thigh to inner, then moved up... I didn't say a word. I just relished the feeling of his fingers playing with my clit.

I didn't *want* to think about why I was allowing him to touch me like this.

My contractual obligation was coming soon enough, sure, but that time hadn't arrived. And yet... here I was.

When his fingers sank into me, I couldn't help letting out

a moan as my eyes drifted closed. He kept a thumb on my clit, teasing and torturing me with it as his middle and pointer stroked.

Stroked.

Stroked.

But wouldn't push me all the way.

"*Nala.*"

His voice came as a low growl in my ear, prompting me to peel open my eyes. I'd been so enthralled with what he was doing between my legs that I hadn't realized he'd shifted position and his face was damn near in line with mine now.

"*This feels good to you?*"

I couldn't lie.

I also couldn't make myself speak, so I just nodded, triggering a smile.

"*Good,*" he murmured, pressing a soft kiss to my lips before his mouth moved back to my ear. "If I ever see another man that close to you…we're all going to have a horrible day."

"I—*ah!*" I moaned, the words snatched from my throat by him pushing his fingers as deep as they could get.

"*Are we clear?*" he asked, lips brushing my ear, and the only response that seemed appropriate was another silent nod, so that's what I did.

"*Good,*" he said, again.

Then finger-fucked me into a whimpering mess in the lukewarm tub.

His thumb on my clit was relentless and so were his fingers, neither letting up. I grabbed his wrist, hoping it would encourage him to lighten up.

Instead, he went harder.

By the time he stopped, I was out of breath and trembling, and it had nothing to do with the temperature of the water.

I expected him to leave me there in the tub, since it was clear our conversation was over. He surprised me by retrieving my robe from the warmer for me, averting his gaze while I stood to be wrapped in it.

As if he hadn't just finished a deep exploration with his fingers.

"Shiloh will contact you with the details for your dress shopping. We'll send you to Freeman's," he said, walking away from the bathroom. "I'm leaving security outside your door tonight, but you'll have your privacy inside."

I nodded, following. "Fine. How long do I have to have a babysitter?"

From my bedroom door, he smirked. "Just tonight. You're moving in with me tomorrow."

EIGHT
ORION

I didn't enjoy "surprises."

Good or bad.

It just wasn't the kind of life I lived.

I thrived on information and order, knowing exactly what was about to happen next. Any spontaneity was because *I* decided on it.

And bore the consequences.

Such as being hopelessly distracted by the news that Nalani had a prior entanglement with a wannabe fucking crime lord, which was being *incredibly* generous.

What *else* did I not know?

"Orion, baby you've gotta eat something…"

Bree's voice in my ear caught me off guard, her tits already pressing into my shoulder as she leaned around me to pick up my fork.

It was so damn ludicrous she had the fork filled with food and halfway to my mouth before I could react by shoving it away, turning to glare.

"Didn't I tell you to stop this shit?" I huffed, but she hadn't moved away.

"I'm just trying to take care of you, like—"

"*Get the fuck out of my face.*"

"Orion, *language.*" A different female voice came across the table, wiping all the ire from my face. I shot another warning frown at Bree before giving my attention to the most important person in my life—my father's mother, my Grandma Calli.

"Yes ma'am," I nodded, sincerely feeling bad for snapping in front of her. She never had played that shit and still didn't now. Age was the only reason she hadn't gone upside my head.

"Lil' girl, get your butt in your seat," she demanded of Bree, who opened her mouth to argue instead of simply following directions. "Remember whose house you're in right now."

That shut her up.

Around the table, Ares and Titan snickered as she sulked back to her own plate. Right on cue, Ms. Wallace, the house manager, breezed through the door carrying a platter of dessert plates, each loaded with a slice of my grandmother's pecan pie, one of the extras from Christmas.

"You've been quiet all through dinner," Grandma Calli spoke up, quickly thanking Ms. Wallace before she gave her attention back to me. "What's going on with you?"

"Yeah, Ri, what's going on with you?" Titan chimed, his smug expression ringing the annoyance bell in my mind.

His ass knew good and well what was *going on.*

"Bailing you out of jail 'cause they're tired of doing you favors?" I countered, making his eyes go wide.

"It was just a little harmless bar fight, nothing to worry about," he told Granny, and I snorted.

"As many stitches as you're reimbursing the other guy for, I think it was more than a *harmless bar fight*."

"Orion got engaged."

Fuck.

"Really?!" I barked at Titan.

He shrugged and started digging into his pie as the heat from Grandma Calli's stare burned into the side of my head.

"Ri, I didn't know you were seeing anybody," Bree said in an accusing tone she truly had no business using with me.

I didn't even bother responding. I met my granny's gaze with a sigh. "I was going to let you know," I assured her. "In a better way than this."

She raised an eyebrow. "This way is just fine. Who is she? Surely not that Jessica girl…"

"*Absolutely* not," I said, shaking my head. "No, it's… Nalani Stark."

Surprise registered on her face first, replaced by a slow smile. "That's a lovely young woman, from what I've observed. Her mother was quite a delight as well. How the hell you get her to say yes to your mean ass?"

Ares and Titan didn't even bother to stifle laughs.

"I bet it's to spite that damn daddy of hers, isn't it?" Grandma Calli added, shaking her head. "I never could stand him, even when he used to run around with Cas."

Cas being *Caspian*, my father.

More than anything, the prior friendship between him and William Stark was an unfortunate coincidence as it related to my imminent contract with Nalani.

Did I enjoy the knowledge that he was suffering a major

loss at my hands, essentially doling out the fatal blow my father had been too upstanding to deliver?

Of course I was.

Was it the *only* — or even the primary—reason I'd taken this course?

No.

"Nalani's worth to me has very little to do with her father," I said, choosing my words carefully. "The wedding will be just after the New Year, in Sugar Valley."

Immediately, Grandma Calli's face lit up, and she leaned in a bit, eyes wide and excited. "Like your Mama and Daddy?"

"Exactly." I nodded. "I thought it would be a good way to honor their memories."

Really though… it was kinda tricky.

On one hand, I questioned how much of an *honor* it could be, considering the utter lack of a "relationship" between Nalani and I. Frankly, I wondered a bit if it was *disrespecting* the real, undeniable love connection between them to follow the footsteps they'd taken to cement *their* bond to seal the deal on what was nothing but a contract.

It ate at me more than most things did.

But it would make my Calli happy and that was the driving factor for a lot of my decisions as of late. And the last of whatever romantic ideals Jess hadn't managed to stomp out of me wondered if continuing a tradition around weddings in Sugar Valley for the Sterling family might actually… plant a seed of the same kind of marital success my parents had found.

Well… maybe not the same, considering the way it ended.

But what they'd had until the untimely end was something to admire.

"You must've knocked the bitch up or something?"

Immediate heat flooded my chest, and I turned to Bree with such ire she sank back in her seat a bit. "First of all, don't *ever* refer to my wife in that manner. Second of all—" I looked to Grandma Calli, shaking my head to dispel the notion that had made her face light up even further. "No, she's not pregnant. *I'm* not that fucking irresponsible. Why would you even go there?" I asked Bree, who shrugged.

"It's the only reason I could see for rushing to marry someone you barely know versus someone whose been around for years."

"Like *Jess*, right?" Ares said and instant discomfort replaced the indignation on Bree's face.

"Well, yes. Of course I'm referring to Jessica."

"*Of course.*" Ares scoffed.

Across the table, I gave him a look that sent his attention back to his plate.

"Can we stop bringing Jessica up?" I asked. "She doesn't have anything to do with anything, so I'm not sure why we're talking about her."

"She was damn near part of the family, Ri," Titan said, with his usual mischievous smirk. "We can't miss our almost sist—"

"What the fuck did I *just* say?"

"Some bullshit."

"*Excuse me*," Ms. Wallace barked, from the kitchen doorway. "Last I checked, this was Calliope's house, and what *she* said was, she didn't want that language at her table."

A chorus of *sorry* and *my bad* went up around the table, catering to the two older women's sensibilities. Ms. Wallace had been with the family long enough that she was basically an extension of Grandma Calli. They were best friends and had been for years and years.

Everybody listened when they spoke.

The conversation shifted to whatever my brothers had going on, prompted by Grandma Calli deciding to take the heat off me and putting it on Titan to ask about his weekend in trouble.

Yet another thing that pissed me off.

He was too old—and too recognizable—to still be getting into the kind of trouble he did. Titan was using his early thirties as a repeat of his twenties, doing dumb shit that annoyed me to no end.

But… there *was* some usefulness to that though.

Once we'd said goodnight to Grandma Calli, and lost Bree somewhere in the house, I was able to pull my brothers aside, to my father's study.

"What do y'all know about this *EJ* nigga, mid-level banger, runs a couple streets in Blackwood…"

Ares shrugged. "I've heard of him, don't know much. Not really my area, you know?"

I nodded.

We all kept our hands fairly clean, but Ares, out of the three of us, was downright squeaky where the things a dude like EJ would be concerned with.

We both looked at Titan.

"You want him shut out?" he asked. "All it takes is a phone call."

"Nah." I shook my head. "I can't have anything blowing back on Nala. Just… keep an eye on him."

Titan smirked. "So you're asking *me* for favors now?"

"I'm asking you to pull your weight, baby brother," I responded. "He might become a problem."

"Why would he become a problem?"

I sighed, letting out a deep huff before I gave a quick explanation of his connection to Nalani.

"Damn, you haven't even hit yet and she's already got you tight?" Titan laughed. "I thought this thing with her was supposed to be cut and dry."

"*Clearly* it's not though, is it?" I snapped. "Just... do what I said."

"Yes, *dad*," was Titan's dry response as he dismissed himself from the office. Ares looked at me, shaking his head.

"What?" I asked.

"You can't keep treating him like he's..."

"Our baby brother?" I filled in and Ares chuckled.

"Nah, like he's a lackey or something," he said. "He does some dumb shit, yeah, but Titan is solid. Give him some credit."

My eyebrows went up. "You really think so?"

"I do," he said. "I know you've been absorbed in your own shit, but... maybe pay a bit more attention to the big picture."

I... didn't know what the fuck that really meant and didn't ask.

Ares was asking for focus I didn't have.

I already had a million things happening in my head, balancing more fragile blocks than I probably should at one time.

Soon though, things would calm down.

I hoped.

In the meantime, I could handle the stress.

I always did.

I left the family house to go back to the quiet and privacy

of my own, ready to immerse myself in my nightly wind-down.

Or so I thought.

Just that quickly, I'd forgotten about the semi-demand I'd placed at Nalani's feet, moving into my house. I'd been gone all day and then gone straight to the family house for our regularly scheduled dinner.

Apparently, a lot had been going on.

Shiloh was the one who'd made all the arrangements—packing, movers, all of that. I didn't want Nalani *having* to lift a finger in effort, since making it convenient would kill a lot of potential excuses or stalling.

Now that I *really* wanted the house to myself... I realized it could've waited.

Exhaustion and frustration laid heavily on me as I navigated my crowded front driveway to access the garage.

Tried to access the garage.

I knew exactly who the two cars obstructing my entry belonged to—one was Nalani's, the other Shiloh's. Before I turned mine off, I checked my phone to see if I had any correspondence from Shi that would've given me some kind of heads up on what I was walking into.

There was none.

Which killed my frustration.

Now I was full-blown pissed off, having to deal with this shit instead of being able to come home and peacefully have a drink and a good cigar. Inside, I found the movers on their asses instead of... *moving*. Leaving ass marks on my exotic leather furniture.

By the time I made it to the door of the room I'd told Shiloh to put Nalani in, I was fuming, ready to lay into the first person who said the wrong thing. I didn't even bother knocking. I heard feminine voices going back and forth, so I simply flung the door open and stepped in.

Nalani and Shiloh looked up, then at each other, and both broke out laughing.

"What the *fuck* is so damn funny?" I growled, crossing my arms.

"*You*," Nalani said, accompanying the words with a head shake and rolled eyes. "It's so predictable that you'd storm in here mad about what *you* put in motion."

My lips parted to counter her accusation, but nothing came out for a moment, until I tamped down my irritation enough to grit out, "I can't even get my goddamn car in my own garage."

"No worries, *boss man*." Shiloh grinned, approaching me with her hand out. "Give me your keys, and I'll do it. The rest of us are all headed out anyway. We're done."

I glared at her for a moment before fishing the key ring from my pocket to drop into her open palm. "Don't scratch my shit."

"Uh, what got up your ass?" she asked, face pulled into a frown. "Besides the obvious…"

"Shi, I'm *really* not in the mood."

She sucked her teeth. "Fine, grouchy. Goodnight, Nala. You have my number, let me know if you need anything."

"Definitely. Thanks, Shi," my fiancée said, giving my assistant way more pleasant warmth than she'd *ever* given me, even with my fingers knuckle deep in her pussy.

Once Shi had left—to send the movers on their way and put my car where it was *supposed* to be—Nalani looked at me, all the missing disdain back on her face.

"Can I help you with something?" she asked. "Otherwise… you can go."

I frowned. "This is *my* house."

"*Our* house," she responded, propping hands on her hips. "*My* room. *My* space. And if that's going to be a problem, I can go catch Shiloh right now, and we can take my shit right back where it was."

I scoffed. "I don't have time for this."

"No time for the nonsense *you* started?" she asked. "The energy here was great until *you* came in acting stank, so…"

"Whatever." I shook my head. "The chef comes by to do breakfast at five. You either need to leave a note with your request or be there to make your requests," I said, already moving to the door—not the one I used to come in, the one between rooms, connecting hers to mine.

To make a point.

"I wake up with music, at four-thirty sharp," I told her, earning another eye roll. "Don't fuck up my routine."

"I thought I'd seen the depths of exactly how insufferable you are," she said, shaking her head. "Clearly I was wrong."

I chuckled, pushing the door open. "I look forward to us getting to know each other."

NINE
NALANI

My alarm went off at four a.m., and I sat up immediately, with a mission in mind.

Shi—who was way too pleasant to be right-hand-woman for a man like Orion—had shown me everything about the room that would be mine for the foreseeable future, so I knew exactly what to do.

I'd slept beautifully on the luxury mattress and sumptuous sheets, so there was no lethargy clouding my movements as I gathered things for a shower, chose my clothes for the day, and then connected my phone to the Bluetooth speaker in the room.

A private smile crept across my face as I navigated to my "Wrong Bitch" playlist and started it up, cranking the volume to an obscene level.

It was four-fifteen.

Perfect.

The same speakers were connected to the bathroom, so my "you got me all the way fucked up" tunes were loud and clear as I stripped down to get in the shower. Moments later, I was enveloped in the embrace of what Shi had referred to as a *sauna shower*, rapping or singing at the top of my lungs to match every word.

It was *great*.

But I wasn't surprised, not even in the slightest, when my music abruptly shut off.

A new grin spread across my face as I tried to finish up my shower, but I heard the bathroom door thrust open while I was still mid-rinse.

"*Why are you fucking with me?*"

Oh.

I knew Orion wouldn't be able to avoid such an aggressive summons, but what I hadn't accounted for was the sleep-imposed rasp and depth of his voice at this time of morning.

My traitorous nipples offered an immediate response, but my mouth offered nothing. I finished rinsing the soap from my body, then shut the shower off.

Before I could reach for it, the glass shower door swung open, letting out enough steam to give a bit of visibility in the cloudy room.

Orion was *definitely* pissed off.

It was all knit into his deep scowl, furrowed brows, arms crossed over his bare chest.

Internally, my confidence faltered. I was nobody's definition of small and his body still easily dwarfed mine. I was in *his* house, no matter how indignantly I insisted otherwise. I was naked and wet. And really, any certainty I had that he wouldn't resort to actual violence against me was more of a *hope* than anything.

I was entirely too vulnerable to keep poking at him.

But much too stubborn not to.

"Good morning, Orion. Can I help you with something?" I asked, coyly crossing an arm over my bare breasts.

"You're not funny, Nala."

"What makes you think I'm trying to be?" This time, I didn't hold back the smirk, held his gaze with it while I stepped out of the shower, despite him not leaving much room to get around him.

I just stood toe to toe with him, not backing down from his glare.

"Keep your fucking... 'girl power' music to yourself moving forward. I don't want to hear that shit."

I shrugged. "That's perfectly fine, as long you keep the 'toxicity as a defense mechanism for your fucking mommy issues' music to *yourself*. I don't want to hear *that* shit."

He pushed out a harsh breath through his nose, then took a step back, shaking his head. Without looking back, he walked off, mumbling something *just* beneath a volume that would indicate he wanted to be heard.

"Of *course* you can't even talk shit with your whole chest," I said to his back, then headed for the mirror to flip the switch that would clear the layer of steam from it. "*Ahh!*" I screamed, clutching a hand to my chest when Orion's face appeared in the reflection, just inches from mine.

He was right behind me.

"That fucking mouth of yours," he warned, leaning over me to plant his hands on the counter, boxing me in. His gaze locked mine in the mirror as he pushed against me. "Is going to get you in trouble."

"People have said that to me all my life, and yet... here I am. *Unchecked thus far.*"

He grinned, then shifted so he was looking at me, and all I saw in the mirror was his profile as he dipped his face to the side of my head, speaking into my ear. "Give me time, Nala, we just met."

He wasn't expecting me to push back against him. His hand immediately went to my waist, holding me there like he thought I was falling. His dick was hard and prominent, enough to give me much-needed ammo I wasn't even looking for.

I was just trying to get him to back off.

"Why don't you just go ahead fuck me?" I asked, turning to face him. Before he could answer, my hand was between us, gripping him through his boxers.

He bit down on his lip, a move I immediately clocked as his way to avoid giving me an audible reaction to what was so clearly written on his face as he looked down at me. My chest was heaving, heart racing as he pushed against me again, forcing me to back up into the cold stone counter.

"I would, if I hadn't decided to no longer fuck women who weren't my wife." He grabbed my left hand, lacing his fingers through it before lifting both in front him.

Fuck.

I had his goddamn ring on.

The grin that crossed his face was equal parts maddening and arousing and I had to believe he knew it.

Of course he knew.

"Soon enough," he said, kissing the back of my hand before he dropped it. "I thought I told you that already."

"This is the reason for the quickie wedding, isn't it?" I asked, grasping for any possible blow. "You've already had your fingers in my pussy, so what's the damn difference, huh? Premarital sex is kinda the standard now, you know?"

"*Standard* is not my go-to," he replied. "And besides that, getting to fuck you has always just been a bonus in this arrangement. I'm marrying you sooner to protect y—my assets."

I raised an eyebrow at his quick attempt at correction, shaking my head. "No, you were about to say it was to protect *me*. Protect me from what?"

"If you just opened your eyes, you wouldn't need me to answer that question for you."

"My eyes are wide open."

He scoffed. "So you know your father is trying to sell *Nectar* before you get him off the executive board, then?"

My mouth dropped.

What?

"Not the building, or the land, 'cause he already did that part. That's why you're in the position you're in now," Orion said, stepping back.

Thank God, 'cause I couldn't breathe.

"The actual *business*," I managed to choke out, staring down at my hands.

They were shaking.

"I can make sure it doesn't happen. If I say it's untouchable, it'll be untouchable," he said. "But it's a move that will raise eyebrows I don't want raised… unless it's a move I'm making for my *wife*."

I didn't have shit else to say.

I was done with the back and forth, at least for now.

I just nodded, and he must've gotten the hint, because he walked away. But just before he left, he stopped in the doorway to the bathroom.

"Don't forget, your dress appointment is at ten."

———

Tears didn't come easily for me.

Not that I *didn't* cry. I certainly did, usually out of mixed emotions.

The recipe always included rage.

What I hated was knowing I'd feel *so* much better if I just let it all out, just let the damn tears fall, instead of keeping the emotions boxed up inside. I hated when I wanted to cry, but just… *couldn't*.

Like now.

It had already been an emotional morning, with anger edging out shock as I put out the appropriate feelers to find out exactly what my father had been up to. Instead of using my morning to *work*, as planned, I was busy unraveling this web of… *duplicity* … that was outright foolish.

I had to come to the conclusion that he simply didn't care if he got found out, which led me to believe he wasn't actually trying to sell.

Or rather, that *selling* wasn't what mattered.

The cruelty was the point.

Instead of causing any confrontation, I just called my brother and had him decommission William Stark's access badge.

He was no longer welcome in the building.

Now, whether or not that would keep him out… chances were right about fifty-fifty.

But it would cause him enough hassle to send a clear message.

For shits and giggles, I had him decommission Alan's too.

Not just access to the building, but access to our online systems and the bank accounts. I could probably get in trouble for it, since this was every bit of *unofficial*, but at this point… I didn't give a fuck anymore.

Sue me.

I had a billion dollars behind me to buy my way out of misbehavior now.

Zero regrets.

And yet, the nagging urge to cry about it all remained, undoubtedly bolstered by the fact that I was sitting alone in a private waiting area at Freeman's Bridal, waiting for my personal sales associate to come back.

I'd already knocked back one glass of the complimentary champagne and was eyeing another. I hadn't looked at a single dress yet and it was already feeling like something I'd need to be half-drunk to get through.

Especially alone.

I closed my eyes, letting out what I intended to be a deep, cleansing breath.

Instead, I just felt even more frustrated.

It wasn't supposed to be like this.

As much as I tried to shake the thought from my mind, it just kept playing, again and again. It wasn't supposed to be like this, and if my mother was alive, it for damn sure wouldn't be like this.

And it wasn't even about me needing to marry Orion, not anymore.

Today's sorrow was about not having my mother next to me, at what was supposed to be one of the most beautiful moments in my life.

The wedding preparations, choosing a dress, the day itself. Announcing pregnancies, giving birth… getting to see her hold her grandbabies.

All those should-be incredible high points … out of reach for me.

Snatched from my grasp way too soon.

"Ms. Stark?"

I looked up from my hands to see the smiling sales associate standing in the doorway. "Yes?"

"If you'll follow me, we have your fitting suite ready for you."

Fitting suite?

Fancy.

"Thank you," I said, pushing up from my seat so she could lead me through the expansive store. Needing to get away from *Nectar*, I'd arrived for my appointment about fifteen minutes early, so I wasn't taken aback about them not quite being ready for me yet. I answered a few questions about my style and measurements so they could pull a few preliminary options for me, then sat and patiently waited for my *actual* appointment time.

As soon as I crossed the threshold for my *fitting suite,* the short wait made even more sense.

The tears I hadn't been able to gather welled up in my eyes as soon as I saw the trio of smiling women waiting for me. I hadn't talked to Morgan, Alexis, *or* my Aunt Lucy about this appointment, thinking it was better to get it over with sans fanfare with the absence of my mother being *so* acute.

But seeing them... I'd never felt such relief before.

"I'll leave you all for a moment while I go grab a few dresses I think you'll like," the sales associate said as they stood to greet me. "And then we can get started."

"What are y'all doing here?" I breathed as soon as she was gone, trying valiantly to keep myself from breaking into sobs. The actual tears were already front and center.

"Orion's assistant called and let us know," Alexis answered, dabbing my face with a tissue she snagged from a box on a nearby side table. "She knew you shouldn't do this alone, but that you probably wouldn't say anything."

I shook my head, accepting hugs from each one of them, the tightest coming from my auntie.

"A wedding *this fast*, baby girl?" she said, keeping her arms around me as she met my gaze. "Does this man have you knocked up?"

"*No*." I laughed, shaking my head as I accepted another tissue, this time from Morgan. "This is his doing. Ceremony in Sugar Valley."

"Oh, we know," Morgan chimed. "Ol' girl filled us in on all the details, arranged transportation and all. Asked us if we wanted to go by *helicopter*."

I rolled my eyes. "Of course they did."

"At least they offered *something*," Aunt Lucy scolded as she finally let me go. "Were you just gonna run off to Sugar Valley to get married and then go on a honeymoon and not say anything?"

"*No*," I denied. "I was going to say something!"

"In time for us to be there for you?" Alexis asked and… I couldn't answer.

"Exactly as I thought, *trash*." Morgan laughed. "But we aren't about to make this little shut down you're trying to pull easy on you. Hoe you're stuck with us. Sorry, Ms. Lucy," she immediately added, seeing my auntie's face. "But Nala knows what's up."

"I do," I confirmed. "And I… I appreciate y'all. More than you know," I said, trying to choke back another wave of emotion.

I failed.

But by the time the sales associate was back with the first dresses for me to try on, I'd managed to pull myself together.

Which was good because we all hated the first few options, several of which I didn't even leave the dressing room to show my little crew. With some feedback, she was able to pull a whole other round of dresses, some of which were better than others.

None of which felt right.

I was right on the verge of chalking it all up to not really being invested in the wedding in the first place when the sales associate asked a question that staggered me a little.

"Would you like to see Mr. Sterling's picks for you?"

All four of us went quiet, stunned by the question. Not the fact that she'd asked, but the fact that he'd made "picks." Honestly, I would have expected those to be the only options I was even shown. But then, when an awkward moment had passed without an answer, she further explained.

"I was instructed not to offer them to you unless you weren't seeing anything that worked for you."

With that additional information, Morgan was the first to speak up.

"Oh yes ma'am, we *need* to see those."

I rolled my eyes, but nodded my affirmation when the sales associate looked to me for approval. "Exactly how naked are we thinking these dresses are going to be?" I asked, re-belting the robe around my waist. "And do we think it's going to be dripping in crystals, so everyone knows how rich he is?"

Alexis laughed. "I'm thinking diamonds, maybe."

"I think it's going to be lace," Aunt Lucy spoke up. "His parents got married in Sugar Valley. I remember the pictures in all the society pages. His mother's dress was a beautiful lace gown, with these sleeves that came over her hands, and that *veil*, edged in all that intricate beading," she gushed, clearly bringing the visual to her mind. "If he decided the wedding venue would be the same as his parents, it wouldn't surprise me if he wanted the bride to look like his mother."

My eyes went wide. "I will jump off the roof of *Nectar* before I play into some sick Oedipus fantasy, oh my *God*," I fussed, worried that she would be right.

That concern was quickly dispelled when the sales associate pulled me back to the dressing room, with three options on display.

They were all… *gorgeous.*

Nothing like what I would've thought to choose for myself, but exquisite all the same – almost scarily so.

There was a classic organza ball gown, a mermaid style with a feathered tulle skirt, and a draped illusion net gown – no beading, lace, crystals or diamonds in sight. I did my best to truly consider each one, but my mind was made up at first glance, honestly.

My little crew collectively gasped when I stepped out in the mermaid gown.

It was unquestionably stunning on the hanger, but even more so on me. I hadn't realized the bodice was made in a way that my deep brown skin would—tastefully—show through, with all the scandalous parts fully covered.

"*That's* the one," Aunt Lucy spoke. A conclusion I'd already come to, but was underlined by the emotion in her voice and tears in her eyes. "Your mother would be a *mess* if she could see you right now."

Immediately, I shook my head. "Don't… don't do that," I pleaded. "I'm trying to keep it together, and if you start, I'm gonna start, and we'll all just be a mess."

"Well go ahead and take the damn dress off so it doesn't get ruined, 'cause I'ma cry." Morgan laughed. True to her word, there were already tears streaking down her cheeks as she lifted her phone to snap pictures.

The sales associate quickly took over, getting snapshots of us all together, toasting, all the customary *found the dress* celebrations.

I hated to admit it, but… it was great.

I *did* take the dress off, and we *did* all cry, like fucking babies.

By the time I made it back to *Nectar*, I was in much better spirits than when I left. I was barely even fazed by the full inbox of store drama waiting for me.

I was ready for whatever came my way.

TEN
ORION

I didn't like doing things fast.

Spur of the moment or last minute—either way made me itch with annoyance that was impossible to scratch.

Thank God for Shi.

Unlike me, she seemed to thrive in situations like the one I'd put her in; another chance to prove exactly why I paid her as I did.

And why there would be a deep orange box gift wrapped and waiting for her at the completion of this.

She knew how to light a fire under people to get them to perform, without being offensive. I didn't have that particular gift, which was why I had *her* handling it.

When I stepped off the helipad in Sugar Valley, my lungs were instantly glad for the clean, crisp fresh air. I was one of the first of my group to arrive, since everyone else had felt safer on the road than in the air.

Good.

It gave me some quiet time.

Someone from the *Maple Leaf* resort, where the helipad was located, came out to greet me, offering lunch and other amenities I didn't want or need. I just needed my Jeep, which had already been brought up for me, so I could make the short drive away from the little town of Sugar Valley to my family's mountain cabin.

I wanted to be settled in and deep in hiding before all the noise began.

Despite what my attention over the last few weeks may have led her to believe, my life did not revolve around Nalani.

I was still top of the food chain in the family business and we were stepping into the plans and processes that would ensure we met our forecasting for Q1 and beyond. Frankly, this whole thing—a wedding and all its accoutrements—was a distraction I didn't need right now.

Some opportunities were just too big to pass up though.

Locked in the master bedroom at the two-story mountain cabin, I buried myself in work calls and returning emails, up to the moment I couldn't put off getting myself together for dinner any longer. Clothes were already settled, so I made the shower quick, got dressed, and finally emerged from my cave.

Nalani was the first thing my eyes landed on.

She was perched at the seating area that overlooked the staircase, into the main entry, talking with Shiloh in low tones. Neither of them noticed my presence at first, which gave me an opportunity to simply observe.

All bullshit aside, Nalani was outright beautiful, and that plentiful, curvy body of hers was well suited by a winter wardrobe. Heeled, thigh-high boots clung to her thick legs, stopping just before the hem of an emerald-toned, oversized sweater. Just that tiny sliver of skin was enticing as fuck, taking my mind on a straightforward journey of what was underneath.

A thought I quickly shook away. There would be time for that later.

I approached the two women; my footsteps across the polished wood floors pulled both of their attention. Nalani glanced and looked away, clearly perturbed by my presence, but Shiloh maintained eye contact with a smirk.

"Has everything been to your liking so far, Mr. Sterling?" she asked, and I chuckled.

Only she and I knew she was fucking with me.

"Almost," I told her. "Her hair," I said, gesturing at Nalani, who had her back turned now, looking at the two-story window view from the balcony. "I want it natural for the wedding."

"I *just* spent the morning at the salon getting a silk press!"

Oh.

So she was paying attention after all.

I shrugged, looking between her and Shiloh, whose expression was a bit stricken as well.

Clearly I'd hit a nerve.

"We'll make sure the expense is reimbursed," I said, not waiting for a response before I headed for the stairs. "Come on. I don't want us late for dinner."

She wasn't that close behind me, but I could *feel* the hot rage emanating from Nalani as we descended the stairs.

I stopped abruptly, turning to face her before she could fix the anger in her expression.

Or maybe she didn't care to fix it.

"Is there a problem?" I asked her.

She let out a dry laugh, her hair swinging quite beautifully across her shoulders as she shook her head. "Not at all," she gritted out. "As a matter of fact, *thank you* for reminding me that you are indeed an asshole."

With that, she walked past me, a blur of intoxicating perfume, silky hair, hypnotic ass, and anger.

I took a deep breath before I followed.

I could not *wait* to fuck the shit out of her.

―――

"Have you been to Sugar Valley before?" I asked, eyes on the road as I broke the silence between us.

It wasn't necessarily awkward, but I couldn't classify it as comfortable either. For any other couple, it would probably be a little alarming to ride fifteen minutes in complete silence with someone you were marrying the next day.

But we weren't "any other couple"… or a couple at all, technically, just two people with a reciprocally advantageous deal.

This was business.

Still, for whatever reason, I couldn't make myself let the silence stand. For a moment, I thought Nalani was going to ignore me, which wouldn't have been surprising considering how angry the hair thing had made her.

Could I have conceded on that?

Of course.

Her hair looked great the way it was, and I was sure tomorrow's stylist would have made sure she presented a perfect bridal picture.

A vision that was likely already planned, for her to have spent precious time having it done today.

The truth was though, in that magazine spread where I

first laid eyes on her, her hair had been in its natural, curly state, and that shit was sexy.

I wanted to bury my fingers in those coils, gripping them by the handfuls while I was balls deep inside her for our wedding night.

Candidly.

And since I was footing the bill for all this shit… why the fuck would I settle for anything else?

"Not since I was a child," she finally said. "We used to come every summer, as a family."

"Why haven't you been back?" I asked. "I would think the winery being reopened would be right up your alley."

"It would be, if this place didn't remind me so intensely of my mother."

Oh.

I glanced at her as she shook her head, like she was clearing some unpleasant thought away. She was staring out the window, into the dark, so I couldn't really see her face.

"Besides," she spoke again. "I'm not really a *great outdoors* kind of bitch, so the only thing here that would appeal to me would be the drinking. And I can do that in Blackwood."

Even though she couldn't see me, I nodded. "That's understandable. Beautiful scenery though. I'm assuming you arrived before dark, got a chance to see it?"

"Yep," she said. "It was insisted upon, actually." My eyes were back on the road, but I felt the shift as she turned to look at me. "Supposedly so I could get settled in."

That had to have been Shiloh's doing, I mused to myself, but didn't say aloud. *My* only concern was that she was present and accounted for at my side when I wanted her there. She could've arrived ten minutes ago for all I cared.

Shi was the one who hadn't left it up to chance.

I turned onto the long road toward the winery, but skipped the turn that would take me to that building. Our destination instead was the house up on the hill that provided a home for the winery's latest owners, who'd done me a personal favor by accommodating this wedding.

Up here in the mountains, the snow was no joke, and the weather could change quickly. It had been clear and beautiful earlier, on the way in, but now the landscape was being blanketed in the fluffy white powder. Not enough to make getting around a problem, but enough that I was glad Nalani didn't snatch away from my offered hand once we'd parked. She let me help her down, avoiding a slip and fall that would have put quite a damper on the festivities for tomorrow.

She revoked that hand as soon as we were at the door, though.

We didn't have to wait long after ringing the bell. Moments later, the front door swung open, sending a comforting rush of warmth and the aroma of dinner.

"Riii, how are you darling?" our host for the evening asked, throwing her arms around me for a hug.

"Eva James, it's been too damn long." I chuckled, returning her warm greeting as I stepped inside, then pulled Nalani with me. "This is my fiancée, Nalani Stark. Nalani, this is—"

"Evangeline James," she spoke over me, extending a hand. "My sales rep handles your account, so I don't think we've formally met, but I'm a huge fan."

"Of the winery?" Eva asked, clasping the hand Nalani offered.

She shook her head. "No. Of you taking half in your

divorce from Leon James. Honey Branch wine is absolutely lovely too though."

Eva's eyes just went big at first, but then a huge grin spread over her face. "Orion... I *love* her." She laughed, discarding Nalani's hand to pull her in for a hug instead. Ignoring me, she helped Nalani out of her coat and then hooked an arm around her waist, leading her toward the dining room. "Tell me you've already got the pre-nup in place, right?"

My mouth dropped open as those two moved on, but I recovered as Eva's *new* partner, Luke, approached.

"How you doing, man?" he asked, and I shook his hand as I took in my surroundings. "Been a while."

"Yeah, it has," I agreed. "I was sorry to hear about your grandmother."

His grandfather had been the most recent passing, but I knew without it being said aloud that there was no love lost *there.* That motherfucker had been mean as shit when my grandmother was coming to visit Georgia Freeman—the original owner of Honey Branch, no relation to the Freemans known for the bridal shop—at the vineyard and was dragging us out here with her.

I couldn't imagine age had softened him, at all.

"Thank you." Luke nodded. "I remember the flowers your family sent," he said, gesturing for me to follow him to the dining room, where the women were already seated and had cracked open a bottle of wine.

I wasn't surprised they were hitting it off.

Eva was a big personality and the one I knew better of the couple. I was familiar with Luke from back in the day, but I knew Eva before she'd come to Sugar Valley.

I was friends with the man Nalani had congratulated Eva on getting a rumored half-billion dollars from in the divorce.

Not that she'd had to fight very hard for it.

Leon loved Eva down to her toes. Honestly, it was a relationship that on the surface, I'd admired. He lost me on his "open marriage" antics, which my father would've been disgusted by, and as it turned out, was how he ended up losing Eva, too.

But their friendship had remained, so *our* friendship had remained. I'd be lying to myself if I tried to claim her approval didn't mean anything to me. She wasn't privy to the arrangement behind it all, but she'd been deeply immersed enough in moneyed circles that she likely suspected this wasn't purely a love connection.

"Sit down," she insisted, when she saw us in the doorway. "Let's eat. This food didn't fix itself."

I took another deep inhale, trying to pinpoint what I was smelling from the covered dishes at the center of the table. "You cooked?" I asked and she and Luke both started laughing.

"You know damn well this woman doesn't cook," Luke said. "I was the chef today."

"And you looked quite sexy in that role, babe," Eva purred, offering her lips as he bent next to her.

Something made me glance at Nalani just in time to catch the wistful look on her face as she watched their affectionate display. Her chest rose and fell in a soft, inaudible sigh before she looked away.

"Thank you again for opening the winery space to us on such short notice," I said as everybody took their seats, and began passing the dishes of food around. "It's appreciated."

"It's not a problem; it's my pleasure, actually," Eva said.

"I've been wanting to see what we could do with a winter wedding, so it gave me an opportunity. That Shiloh you've got on your team? I might have to poach her from you."

I chuckled. "She's an expensive pain in my ass, but she does get things done, doesn't she?"

"Mmmhmm. Especially pulling together a wedding to... what?" she asked, looking between me and Nalani. "Get inheritance money? Secure a business deal? Hide a baby?"

Nalani's eyes went wide, but she didn't say anything, focusing a little too hard on moving food around on her plate.

"Why does it have to be something like that?" I asked.

Eva smirked as she met my gaze. "Because *I know* how you operate. And it's convenient, right? Nalani is HBIC at *Nectar*, you're HNIC at *Wholesome Foods*. It makes too much sense for a little mutually assured success to *not* be at play," she said. "Listen, I'm not judging. I understand the game. Luke is only hanging around to make sure I don't ruin his grandmother's winery."

"What?" Luke asked, choking on a mouthful of food as Eva laughed.

"I'm just playing with you baby. I know you're here for the pussy."

Luke gave her the "stop fucking around" look, even though we all knew she wouldn't, and nobody expected her to, really. She was a well-known "say whatever was on her mind" kind of woman, so it made no sense to get upset over it.

Which, he didn't, 'cause he knew what he was in for.

As did I, with Nalani.

Somehow, we got out of dinner without answering the question Eva had levied, which could be considered an answer, but one that was unnecessary. As she'd said... she knew the game.

At this level, *love* wasn't always a primary reason a couple decided on marriage. Hell, it might not even rank top five. Sometimes you had to make a decision that was just… *smart*. Purely strategic.

And that had to be okay.

"Can you drop me off at the lodge?" Nalani asked after we'd loaded up again, as we came to the stop sign at the end of the Honey Branch driveway. "It's barely out of the way, just right up the street."

I raised an eyebrow at her. "Drop you off? This late?" I asked, glancing at the clock display.

"It's not *that* late," she argued. "And the bride typically spends the night before the wedding with her friends. Is that a problem for you?"

"It's not a problem, I just didn't know."

"Okay, well… now you do."

My jaw clenched as I considered my options.

I *could* drop her off to stay with her friends who were at Maple Leaf Lodge after driving up for the wedding.

Or…I could simply drive back to the cabin, purely to piss her off.

Decisions, decisions.

She was sitting over there stewing, staring a hole in the side of my head as she kept a lid on whatever diatribe she was going to hurl at me if she didn't get her way.

Part of me wanted to make the right turn just so I could hear it.

Decency prevailed, though.

I made the left turn, taking her to the lodge as requested, and I even helped her up to the door.

"You're sure they're in there?" I asked before I walked

away, and she rolled her eyes, holding her phone up in front of us.

"Yeah, I just confirmed."

"Okay," I nodded, taking a step back. "Don't do anything crazy."

She looked me right in the face, her expression and voice both deadpan as she snapped her fingers. "Damn. There goes my plan to sneak into the back of somebody's car and get whisked away. Or maybe one last hoorah with a handsome local. Oh, or a tourist even."

"Cute." I chuckled, starting back to the vehicle. "But just so we're clear…"

"What?" she called when I didn't finish the statement.

I took a deep breath, turning back to look her right in the face. "Do not make me come looking for you."

ELEVEN
NALANI

I understand the game.

That's all this was to them.

A damn game.

I honestly liked Eva, not just because she'd left her marriage with obscene money, or even what she'd turned Honey Branch into, which was admirable.

She was just *likeable*.

But the truth of the matter was, she was very much part of a class of people so stupidly rich that the rules the rest of us governed ourselves by only *barely* applied to them.

If at all.

And technically... I would soon be a part of it.

Which I wasn't sure how to feel about.

I understand the game.

I couldn't get that shit off my mind, even once I was three drinks deep with my homegirls.

"Naaaala," Morgan urged. "I know this isn't exactly everything you dreamed the night before your wedding would be, but...damn, bitch. Perk up. You've got us up here now, and we're in it, we're celebrating. The least you can do is look on the bright side. Where did you say you guys were honeymooning again?"

"Some private resort off the Pacific coast," I answered. "But did you hear what those guys in the booth behind us were talking about earlier? They said it was looking like blizzard conditions were possible tomorrow, so who's to say I could get out of here even if I wanted to? What if you guys aren't able to get home?"

"It's a mountain, sis," Alexis assured. "They get heaps and heaps of snow every year and I am quite sure they know how to handle a snow plow or something. And if we *are* stuck up here... they've got good food and liquor and these cabins are quite cozy."

"Until the food runs out and we have to consider cannibalism."

"Stop." Alexis laughed. "Either way, I'm with Morgan. You're about to marry a fucking billionaire. A fine, generous one."

"That generosity is limited solely to what makes him look good," I reminded her. "Don't let this little all-expenses-paid getaway fool you. He's an asshole. You know he told me I had to wash my damn hair?"

Morgan gasped. "*Excuse me*?! Baby the press is giving finest mulberry silk, so what makes him think your hair needs washing? He thinks it looks dirty?!"

I blew out a sigh. "*Fine.* Let me not make it out to be something it wasn't. He wants my hair back natural, *after* I spent two hours this morning getting it silked out. Like damn... if you had stipulations on what my hair was supposed to look like, you couldn't have said that shit earlier? I could have been doing something else."

"Okay, I hear you, but… on the bright side," Alexis started, "Can we appreciate for a moment that this Black man loves and wants his Black woman's natural hair? Bare minimum award, sure, but… I kinda like that he wants that. He *is* reimbursing you for the visit to the salon though right?"

"He sure the hell is," I countered. "It's the least he can do for inconveniencing me. That's probably about to be the theme of the whole weekend, inconvenience Nalani. Get on her last possible nerve."

I glared at my empty cocktail glass, annoyed that it hadn't somehow filled itself.

"I don't know, y'all. I'm just…over it."

"Is it too late to not go through with it?" Morgan asked and my face curled into a frown.

"Girl, hell yeah." I laughed. "I signed the damn contract. And besides that—remember what's at stake for me. I am… going to have to do like Alexis said and get my shit together to just tough it out. Grin and bear it," I told myself, nodding. "And at least I'll look pretty doing so. Right?"

"You're gonna be downright gorgeous honey," Alexis crooned from beside me, throwing an arm around my shoulders. "Now, let's get another round and change the damn subject."

"To what?"

"Ooooh… to what Orion's dick is gonna be like."

I groaned, shaking my head as they laughed, deciding without me that Orion's penis would indeed be the topic.

"It's probably wack," I huffed.

I couldn't say it was *small* because I already knew better.

Morgan squinted across the table at me. "Not if the dick skills run in the family."

"Ooooh," Alexis gushed. "That's right, you used to bump uglies with Ares."

"Do we have to talk about that?"

I sucked my teeth. "Ma'am, *you* brought it up."

"Did I?"

"Okay, you're done." I laughed as our server approached. "No more for *her*, but one more for me."

"And me," Alexis chimed. "My first sip will be for you, babe," she told Morgan, who gave her a little salute.

"Since we're on the topic… *yes*, I used to swap bodily fluids with Ares Sterling, *fine*… Is it going to be awkward to see him tomorrow though?! Well… yes, probably. But still I rise."

"Still I… *bitch*." I laughed. "Why in the world would you say that?"

"Hell, somebody has to do some encouraging, it may as well be me!"

The conversation—and laughs, so many laughs—went on from there, our drunk asses devolving into very, very silly. Morgan and Alexis were both staying at the Maple property, but still made a point of accompanying me in the ride share to get back to the luxe modern cabin in the woods that was the Sterling property.

I was just about to knock on the door when someone opened the door for me.

"Ms. Stark," the suited man who'd let me in greeted me, before closing and locking the door, and returning to his post nearby.

Security.

There was no way they were here around the clock, right?

I shrugged it off, chalking it up to the fact that there were so many people in the house, all Sterling-related, all arriving for the wedding.

Shiloh had introduced me to a few people, all of whom had been fine, but... settling into the family was of very little interest to me. There were lights on all over the place, signaling activity I had no plans of getting involved in.

I rushed up the stairs as fast I still could carefully, heading straight for my cute little reserved suite.

Not fast enough.

My attention snagged on a woman slipping out of the same room Orion had exited before dinner. I didn't look away soon enough to not meet her gaze.

She smiled at me, slinking my way in fuzzy slippers and a soft pink loungewear outfit that was more fit for meeting your man at the door than creeping out of *my* man's room at two in the morning.

"Hiii," she gushed, extending the hand that wasn't carrying a half-empty wine glass in my direction. "I think I missed you earlier, you're Nalani, right?"

"Yes," I answered, looking at her hand before I brought my eyes back to her face. A very, *very* pretty face. "Who might you be?"

"The dirty-little-secret." She laughed, leaning toward me like we were sharing a joke. "Kidding, of course—Jessica Givens, head of marketing for *Wholesome Foods*. I'm sure you've heard my name."

"No, I haven't. And I wouldn't think... *this*... was in your job description as head of marketing," I said. "The head of human resources isn't there too, I hope?"

She let out another—obnoxious—laugh. "Oh I like you, you're funny. And quite beautiful," she added. "I can absolutely see why Ri is locking you down. You have to tell me where these bundles came from," she said, finding the *fucking audacity* from God knows where to raise her hand, swiping it through my hair.

I was too shocked that a Black woman would engage in such weirdo behavior to stop it before it happened. I was *not* too shocked to push that damn hand away from me as she tried to make her way up to my roots. I took a step back, trying to gather my composure.

I am way too fucking tipsy for this.

"Don't be stingy, sis. What are those, tape-ins?" she insisted, pushing the issue.

"I don't have any extensions, this is just my fucking hair. Why is this even a conversation?"

Her gaze flicked to the top of my head, then my face.

She didn't believe me.

But I wasn't about to prove shit.

"You don't have to get defensive," she said, still wearing that same creepy grin.

I narrowed my eyes. "I'm not getting defensive, I'm getting ready to call on Jesus because you're acting like you want to wear my damn skin."

"Jessica. I said *goodnight*."

Orion's voice behind me was lowkey comforting. At least his presence meant I wasn't witnessing this weird shit by myself.

"I'm *going*." Jessica smirked at him, biting her lip before she looked back to me. "And goodnight to you as well, Nalani."

"Who is the oddball chick?" I asked once she'd walked off. "And why is she coming out of your room?"

Instead of answering, he pulled the door open wider, gesturing for me to come inside.

Only out of curiosity did I obey that directive and the first thing I did was take a deep breath in.

It didn't *smell* like sex in here.

"I'm not doing the open marriage thing," I said, turning to face Orion.

He'd closed the door behind us, but hadn't stepped back into the main area of the room yet. "What makes you think I'm suggesting you should?"

"Your *head of marketing* coming out of your room in booty shorts the night before we get married," I explained, shaking my head. "With a glass of wine and a smug look. What *should* I assume?"

"That I'm a man of my word and I already told you; I don't fuck women I'm not married to. Did you think I was just saying that just to say it?"

"I think you say whatever you want," I answered.

"Okay, so let me make myself clear again," he said, fully stepping up to me. He was shirtless, which definitely did not help his "I am not fucking that woman" claims, but I was distracted from that by lots of deep caramel skin, and thick arms, and the fact that he smelled quite good. "I do not fuck women I am not married to. Including you."

He smirked after that statement, making me wonder if I was giving off a vibe.

Alcohol did have a tendency to put me in a certain… *mood*.

And at this point… I probably wouldn't have said no.

I shook my hair back over my shoulders, so I could look him right in the face as I asked, "Then what am I doing here in your room?"

"Come on. Let me show you."

He moved past me, to a set of big double doors that at first glance I'd assumed were windows. He pushed them open though, revealing a covered balcony space before he looked back, motioning with his head for me to follow him.

"It's snowing."

"Barely, right now."

I crossed my arms. "It's cold, and you don't have a shirt on."

He raised an eyebrow, grinning. "Are you worried about me, Ms. Stark?"

I scoffed and started moving toward the open doors. "Listen, if *you* want to end up with hypothermia the night before our wedding that's fine. Just make sure you don't try to get mad at *me* for it, okay?" I shrugged, following him out onto the cold, snowy balcony.

"Look out there." He pointed. "At the sky. I know there's a little snow still coming down, but there's barely any light pollution out here and you can see it even better than usual in the cold. If you're looking hard enough."

I looked, just as he was directing, but couldn't figure out what the fuck he was talking about. A question about if he'd been drinking too was right on the tip of my tongue, but then it hit me, very suddenly, a moment later.

The stars.

He was talking about the stars.

And he was right.

Even with the occasional fat flakes of snow cascading down, far up in the sky was inky dark. The stars glittered like jewels against the midnight blue and I shivered a little as Orion moved to stand behind me.

I didn't know what was going on.

But, I didn't fight him as he positioned his hands at the back of my head, guiding me to look where he wanted. Once I was looking in the right place, he reached past me, using a thick finger to make an outline, bringing my attention to specific stars.

"That right there," he said. "That's my father's constellation. *Leo Caspian.* The constellation is Leo, but he went by Caspian."

I didn't say anything. I just listened, cooperating as he moved me around, pointing things out.

"Over there, that's my grandmother. *Calliope Columba.* The constellation is *Columba.*"

He pulled me further out onto the balcony, from underneath the sheltered roof to steer me to a different place. "There are my brothers. Ares, or *Aries.* And Titan *Cetus.* The constellation is *Cetus.*"

"So... is that a thing for the whole family?" I asked. "Everyone has a constellation in their name?"

He nodded. "First or middle. And when we need to, we'll repeat."

"How long will that take?"

"Well... there are eighty-eight officially recognized constellations. Some of the names are a little wilder than others, so nobody chooses them. So... maybe not that long."

"Interesting. Where's yours?"

"Right over here," he said, tightening an arm around my waist as I stumbled a little in my heeled boots. His mouth was right against my ear. "*That* is mine."

This...could have been romantic.

Would have been romantic, if that kind of connection existed between us.

Instead I just felt... uncomfortably comfortable with his

arms around me, a realization I quickly chalked up to the liquor I'd consumed earlier in the night.

I stepped away, breaking the contact between us before I turned to face him. "That is…pretty cool," I admitted, nodding. "A little strange to need to show me at two in the morning."

"I would've shown you earlier, but you were out with your friends."

I raised an eyebrow. "So you were waiting up for me, all this time?"

"All of it? No," he said, pushing his hands into the pockets of the pajama pants he was wearing. "I had things to keep me occupied."

"Like Jessica?"

He chuckled at me, then turned to walk inside. "If I didn't know better, I'd think what you were showing me right now was jealousy."

"I'm glad you know better then," I chimed, following right behind him. The heat inside the room instantly gave me that *unthawing* feeling I ignored in favor of setting him straight. "I'm just making sure you plan to uphold the terms we negotiated. A *key* one of which was, *do not fucking embarrass me.*"

He crossed his arms. "Did something embarrassing happen?"

"Not yet, but I see the potential for it," I answered, choosing to speak plainly instead of trying to swallow my feelings. "I didn't like the vibe of whatever that was."

"All that was, was my head of marketing congratulating me on our pending nuptials. Forgive any awkwardness on her end, please. She'd had a little too much to drink."

My eyes narrowed, and I propped my hands on my hips.

"Stop treating me like I'm an idiot," I demanded. "What is she to you? Or… what was she, previously?"

He blew out through his nose. "Fiancée."

"There it is,.." I smiled. "Thank you, for your honesty. Now… care to tell me why it seemed like a good idea for your former fiancée to be spending the night in the same house with us right now?"

"Because she is a family friend still and because she is indeed my head of marketing. And she's invited to the wedding. There are a lot of c-suite people from *Wholesome Foods* staying in the house for the wedding."

"How many of them have you fucked?"

"Just her."

"Just her. So… the rule about not sleeping with women you aren't married to, that was… after her?"

"It was several women after her," he answered. "You finished interrogating me?"

"For now."

"*Forever*," he countered, moving to his door. "Unless you want to talk to me about EJ?"

Nope.

That was a great way to get me to leave.

He opened the door to usher me out, even though that was already my plan anyway. I was barely over the threshold when he grabbed me by the arm, pulling me close.

"Get some sleep, *my love*," he told me. "You're gonna need it."

TWELVE
ORION

Where the hell is Calli?

    I'd been peeking out into the small crowd at regular intervals, waiting for my grandmother to take her place of honor up front. Because we didn't want a big ordeal, there was no bride's side or groom's side—just the first two aisles of seating, side by side, reserved for treasured friends and family members.

    Nalani's Aunt Lucinda was there, as well as her lawyer, Demetria Byers. There was space for her father and brother, but I'd be shocked if the former showed his face today. I had no doubt Soren would show up for his sister and her friends were already in the building, in the bridal suite doing whatever the bride did before the wedding.

    Last minute touchups on makeup?

    Hair?

    Shots?

    Talking her into running away from this shit or not?

Who knew?

Then there was my side. The only people currently seated in my *VIP* row were Ares and fucking *Bree,* whose silly ass had dressed in black.

Shiloh must not have seen that in time to do much about it.

Titan was in the back with me. My brothers had flipped a coin for the privilege —my word choice—of standing with me as best man, and the young knucklehead had won.

The only people I *truly* cared to see were all accounted for, except Grandma Calli and Ms. Wallace.

I'd reached into my pocket for the phone I wasn't supposed to have right now, intending to hit Shiloh up. I knew she was stressed with making everything work, but if Calli wasn't here… as far as I was concerned every ounce of this shit may as well be for nothing.

A buzz of activity in the main room pulled my attention before I could initiate the call, prompting me to look out the door into the event space one more time.

This time, I locked eyes with Shiloh, heading up the aisle.

She looked… *worried.*

But Calli was behind her, looking beautiful in the midnight blue gown she'd chosen for today. Ms. Wallace was right at her elbow, helping support her weight down the aisle to her seat. My most trusted security, Henry, was behind them, ready to step in if needed, but I could imagine how the conversation about that arrangement had gone.

Shiloh insisting that Henry be the one to assist and Calli telling him to, *"Get his big overgrown ass off her."*

Even with her age and health status, she was independent to a fault, which I hated.

This should've been her time to relax, to be pampered and taken care of.

If only we could convince her.

Once Calli and Ms. Wallace were seated, Shiloh made a beeline in my direction, slipping into the room designated as the "groom's suite" with me and Titan.

"Okay, I think we're ready to get started," she said, taking a deep, cleansing breath. "Everything is in place. The photographers have all their pre-ceremony shots for the Sugar&Spice spread, unless you've changed your mind about the first look?"

I shook my head. "No. My family has never done that, and we aren't starting now," I told her.

My grandfather saw Calli for the first time coming down the aisle. My father had seen my mother as his bride for the first time coming down the aisle.

I would do the same.

Calli showed my grandfather the constellations at the cabin in the mountains the night before their wedding. My father showed my mother the constellations at the cabin in the mountains the night before *their* wedding.

I'd done the same.

Marrying Nalani in this way, this damn business arrangement... I'd fucked up family tradition enough by marrying for what they'd all undoubtedly see as wrong reasons.

I could at least do *these* things in the right way.

"How is Calli?" I asked and from the stricken look on Shiloh's face before she hurriedly schooled her expression to neutral, I knew there was something.

"She's fine."

That answer came *entirely* too quickly for me to believe shit that was coming out of her mouth.

"Shiloh do not lie to me to right now. *How is she*?"

"Let's talk about it after."

"Goddamnit Shi…"

"*Fine*," she huffed. "Calli… fell this morning. Slipped on ice. But we had the doctor here check her out. She's *okay*. Nothing broken or anything like that, just a little bruising."

I… heard everything Shiloh told me after "Calli fell this morning," but my brain stayed stuck right there for a moment, processing before I caught up.

"What doctor? Some small town—"

"Kyle Desmond," Shiloh spoke over me, hands up to calm me down. "World-renowned surgeon, used to be head of her department at Blackwood General. A fantastic doctor."

I blew out a relieved breath, but still… "I need to go talk to her," I insisted, already moving past Shi towards the door before she caught me by the arm.

"Orion, you're *getting married* in like five minutes!"

"Okay, then I have at least three to go talk to her," I insisted, shrugging her off and pushing my way through the doors.

A bit of a hush went around the room at my presence, but I tossed up a hand to give a brief wave and a smile, then set my sights right on Calli, who was seated now.

I went straight to her, kneeling in front of her to ask for myself. "How you doing, gorgeous?"

She smiled. "You look so handsome," she gushed, cupping my face in her hands. "What are you doing out here right now?"

"I had to come check on my favorite girl," I told her. "Now don't ignore the question, how are you?"

"I'm doing just fine, nothing a stiff drink and a little rest won't fix. How are *you?*"

I raised an eyebrow. "I'm good."

"You sure?" she countered. "Are you *sure* this is what you want to do?"

"Why wouldn't I be sure?" I asked, and she gave me a look—a look I knew all too well from growing up under her thumb through the years. The same "don't bullshit me right now" look I'd just given Shiloh a few moments before.

"You know you don't have to do this on my account? You could take your time, make sure it's right. I'm going to be here a good long time, you know?"

I just smiled.

She was much more certain about *that* than I was.

"I promised you I would, didn't I?" I reminded her. "I promised you'd get to see it and here we are."

"But—"

"But *nothing*." I chuckled as I stood, giving her a quick kiss on the forehead before I fully straightened. "Shiloh is going to start spitting fire at me if I delay the ceremony starting. I want you at *your* doctor's office for full checkup first thing Monday morning, all right?"

"You don't tell me what to do, boy," she huffed, and I gave her *her* no bullshit look right back.

"Don't play with me, old woman," I told her, making her laugh as I quickly made my way behind the scenes. As soon as I was on the other side of that door, I took a deep breath, trying to calm the maelstrom of twisting emotions working their way through me.

"You know you don't have to do this on my account right?"

No.

I didn't *have* to.

But all things considered, I was certain enough I was

making the right move to pull the trigger. I never doubted my gut—something deeply ingrained in me by my father—and I wasn't about to start questioning it now.

"Ay man, you good?" Titan asked, clapping me on the shoulders as he came to stand in front of me .

"Yeah." I nodded. "Ready to get this done."

Titan chuckled. "You make it sound like a damn colonoscopy, man. Nalani is bad as fuck. It can't be that hard to swallow."

"Nah, it's not about that. *Bad as fuck* isn't a foundation to build a marriage and family on."

"Shit, maybe not for *you*."

"And shouldn't be for you either." I laughed, giving him a playful shove. "Don't be dumb."

"When am I eve—don't answer that." He caught himself, stepping back as the door opened again.

"Y'all ready?" Shi asked. "Everything is place."

Titan looked at me, eyebrows raised. "Last chance to escape."

"Not necessary." I shook my head. "Let's do it."

―――――

Nalani

"Last chance to escape," Morgan teased, as she was still moving around, fussing over my veil.

There was nothing to fix. Everything looked perfect, which for some reason made the urge for tears even stronger.

Everything *looked* perfect, sure. The dress fit like a glove, my makeup was flawless, and the stylist for my hair had styled my coils into an updo more regal than anything I could have imagined. The venue was breathtaking. It wasn't snowing now, but outside there was a heavy blanket reflecting the sun through the big windows, making the inside of the ceremony look ethereal and bright.

Everything that *really* mattered though?

It was in shambles.

"You should've made that nigga marry you in a garbage bag."

My eyes went wide, heart leaping up into my throat as I turned to the doorway. A grin spread across my face, mirroring my brother's as he came in taking off his coat.

"Soren, what happened?" I asked, accepting his hug while trying to make sure I didn't smudge any of my makeup. "You were supposed to be here ages ago."

"Snow happened," he explained. "The roads are open, but it was slow. And… I ended up leaving Blackwood a bit later than planned. Trying to talk some sense into that damn daddy of ours."

I rolled my eyes, moving my shoulders to shake off the flush of negative energy that hit me at just the mention of him. "You didn't have to bother. I already knew what that situation was going to be."

"Yeah," he agreed. "But still. I figured it was at least worth an honest shot." There was genuine remorse in his eyes —for something that wasn't even his fault—as he met my gaze before it shifted to Alexis and Morgan. "Damn, here y'all go, looking like you do."

Both of my friends humored him—just a little—for a few moments before Shiloh came in, rushing him off to change into his tux. Soren was a later-in-life baby for my parents, with damn near a decade age difference between us.

As much as he tried, My friends had never given him any real attention, which I thanked them for.

He was handsome, intelligent, and way too talented with tech for his own good.

A woman to impress was the last thing anybody needed on his mind.

His ass would be somewhere hacking bank accounts and deleting loans.

It didn't take him long to get back. He showed up at the same time as Shiloh, letting us know it was time to start. Morgan left to take her seat and Alexis moved to get in place to accompany my soon-to-be brother-in-law down the aisle.

It was just me and Soren now.

"You're really doing this, huh?" he asked, taking my hand to escort me to the dressing room door.

"I am." I nodded. "You know I have to… right?"

He shook his head. "Nah, I *don't* know that. You don't *have* to."

"The other option is lose the store."

"Or I can put a back door in the *Stellar Foods* system. Fuck up everything. If they want it fixed, we can trade. One business for another."

I smiled. "That sounds amazing. But… you know what these people would do to you, right?"

"I'm not scared."

"But I am," I told him. "Not just for me, or even you. But our family… everybody we love. I don't want to be on their bad side. And, I want the insurance—*assurance*—that they can provide," I said. "For the store to always be ours."

"I understand." He nodded. "Just… keep it in mind."

I met his gaze. "Absolutely. We're keeping it in the chamber."

A moment later, we got the signal that it was our time. I swallowed the last bundle of nerves keeping my feet from moving and... walked. Through the halls to get to the entry doors where attendants were waiting to give my grand reveal, and then... down the aisle, on my brother's arm.

I hated that it was so beautiful.

Every single detail, every little touch, was impeccably done.

From the fabric draped along the exposed wood beam ceiling to the fairy lights to the sun starting to set in the background, the timing we'd been waiting for.

It was gorgeous.

And... *grudgingly* ... so was my husband.

In a different life, I would've *run* down the aisle to marry a man standing there looking like he did—immaculately groomed, wide-shouldered, in a bespoke charcoal suit whose fabric just *screamed* luxury.

Once I saw him, I saw *only* him, and the attention was mutual. His gaze was intense, drinking me in, his expression one of pure admiration.

And then our eyes met, and... things got really, *really* still.

I was moving, somehow, but it was like... nobody there but me and him.

Which was an *insane* thing to feel.

I blinked, taking the opportunity to look away as Soren and I reached the exquisitely decorated arch where Orion and the officiant waited.

I had to chalk this strange sensation up to being swept into the moment.

It was a wedding, after all.

And I loved weddings.

I just happened to be in a starring role in this one.

"Beloved family and friends and board members," the officiant started, garnering a little round of laughter. He was a man probably the same age as our fathers, maybe a little older. With an opening like that, I had to assume he was very familiar to the Sterlings. "We are gathered here today in the snow, among the vines to witness the matrimony of Ms. Nalani Stark and Mr. Orion Sterling. Who affirms this union today?"

Soren shifted a little beside me, stepping slightly forward as he spoke. "With the blessing of our late mother's legacy and our ancestors before us… I do."

I glance at him, surprised by that wording, but… pleased.

I accepted his hand again to walk me forward to face Orion head on.

So we could get married.

Orion pinned me with a new gaze, a self-satisfied smirk that made me want to roll my eyes, but I decided not to. I knew when and where to exercise a bit of decorum.

The ceremony itself wasn't long—they never were—and it didn't escape my notice that neither the generic vows nor the declaration of intent was very… traditional.

Probably because we both knew we weren't planning to be in this very long.

Before I knew it, we'd said the "*I dos*", and were slipping rings onto each other's hands.

And he was kissing me.

Like we were really in love.

It was… *crazy*.

"With full authority, I now pronounce you Mr. and Mrs. Orion Sterling," the officiant said as we turned to face the crowd.

Everybody stood, cheering and smiling and… *happy*.

Orion hooked his fingers through mine so we could take our first steps back down the aisle.

As newlyweds.

There was truly no turning back now.

THIRTEEN
NALANI

"I knew your grandmother; did you know that already?" Calliope Sterling asked me, after flagging me down to insist I come sit next to her.

Our — also untraditional — wedding reception was in full swing—food everywhere, wine flowing, and there were no signs of cutting a cake or tossing a bouquet.

I actually… kinda loved it.

No awkward speeches or dances, none of that, just congratulations and a fancy party.

I'd taken Shiloh up on the suggestion for a reception outfit, choosing a beautiful white silk jumpsuit that my friends had oohed and aahed over. I felt great in it now, able to move and dance and apparently… really meet the family.

Morgan was keeping a wide berth from him, but Ares, the middle brother, was nowhere near the stuffy bastard I'd expected from her description. Of course, her opinion was formed from heartbreak and assumptions that may not be fair to hold against a man decades later.

But still.

She was the homey, and he was the brother in law I'd gotten as a package deal in an offer I'd only grudgingly taken. Finding solidarity with her and being a little cold to him—not enough to be rude, but enough to know I was onto him—was easy.

Titan, on the other hand... that was the wild child.

I could see why Alexis was friends with him. It was hard not to be when his energy and charm were so infectious. He was dancing, drinking, talking to everybody who'd listen, including a full fifteen minutes spent talking about dough technology with my Aunt Lucy.

Both men struck me as wholly different from the Sterling brother my unlucky spin had landed on.

Jessica Givens, head of marketing, made a whole point of coming to offer her congratulations; much less erratically than she'd been last night. She was distinctly more put together—and covered up—and while her compliments still felt like sitting on fake leather a little too long, I gave her the courtesy of being polite.

Breana Sterling, though.

Well.

That one was...

Shit.

I wasn't even sure what to say.

I'd heard her name and assumed family, for obvious reasons. But her interactions with the men—*any* man—around her were just a little... unnerving. It was especially evident in the way she spoke to the brothers—way too close, hands in the wrong place, lingering a bit too long.

Even when she introduced herself to me, she hadn't told

me her relation to them, just that she and Orion had a "special bond" she expected me not to get in the way of.

Which... I didn't give a fuck about this man kicking it with his weird second cousin or whoever the hell she was.

A fact I communicated, confused, to a wide-eyed Shiloh who explained to me that Breana was, in fact, not blood related to this family at all.

She was Caspian Sterling's widow.

Some might say... Orion's *stepmother.*

Which was the final seal on my conclusion that the whole family was a bit... off.

Not Calliope though.

As their matriarch, they held her in clear esteem, and it was easy to see why beyond her being the oldest. Everybody that approached her spent the whole time smiling, and not the fake shit either, genuine joy. I could hear her speaking sometimes as I moved around the room. She still had all her sharpness and wit, knew exactly what was going on.

She was one of *those*.

Which made me a little sad all over again because all my family I'd held in the kind of regard the Sterlings so obviously held for Calli... they were gone.

I loved that they doted on her though. There was always someone close by, making sure she was good. I even saw her charming Soren at one point.

Because Orion hadn't introduced me to her, I'd made it a specific effort to keep my distance. I didn't want to end up saying the wrong thing and breaking her heart or something 'cause she could clearly see through this lie of a marriage.

Apparently, she wasn't letting that ride.

"I *didn't* know you knew my grandmother, but it's not a

surprise. Probably a generation or two before that as well?" I asked, accepting her offer of her hand.

She smiled as she met my gaze and nodded. "You already know the founding dates for *Stellar Foods* and *Joyce Groceries* are maybe a year or two apart?"

"*Joyce Groceries?*"

"That's way, *way* back, before your time or mine," she explained. "But our families have *been* in the same business —coexisted beautifully for a nice little while. *Cooperatively*," she added, with a pointed look I didn't quite understand.

"I… have personally only ever understood *Stellar Foods* to be… uh… competition," I responded, choosing a less offensive way of describing how they'd been positioned in my mind. "Of course, until now."

"You don't have to clean it up for me." Calli laughed. "I'm sure your father has called this company and this family *everything* but children of God. But the truth is… there was no rivalry until he made it one."

My eyebrows lifted. "Excuse me?"

Calli nodded. "Mmmhmm. Larena, Caspian, William, Daneitha, that's Orion's mother, if you didn't know. And there were a couple others in the little group, all friends. We'd do neighborhood potlucks whenever they came home from school for the summer and they were all inseparable. Until William decided he wanted to be *separate*. Took Larena with him."

I frowned. "Wait a minute… you're saying our parents… were friends?"

"I fed your mother right at my table more times than I can count. That was before any of y'all were born though. Like I said, they were kids themselves back then."

"Not Lucy though?" I asked, gesturing to my aunt a few tables away.

"Different ages," she explained. "But I'm sure she remembers all this. You should ask her."

I certainly plan to.

"I sure do hate that your father made that rift happen. All you kids could've grown up together. Maybe you and Orion would've gotten married sooner."

My eyes went wide. "That would've certainly been something, wouldn't it?"

"You're such a lovely young woman. I told that grandson of mine he'd better do right by you, okay?"

"Yes ma'am." I smiled. "I appreciate that."

"I appreciate *you*. Lord knows that boy needed something other than work and working my nerves on his mind. He's not always the easiest to get along with, but now that he's put his name on you, you'll never have certain things to worry about."

"Things like what?" I asked, leaning in for the answer.

One that never came, because of Orion's approach.

"You're not over here scaring my wife are you?" he asked, in a stern voice that took none of the amused light from Calli's eyes.

If anything, she was *more* entertained.

"Boy I'm sure you do enough of that just fine on your own," she said, grinning as he leaned down to kiss the top of her head. "I was just making sure she knew, *I'm* not scared of you. Anytime you need him put in line, you just let me know baby, you hear me?" she said, squeezing my hand again. "I used to wear his little ass out and I still will if I need to."

"I can outrun you now," Orion said, unperturbed.

"You can't outrun a pistol."

"Damn girl, you shooting now?" He chuckled, kneeling beside her. "I thought I was the favorite?"

She nodded. "You *were*... until you got married. I'm a girl's girl through and through. Your *wife* is my favorite now."

"That's cold." He laughed, straightening up. "Now I don't even feel bad about it being time for you to go." He stepped back as another older woman approached, along with a big ass side of beef I recognized as his bodyguard. "Henry and Ms. Wallace are going to get you bundled up and out of here. I don't want you stuck on this mountain before the weather turns."

She glared at him. "I told you I wanted to stay until the party was over!"

"The party *is* over, gorgeous," Orion said, his voice soothing as he planted a hand on her shoulder. "We're getting you out of here first so you're not caught up in the crowd."

Sure enough, a little after Calli and the little crew he'd assigned her had made their way out, the announcement came that it was time to shut everything down. I made my way to my people, checking in to see what their plans to travel back to Blackwood were.

Apparently, *everybody* was trying to get back down the mountain.

Except me and Orion.

We took the opposite route, back up to the cabin.

I wasn't sure exactly what I expected the vibe between to be now that we'd officially executed this contract, but I hadn't projected it to be so... *quiet.*

Questionable road conditions made the ride to the cabin tense. Orion's Jeep was specifically fitted to handle the terrain, but his focus out the windshield and grip on the steering wheel kept my mouth closed. I had plans to live a good long life, so I wanted him to get us there in one piece.

I didn't breathe easy until we were inside the cabin.

"Excuse me. I have a few things to handle," Orion told me as soon as he'd locked the door, branching off to leave me standing there in the foyer to unbundle myself from my winter gear.

With zero instruction on what I was supposed to be doing next.

I just nodded at his turned back because he'd already given his attention to whatever was so important on his phone and took myself upstairs to the room I'd stayed in the night before.

There was a big, white satin box on the bed, tied with ribbon.

It *definitely* hadn't been there when I left; all my bridal preparations had happened at the winery.

There was no note.

Inside the box, folded into layers and layers of luxurious tissue paper, was the absolute most gorgeous lingerie I'd ever seen. Delicate hand beaded florals, translucent tulle, and silk ribbons, all black.

Considering the circumstances, I shouldn't have been excited to put it on.

But my friends had urged me to look for silver linings in the situation and getting to wrap myself in *Scantilily Reserve* was absolutely one.

I practically skipped my ass to the shower.

Things were different in the bathroom too—specific body wash, body butter, perfume. It all smelled divine, so I went with it, scrubbing off the stress and fatigue of the long ass day before pampering my skin with the available toiletries, unpinning my hair to fluff around my shoulders, and then putting that exquisite lingerie on.

I didn't realize quite how scandalous it was until I saw myself in the mirror.

That ultra-soft translucent tulle hid nothing. My nipples and freshly waxed pussy were right there in full sight, even with the ruffle-trimmed "robe" on. Absolutely zero imagination needed and the idea that the ribbon closures were doing anything more than being pretty was ridiculous.

They certainly weren't barriers to access.

Which, I guess, was… what Orion wanted.

And I couldn't back out of giving it now.

I left my face makeup free, but slipped my feet into the little fuzzy sandals that had been the last thing in the box. One more deep breath to clear any lingering nerves, and then… I headed out of the room.

To find and fuck my… *husband.*

The cabin was quiet, reminding me again that all the other guests had been sent off. The most obvious place to look for him was the big room from last night, but it was empty when I stepped in. The fireplace was crackling with a fire he had to have started after we arrived, but I was alone.

And now it was storming.

The strangest storm I'd ever experienced, stepping up to those big double doors to peer outside. The snow swirling in high winds made it hard to see, but I could hear the sleet mixed in with it, pelting against the glass. An eerie rumble started up, loud but simultaneously muffled, so unfamiliar that I didn't clock it as thunder until a moment later, when a peal of lightning lit up the sky. The jagged streak of light made me jump. I hadn't experienced the phenomenon of lightning in the snow before.

It was beautiful, yes, but scary as well. Yet I couldn't tear my eyes from the window, ears keen for the next rumble of thunder so I could witness it again.

"Were you looking for something?"

Panic snatched me by the chest over the sudden sound of Orion's voice over my shoulder. I whipped toward him, quickly finding there was barely any space to do so with him standing so close. With my back pressed to the frigid glass of the balcony door, I took him in.

Shirtless.

Wet.

A towel around his hips.

Clearly he'd been in the shower, which explained the empty room.

I swallowed the anxiety he'd inspired with his sudden appearance, channeling it into annoyance over him sneaking up on me the way he had. Looking him the face, eyes narrowed, I explained.

"Just here to fulfill my marital duties," I told him. "That's what the lingerie was for, right?"

Instead of answering me, he just held my gaze a moment before his eyes dropped down. He stepped back to fully drink me in, then carefully unbelted the robe.

As if it made a difference.

Breathe, bitch, I told myself over and over again, not wanting to be turned on by his scrutiny.

My nipples betrayed me though.

They hardened to achy little peaks under the heat of his attention and he wasn't even touching me.

I held my breath as he reached out, thinking it was about to happen.

Instead, he grabbed a pillow from a decorative chair nearby, tossing it onto the ground between us.

"I need you on your knees, Mrs. Sterling."

I wanted *so badly* to at least hesitate, to offer even a shred of rebellion against that directive.

But I couldn't.

It was as if the synapses that controlled my movement were connected to *his* brain instead of my own. My knees bent, one after the other, using the hands he offered for support as I dropped down onto the pillow.

He didn't take the towel off.

He just gave me an expectant look.

Okay.

Apparently it was my job.

I decided my objective right then, to make him regret putting me in a position to suck out every last drop of his willpower. I grabbed the front of the towel, untucking it to let it drop.

I was immediately confronted by… copious amounts dick was the only way I could describe it — smooth skin slightly darker than the rest of him, long and thick, richly veined, staring right at me.

I wasn't intimidated though.

I looked up, staring him right in the eyes as I spit in my hands then grabbed it. A subtle grunt escaped from his lips as I squeezed it in my palms, a little harder than what should have been pleasurable.

"Is this what you wanted?" I asked, smirking as I held his gaze.

Instead of any undercurrent of annoyance or anger as I

might have expected, he looked me dead in the eyes and shrugged. "It's yours now, Nala. Do whatever you feel."

Now why in the world would a statement like that hit me between the legs?

It *should* have rubbed me wrong, but his unbothered reaction to my attempt at bratty behavior caressed me just right, making my pussy throb as I slowly jacked him off.

Remember the objective, I told myself, knowing what I needed to do next.

I shifted my two-handed job to just one, using the free hand as a counterbalance against his thigh for support before I leaned in to take him into my mouth. The satisfaction in the moan he let out was exactly what I was looking for.

That little grunt of pleasure bolstered me to take him even deeper, relaxing my throat to avoid gagging—that was a tool I'd pull out later.

For now I was content to deep throat him like the key to life required the tip of his dick to hit the very bottom of my esophagus.

"*Fuuuck*," he grunted, his hips surging to push himself deeper down my throat after I'd moved my hand to caress his balls. I closed my mouth tight around him, funneling all my breath through my nose as I sucked him harder, not wanting to relinquish control.

He grabbed a handful of my hair, pulling my head back so he could see my face. I acquiesced, without stopping what I was doing. My jaws were starting to hurt, eyes watering from lack of practice. This kind of performance was reserved for a very, *very* select few.

I couldn't throw in the towel though.

I swirled my tongue around him, lapping at a particularly thick vein on the underside of his dick with every inward pull of my mouth. As I did, I slid a finger behind his balls, putting pressure on that sensitive line of nerves.

The instant tension in his hips, the tighter grip on my hair, let me know.

That was the move that was going to make him crazy.

At least it would've, if I'd been more focused.

Another surge of his hips caught me off guard and the next thing I knew he was using handfuls of my hair to hold me still while he fucked my throat.

"*Look at me*," he demanded, and my eyes flicked up, taking in his intense, concentrated expression as he surged deep enough for his balls to pat against my chin. "You're so fuckin' beautiful," he growled at me as I gagged on him, tears streaming down my face. "Keep your eyes open for me, baby."

What.

The fuck.

Is this?

A surge of wetness dripped down my thighs, unobstructed by those skimpy panties. I followed his directions, eyes locked on him as he used my mouth and throat like his personal toys.

Faster, harder, until with one last surge of his hips and a deep, animalistic grunt, he used my hair to force my mouth directly to his groin, restricting any possibility of breathing as he nutted directly in my throat.

Swallowing was my only possibility.

He freed me from the obstruction of his dick as soon as he was done, and I fell back, gasping for air.

I didn't get to stay there long.

He reached down and scooped me up like I didn't weigh a thing, striding across the room to deposit me on the bed. My chest was still heaving when he spread my legs wide open and dove face first between them.

He didn't even bother to take the panties off.

His lips brushed my vulva, then his tongue, barely muted by the skimpy fabric. His mouth closed over my clit and he sucked me there, hard, making me sit up on my elbows.

I wanted to see what he was doing.

Past my breasts, past the soft curve of my stomach, I met his gaze.

He smirked.

"Your pussy is even prettier than expected Mrs. Sterling."

My brow furrowed. "Does calling me that get you off of or something?"

He shrugged. "A little."

With his gaze still locked to mine, he pushed fingers into me. I didn't know or care how many, the stretch just felt *good*. His free hand went for those little delicate ribbons at my hips, undoing them with a tug on one side, then the other. It barely made a difference in my level of exposure, but he broke our eye contact to observe my pussy with such reverence, as he spread me open like a flower, it certainly *felt* different.

He flicked the tip of his tongue out to just *barely* run the length of my clit and that small action sent a ripple of pleasure right up my spine. Then it was wider, flatter, touching everything in reach for a slow, firm swipe, followed in quick succession by his mouth on my clit again.

No obstruction this time.

And he kept it right there, alternating between constant and rhythmic pressure as he finger-fucked me at the same time. He matched the pace of his fingers to the pace of his mouth—slow and steady, then fast and firm, keeping me off kilter until I was right on the edge of losing my mind.

And then he stopped.

"You seemed to be enjoying that," he murmured into the soft skin of my inner thigh, biting me there as my eyes popped open, wondering what the hell was going on.

"Don't play with me right now, *please*," was the unabashed request I didn't hesitate to offer.

I was way too close for ego to be a factor.

He smirked, then kissed his way back to my clit. "Anything for my wife."

I was still processing *that* when he started devouring me again, with even more passion this time.

And not just for my pussy.

I almost came off the bed when I felt his tongue on my asshole, licking and lapping like he'd found dessert. Any restraint I'd had melted away as he licked me into a state of bliss. I wasn't burdened by the thought of anyone hearing, so I gladly screamed myself hoarse. When he finally moved back to my clit, pushing a finger in my ass to stroke me there too, I just…

Fuck.

There wasn't anything I could do.

There wasn't anything I wouldn't *let him* do to me, at that point.

He took me to the peak of orgasm and then shoved me right off, barely giving me time to recover before he settled between my legs and buried himself balls deep in my pussy.

One leg spread on the bed, the other up over his shoulder.

One hand caressing my breast, the other pushing a finger back in my ass.

The kind of eye contact that dared me to look away, at *anything* else, to close my eyes.

Then, he started stroking.

Deep, punishing strokes that took my breath away, had me seeing those fucking constellations all over again.

"You know how long I've been waiting for this, Nala?" he asked, stopping to sit at the bottom of a stroke while he waited for my answer.

"I... I... *fuck*, I don't know," I whined, squirming against his dick.

He smirked at me, pushing his weight down against mine, crushing my thigh against my breast so he could speak right against my lips. The movement opened me wider, gave him room to sink just the slightest bit deeper, and he took full advantage, grinding his hips against mine.

"Too long."

Fuck.

Fuck.

Fuck.

I lost any semblance of coherent thoughts about anything outside of the way he felt when he started moving again. Emptying and then filling me up.

My mouth fell open, but there was no capacity for real sound. I was just mouthing my pleasure as he dug into me, fucking me harder and deeper until there was nothing left for me to do except... *melt.*

Into the bed, into the floor, into... nothing.

There was only the pressure of his body on top of me, the weight of his dick inside me, the warmth and wetness of his mouth as he moved his head to suck my nipple.

I came unglued beneath him with his tongue in my mouth, nothing but a whimpering mess of post-orgasm bliss by the time he nutted again, so deep I'd probably be seeing him in my panties for days after.

I loved every.single.second of it.

He extricated himself little by little, leaving me feeling void.

His finger, his dick, his tongue left me one by one, all having served a shared purpose of making me understand exactly why he'd told me I was going to need my sleep.

Even now, all I could do was close my eyes.

FOURTEEN
ORION

Was waking up married supposed to feel different?

That was one among many questions bouncing around my mind when I opened my eyes the morning after the wedding. Nalani was beside me in the oversized bed, peacefully dozing.

Was there some specific emotion that should be invoked in me right now?

I wasn't sure.

And I couldn't help the nagging admonition in the back of my mind that anything I was supposed to be feeling, but wasn't, was a direct result of me not going about this shit the "right" way.

I needed to talk this shit through with somebody.

The person who would've been the obvious choice wasn't; not that I hadn't dialed my father's private line hundreds, maybe thousands of times, just to hear his voicemail greeting, knowing an answer couldn't happen anymore. My brothers were fine to talk to about some things, but they were both younger than me, and couldn't work together to string more than two serious relationship experiences.

As my thoughts kept rolling with possibilities... a good one clicked in my mind.

I crept out of bed quietly, leaving Nalani to sleep off the rigors of last night. If I hung around too long, knowing what was underneath the warm bedding covering her... I was going to wake her ass up for a few more rounds.

I was trying to maintain some decorum though.

I got dressed pretty quickly, in weather-appropriate gear, then made sure I had my phone and earbuds before I ventured outside.

The blizzard had done quite a number on the terrain.

The only reason I could pinpoint the road was because I could see the garage. Snow was piled against it though, damn near up to my knees. I surveyed the damage of limbs snapped off trees from the weight of the snow and ice, looking specifically for any that might've hit the cabin.

When I was satisfied that there was nothing significant, I looked around for the mountain trail.

I was familiar enough with the land in all weather conditions that I wasn't afraid to venture off. Nalani was alone in the house, but safe. The cabin had its own generator, internet and cell service, and had been stocked with enough food to feed a lot of people for several days, by which time we'd probably be able to get out anyway.

If she woke up scared, she'd call me.

I made my way up the private trail, marked by bright red reflective markers the family had installed years ago. I didn't go far, just enough to make it to the tree house me, my brothers, and father had built... damn... thirty years ago, maybe? I stared up at it, half buried in snow and winter foliage, wondering if it was still as sturdy as the last time I'd come up here, after my father's death.

It only took a moment to decide I was trying it.

The opening was icy for sure, but with the way we'd built the roof there wasn't much snow accumulation. Inside, I checked for any wild fauna that might have sharp claws or teeth, and when I didn't see any, I finally took a seat on the cold, rugged wood plank floor and pulled my phone out.

He answered pretty quickly.

"Boy, shouldn't you be somewhere rubbing up on your pretty new wife?" Leon James asked, chuckling over the line.

I shook my head, unsurprised by that opening greeting from him.

Honestly… it was something my father would've said.

Leon wasn't *that* much older than me, but he'd been my father's friend before mine, with a solid ten-year age gap over me. He'd become something of… an uncle figure, maybe. The only reason he wasn't present at the wedding was because of my impatience. I didn't want to wait until he could get back from a business trip overseas.

Couldn't wait, with the shit Nalani's father was on.

But anyway.

"I'm sure she's probably glad to get a break from me." I laughed. "And that's not—"

"Oh I *know* what it is." He cackled.

"No, seriously." I shook my head. "It's not that type of comment. She… genuinely does not fucking like me."

It was quiet on his end for a moment and then, "Uh… I don't think that's supposed to come until much later, my man. Right now it should still be lovey-dovey."

"It was never lovey-dovey," I explained. "This wasn't… we're not…"

"*That's* why you couldn't give an old man a few weeks to head back your way. This was a corporate politics thing?"

I didn't answer, which was an obvious answer.

I closed my eyes as Leon let out a low whistle.

"Okay. *Okay.* You got a contract in place, right?" he asked, immediately settling into business mode with me. "You know I love me some Evangeline James, but—"

"No *but*," I interrupted. "That's the part I want to talk about. The contract is airtight."

"You want to talk about me loving Eva?"

"Yes. Well… not exactly. I mean, y'all are divorced, have been that way for a while. But the divorce took time, right?"

He chuckled. "Yeah, it typically does. Get to your point."

"I… *shit*." I laughed at myself. "I'm… so, we're not in love, you know? She barely tolerates me, actually. Which…"

"Seems like the kinda thing your ass would enjoy."

I couldn't do anything but laugh about that, because… he wasn't wrong.

But still.

"I guess more than anything, what's troubling me right now, is making sure that… even though this is business, even though I kinda forced her hand…"

"You want to make her fall in love or something? Put a card in her hand with no limit."

I scoffed. "No, it's not about that. And she's not even impressed with that."

"All women are impressed with it. Why do you think your lil friend Eva took half of mine."

"Because you couldn't keep your dick to yourself."

"And you plan to?"

"I do, actually," I explained. "That's part of all this. I want what I want from her, and I have no doubts that I'll get it, but

I… I don't want her to have a negative experience. I want her to feel like it was worth it, despite how she feels about *me*."

"What is she getting in the deal? What was her incentive?"

"Getting to keep her family's store, which never should've been up for grabs in the first place."

Leon snorted. "Okay, give the woman her shit then. Problem solved, early. You're welcome."

"That's already in the works," I assured. "I just wonder if it's enough."

"So you like her then?"

I frowned. "Where the hell would you get that from?"

"If this was *all business* the way you seem to want to claim, you wouldn't give a shit about her experience, or if she was getting enough. Are you worried about the other side *getting enough* in any other deal?"

"They don't look like Nalani."

"Nigga, *exactly*." He chuckled. "You can *it's business, it's business* all you want, but it's clearly personal. And there's nothing wrong with it being personal because that's your damn wife. Unless… you're thinking she's got some ulterior motives or something?"

I blew out a sigh. "I think there are moments she'd welcome the opportunity to put a knife in my back."

"Offense or defense?"

That question struck me right in the chest, making my eyes go wide.

But I told the truth.

"I'm sure it would feel like defense to her. I put her on the ropes to make this happen."

"So how she feels about you is your own doing?"

"Unfortunately."

"Well... you gotta get her off the ropes then. Can't ever start building a real relationship unless you've done that."

"Real relationship? Who said that?"

"Nigga, *you* said that." Leon chuckled. "Since my divorce, I've learned to read between the lines. I'll never get married again, but if I did... I'd know how to do it right this time."

"I would hope you weren't enough of a loser to fumble *two* wives."

"You just make sure you keep ahold of the first one, how about that?"

"That's the plan," I told him.

Truthfully.

I wasn't an idiot. I knew the possibility that Nalani would tolerate me for the required five years and then bounce was sky high.

I should've pushed for longer.

But as it stood, by my estimations, I had a solid two years to make remaining married seem worth her while. Nalani was a smart woman, enough to know *love* wasn't the only—or even primary—thing that made a long term relationship work. And we both knew finding a spouse that really checked off all the boxes was... a treasure hunt, to be optimistic about it.

We could *both* do much, much worse than each other, but the opposite?

Doing *better* than each other?

... I wasn't that sure about.

More than any of that, chief on my mind was the reality that I'd already fucked up enough. Calli and my grandfather were in love.

My mother and father were in love.

Ares was stuffy, but romantic at heart. His ass never recovered from my parents acting an ass about his high school sweetheart. There was no chance he was marrying for anything *but* love. The odds of Titan settling down any time soon were low, but if he did, there was no doubt in my mind that he'd be in it for the long haul.

And here I was… making business arrangements.

Well… not *only* that, but… it was what everybody would see and remember.

The least I could do was not add a fucking divorce to the mix too.

When I got off the phone with Leon, I made my way back to the cabin just as it began snowing again. I made a mental note to check the weather as I stopped in the foyer to strip out of my outdoor gear.

I could smell coffee.

There was still too much on my mind for an in-person conversation right now, so I purposely bypassed the kitchen to make my way upstairs. In my—*our*—room, I stripped the rest of the way down and got in the shower.

Afterwards, I didn't bother putting anything on once I'd dried off.

Nalani must've found the manual temperature controls because it was comfortably toasty throughout the whole house. I located her in the kitchen as expected, sitting at the bar counter with a cup of coffee and a bagel beside her laptop.

My wife was fine as hell.

She'd styled her natural hair into a puff on top of her head, and paired that with her fresh, makeup free face and silky lounge robe — not the one from last night's lingerie — and she looked… *comfortable*.

Until she noticed my presence in the door.

"Why don't you have any clothes on?" she asked, eyes on my dick before she forced her attention to my face.

"Why would I?" I asked, sauntering toward her. "There's nobody here."

"Uh, *I'm* here," she said, frowning as I stepped into her space. "And I don't want to look at your dick all day."

"You sure? Your nipples are telling a different story," I teased.

She glanced down, noticing the way they were indeed straining against the buttery fabric. Her arms went up immediately, covering them. "It's cold," she lied.

"You know we're *supposed* to be attracted to each other, right?"

"Why?" she countered. "This is just business, remember?"

"You were singing a *much* different tune last night, Mrs. Sterling."

She rolled her eyes, slipping off her barstool as she pushed her laptop closed. "To fulfill my contractual wedding night obligations. And I believe I have… what, at least another ten hours before you should be bothering me again."

"I'm bothering you?" I asked, using a hand pressed to the counter on either side of her hips to box her in. "That's really how you feel?"

"I'm *bothered*," she answered, wetting her lips with her tongue before glancing down. "Can you put that thing away please?"

"Anything for my wife." I smirked. "I know exactly where I'm gonna put it."

Before she could protest, I'd grabbed her by the thighs, parking her up on the counter. The action loosened her robe at the waist, and it spilled open, revealing what was underneath.

Nothing but pretty dark skin.

"Now… I admit to not knowing *everything*," I said, slipping the robe off her shoulders. "But I *know* that if you didn't want me to fuck you again... you would've put on some clothes."

Her eyes narrowed. "Do you even hear yourself? You sound like a fucking predator."

"Tell me I'm wrong," I dared, pushing her legs open to step between them. "Just say the word, and I will leave you alone... no questions."

She glared at me, eyes full of fire, but... she did *not* open her mouth.

Taking that as a sign, I pulled her a bit closer, lining my dick up to sink into her. She *opened* her mouth then, to welcome my tongue as I brought my lips to hers.

Exactly as I thought.

FIFTEEN
NALANI

I AM GOING to kill this man if I don't get off this mountain soon.

Not even a full second had passed after that thought before my potential victim came striding from the bathroom, fresh from the shower.

After yet again fucking me within an inch of my life.

I knew better than to bother complaining about such a thing to my friends; they'd fail to see the problem.

There wasn't an issue with consent. No, my legs parted themselves with little input from anyone, including myself, every time his ass even looked at me.

And *that* was the thing threatening to send me into a mental crisis.

I didn't *want* to be well-fucked and well-protected and well-fed coming off this mountain. I didn't *want* a shred of my perception of this man changed. I didn't want the blinders that came with full acceptance of my situation, because I couldn't afford to be tricked by it.

It would be foolish, to say the least, to fall underneath the spell of, "Well… maybe…"

I could *not* let myself forget what this man had unleashed when he showed up at *Nectar* that day.

He was no hero.

Not to me.

"You hungry?" he asked, whipping the towel from around his waist to reveal all six-foot-something, two-hundred-something pounds of himself and I forced my gaze away, staring up at the ceiling.

Stay focused, bitch.

A demand on myself that would probably be a lot easier if my thighs and jaw weren't so deliciously sore and he hadn't been pumping me full of cum from both ends for the last three days.

Two days?

No, three days.

Shit.

I didn't even know what damn day it was, and wasn't sure it mattered, either.

Of course it matters, the fuck?

I sat up, pulling the luxurious sheets with me to cover myself from his hungry eyes as he looked to me for an answer to his question.

I *was* hungry, but hesitated to say yes, because who the fuck knew what that would entail?

"Nala… you good?"

"*I'm fine,*" I snapped, but he was already striding in the direction of the bed, dick swaying in front of him with every move.

He pressed his hands to the bed as he leaned onto it, getting into my space. "You sure? 'Cause you seem a little grumpy and I thought I'd already fucked all of that out of you."

I rolled my eyes, moving away as he laughed. "Trust me, I'll always find some vexation from *somewhere* just for you, *husband*."

"Don't be like that."

"How in the world else should I be?" I asked, looking back to find he'd fully climbed on the bed now and was barely inches away from me.

"You could settle in and get comfortable. Take advantage of the perks. *Relax*."

"Last time I thought I could relax, I ended up having to get married to keep something that was supposed to belong to me anyway," I reminded him.

He sighed. "Okay. I get that. *But…* you don't have to worry about that kind of shit now. Nobody is fucking you over while you belong to me."

"The fact that I *belong to you* is part of my *current* fucking over, are you crazy?"

"You're surrounded by luxury and peace, with an unlimited bank account at your disposal, and have a man willing lick any and all parts of your body at your discretion. A lot of people would kill to be 'fucked over' this way."

I rolled my eyes.

Again.

"Is this the billionaire's wife version of 'there's a kid in the world starving somewhere while you complain about the meatloaf'?"

He grinned and nodded. "Yes, Mrs. Sterling. It is. Now, I ask you again, before I go downstairs to prepare something for myself, *are you hungry*?"

He held my gaze, unwavering, while moisture built between my legs again.

"Yes," I answered, more to get him away from me than anything.

Before he smelled the arousal on me and pounced.

I ignored his whistled appreciation of my naked body, hurriedly closing the door behind me once I'd successfully made it to the bathroom. And it took entirely too much effort not to smile.

Literally disgusting.

I took my time in the bathroom, showering away the smell of him, brushing the taste of him from my mouth. The lingering feeling?

I couldn't do anything about that.

Once the rest of my routine was done, I took a little inventory of my hair.

It would've been so much simpler to keep it pressed.

I couldn't front though, his admiration of that particular feature *had* been thrilling in those moments. Yet another reason to be disgusted with myself.

Instead of leaving it out, I braided it into two thick cornrows to pin up at the back of my head.

Petty?

Probably.

But whatever.

Fuck him.

When I re-entered the bedroom, it was blessedly empty. I immediately noted the linen change on the now-made bed. That was one thing I could appreciate; the man was clean on his own, without waiting for a housekeeper to come behind him.

I made a point of dressing quickly, in leggings and an

oversized sweater I was glad I'd had the foresight to bring. We weren't supposed to be at the cabin this long. We should've been in a beach bungalow by now, but the weather had different plans.

It kinda felt like a conspiracy against me.

At a resort, I could get away from him. I could go to spas, drink alone, escape in clubs. Here? I was stuck in the same house, seeing and smelling him, nowhere else to go.

Of course I couldn't keep my pussy off him, what else was there to do?

Grudgingly, I left the bedroom to head for the kitchen, which I found empty. There was a covered plate left for me on the counter, which I nibbled at for a while before curiosity got the best of me.

Where the hell was he?

He'd disappeared every morning since the wedding. This was morning three, I remembered now. I'd never asked him about it, but couldn't find him in the house, so deductive reasoning said he had to be outside.

In the freezing cold.

Shit.

I just *had* to be nosy.

I slipped on all my winter gear and made my way outside. The first thirty seconds of frigid mountain air was more than enough for me, but I committed to at least making a full round outside. I avoided the potential icy conditions of the paved walkway, choosing to trudge through the snow. When I made it around to the garage, it was clear Orion had been there.

Now, he was nowhere to be seen.

There was a big shovel planted in the snow, near a pile he'd been making, clearing the garage opening.

I laughed.

Maybe he was sick of me too and trying to get us off this damn mountain.

A girl can certainly dream.

Wherever he'd gotten off to now wasn't clear, but my next guess was that he'd gone inside to take a break. Instead of finishing my path around the house, I turned around to head back the way I came.

And… there he was.

Just standing there.

Grinning at me.

An uneasy feeling spread through me, driven purely by the look of wickedness he wore, and I was stuck where I stood, not knowing what was happening or what to do.

I didn't see the snowball until it was already coming at my face.

"*What the fuck?!*" I shrieked, temporarily blinded by the attack as his snowy missile burst into soft powder, going up my nose. Even without being able to see, I knew enough to immediately get low, listening for the sound of his laughter and heavy boots trudging through the snow.

"I'll give you a moment to recover," he shouted, from somewhere behind me.

I finally got the snow scrubbed from my eyes, enough to pull myself back to a standing position before I looked around to clock his location.

"Time's up."

"*Ouch!*" I shrieked, more out of surprise than actual pain.

That time, he'd struck me right in the ass.

"You motherfucker," I muttered, leaning to grab two gloved handfuls of snow. I was well beyond the years of snowball fights with my friends growing up, or out in the yard with Soren, but not far enough that I didn't remember the techniques that used to send him crying inside to Mama.

Orion's next snowball hit me square in the back of the head and I made a big show of how bad that one hurt.

"*Dumbass*!" I yelled when he fell for it, trudging in my direction to check on me. His eyes went wide when I straightened up, launching my oversized snowball directly at his face.

I'd waited till he was too close to duck it.

"You know your ass is mine now, right?" he asked, before he was even done clearing his face.

"Gotta catch me first!"

I took off towards the house, thinking I had some advantage. A belief he quickly put to rest by almost immediately catching up.

I shrieked, *loud*, my voice echoing off the surroundings as he grabbed me at the waist, easily pulling me down. He flipped me over on the snow, planting a hand on either side of my head.

"Caught you," he jeered, and I threw a handful of snow at him, my only possible recourse.

All that did was make him laugh before he grabbed me at both wrists, pinning me into the snow.

"Now what?" I asked, still trying to catch my breath.

He shrugged. "You tell me."

"You're the one who started this."

"Just trying to have a little fun."

Fun.

Is that what this was?

The moments before this, from first getting hit with the snowball to him catching and pinning me down... when I played it in my head, once again, I was fighting a smile.

So maybe it was.

"It's okay for us to have a good time together… you know that, right?" he asked, with his face much closer to mine than it had been a moment ago.

As well I could, I shrugged. "You're more convinced of that than I am."

"That we've been having a good time, or that it's okay?"

"Either. Both."

He chuckled, his lips barely an inch from mine. "You can pretend about a lot of things, Nala. But don't you dare look me in the face and fictionalize the chemistry. It's there. You can't deny it."

"I can try."

As soon as he smirked, I knew what was coming.

And of course he was right. I couldn't refute the chemistry, and I hated it so bad. My brain outright refused the signal to turn my head away. I welcomed the warmth of his lips on mine, the rasp of his tongue when he slipped past them, the lingering sweetness of fruit juice as he kissed me like we were…

Fuck.

Even though it was bitterly cold, and my leggings were weather-inappropriate as hell, I was perfectly content to stay half buried in snow, warmed by the weight of Orion's body as he kissed me like we were exactly what we were.

A couple.

Genesis aside, that was the fact.

It was very hard to tell myself otherwise while we were full-blown making out.

We probably would've been there a while if his phone hadn't rang.

A confusing sense of frustration lit in me as he pulled back, holding my gaze while he fished in the pocket of his coat for his phone. But something about the look on his face as he checked the screen before answering doused water over that particular fire.

"Hello?" he answered, then listened intently to the muffled female voice over the line. I guessed it was probably Shiloh. "How did the doctor she saw here not notice?" he barked into the phone, then immediately sighed over whatever the answer to that question was. "Of course she did," he replied, sounding defeated as he pulled himself to a standing position. He tucked the phone against his ear, then held out his hands for me.

Five minutes ago, I would've tried to pull him back down into the snow.

The anxiety on his face now let me know it wasn't the time.

Instead of playing around, I accepted his help getting up and then waited for him to end the call. A moment later, he did, but then he just… stood there, looking lost.

"Orion… what's going on?" I asked, after I'd waited as long as I could in the increasing cold.

The sound of my voice seemed to pull him from his thoughts, and he turned to look at me. "Uh… Calli," he said. "She had… uh… an episode."

"An episode?"

"She's at the hospital now, waiting for answers. But um… we need to go. I've gotta…"

He didn't finish that statement, just headed back to the garage where he yanked up the shovel and started moving like a madman, clearing the snow.

"How can I help?!" I yelled. "Is there another shovel, or…?"

"I just need enough clearance to get the Jeep out of the

garage; it can handle the snow," he answered, shaking his head. "You're my wife. I don't want you out here with a shovel."

"Okay, but what *can* I do?" I asked, ignoring the look of frustration he sent my way over another interruption. "You know what, never mind. I'll get us packed up," I said, instead of waiting for an instruction he probably wasn't in a space to offer.

I rushed back into the house, changing into dry pants first, then set about the task of shutting the house down the best I knew how, then repacking our bags. I did a mental inventory, making sure I located cell phone chargers, laptops, everything. There wasn't anything that couldn't be replaced, but in absence of anything else useful, I could at least mitigate the chances of later annoyance.

Down in the kitchen, I made sure everything was clean and dry, and did the same in the bathroom. There wasn't a lot I could do about the linens that were still wet, but at least tossed them in the dryer.

I was just heading back downstairs when I heard the garage door machinery engaged, which I took as a good sign. I grabbed all the bags, walking them out to see that Orion had already backed out into the driveway and was getting out of the vehicle, presumably to come looking for me.

He seemed relieved when he saw me in the door.

Instead of getting back inside, he helped with the bags, then thanked me for the thermos of coffee I put in his hands. He'd been out in the frigid weather much longer than I had and I'd spent a good fifteen minutes with my limbs tingling from the warmth inside.

He had to be freezing.

Orion didn't say much, and neither did I. I wanted him

focused as he maneuvered in the snow. He must've picked up on my anxiety because he muttered something to me about special tires and terrain capability, stuff that was too far into the details for me to care about.

I just wanted off the damn mountain alive.

Which he gave me.

It was much slower getting back down than it had been coming up and I had a sneaking suspicion he would've been much more reckless about it if I wasn't in the car. Nearly an hour after we set off, we pulled into Sugar Valley proper, but only to fill up with gas and take the chains off the tires.

The weather wasn't clear enough for a helicopter ride, so we were driving back to Blackwood.

Stress laid so heavily on Orion by the time we left Sugar Valley it was impossible not to feel bad for him.

"Do you... want to talk about it?" I asked, feeling awkward about it, but knowing I shouldn't let the radio be the only thing filling the silence.

"Not really," he answered, and I nodded, a bit relieved.

Sure, we'd connected through sex, but this was something else, something way deeper. Something that required a relationship capacity we hadn't arrived at yet.

When a chime started up, signaling a phone call, he answered immediately, with an apprehensive quality I'd never heard before in his voice.

"She's stable," were the first words out of Shiloh's mouth. "And she's resting now. Ares was able to talk to her for a few minutes. She swore she was fine and wanted to go home."

"But she's *not* home," Orion countered. "So... what was it? What happened?"

For a moment, she didn't answer, clearly not wanting to

say it, but then she pushed out a breath. "They're confirming a stroke."

Orion's eyes closed for a moment before he glued them back to the road, his hands gripping the steering wheel so tight I could see the strain in his knuckles. "So… when she got dizzy the morning before the wedding and fell, but let everybody think she'd just slipped…?"

"They think it may have been a ministroke. Which could've led to this full blown one. Ri… if she'd been honest with the doctor initially…"

"Yeah." Orion nodded. "I know. We'll be there in about an hour," he said.

"Okay. Nobody is leaving her side."

"Thank you, Shi."

"Of course. Calli is family."

When the call ended, it was very, *very* quiet.

And then — "Calli raised us, basically," Orion started, unprompted. "Our mother was ill, for a long time, so Calli retired from the business and moved in. She took care of Mama and took care of us. There was a period where she seemed to get better, and it was hopeful, but then… I was just about to graduate college when she passed."

"That's… still practically a baby," I said. "I'm sorry."

"I appreciate that. You're right though; that was young as hell to lose her like that, to cancer. I know you're familiar with what that looks like."

I nodded. "Yeah."

"So… after that, it was just my father and Grandma Calli, and eventually… we were okay. We missed her like hell, but we were okay. My father remarried and things were cool. Then *he* had a heart attack and didn't get medical attention soon enough. The heart attack itself didn't take him, but the sickness after... you know the rest. But that damn Calli... outliving everybody."

And now there was a chance she might be lost soon too.

He didn't have to say it.

I could tell exactly what was on his mind without another word.

My father was still bouncing around healthy as ever, but losing my mother was still vivid in my head.

Without thinking about it, I reached across the console, putting a hand on his leg.

It wasn't much, but... it was something.

One of his hands loosened on the steering wheel and, a moment later, covered mine.

SIXTEEN
ORION

The fear of losing something that mattered was at the root of everything that enraged me. Not a conclusion I'd arrived at passively, or without evidence, it just *was*.

When I peeled back the layers, especially on the things that made me act "irrationally" so I could get to the core of it, and do something about it, there it was.

Sometimes, though, I couldn't do anything about it.

And in *those* moments… man.

I scared my damn self.

So I tried to avoid moments like that.

Moments like *this*, where protestors were choosing the worst possible fucking time to interrupt the building process at one of the new *Wholesome Foods* locations.

The *worst* location to pull this shit.

Why?

Because it was actually an important one.

I didn't make certain moves without a research team's approval and this was one of them. That location was strategically planned to accommodate a close-enough metro area and simultaneously solve a food desert situation. Black residents of the city had organized a whole letter-writing campaign, asking for our attention to their area, and we'd listened.

In a way that made financial sense for the business as well, absolutely.

We were in it for profit.

But, if we *could* help some people out at the same time, it would be a win-win situation for all involved.

As long as nothing got in the way of it.

"What if we just sent a team out there for the duration of construction," I suggested, frustrated that I had to deal with this at all. "We knew we'd need a certain level of security for the location anyway, so let's just pay the money and get them out there early. Aggressively."

Stanford Reese sat forward in his chair with a chuckle, scrubbing a hand over his gray beard. "Violence is not always the answer."

"And sometimes, it absolutely *is*," I countered.

Lightly.

Stanford Reese was the manager for that whole region. The new store would fall under his purview once it was done. He was the one who'd brought the community proposal to the executive level for approval, and because I trusted the man implicitly, it was a no-brainer to say yes to a couple of the new stores going to him.

He'd served my father well as both a friend and trusted executive, and so far, my experience with him had been the same.

"Yes." He chuckled. "There are occasions that warrant a little tactful aggression, but *others*… you can end up making the situation much worse than it ever needed to be. There's no harm in putting ego to the back-burner and taking a moment to think before acting. Especially if we're already on edge about unrelated things."

I raised an eyebrow. "Are you saying you don't believe I'm thinking rationally right now?"

"I know you're not thinking rationally right now," he scoffed. "Not with Calli being ill and you fresh off your clipped honeymoon. Which is why I'm trying to assure you. As bad as the news stories might look, we've already got this covered. You know better than to lean into the propaganda," he scolded, and I pushed out a deep sigh.

He was right.

I didn't even say anything before he continued.

"These people—agitators—doing this supposed protesting aren't even a part of the community who petitioned us for help. All we have to do is remind the general public of that. They *asked us* for that store."

I sat forward, hands clasped under my chin. "I thought the agreed-upon approach was *not* putting forth anything that presented us as some kind of saviors of the neighborhood?" I asked. "*You* were the one who made a big point of that."

"And I stand by that methodology," Stanford assured. "*Until* something gives me a reason not to. Which is exactly what these 'protests' do. We remind these people of all the positive things we're bringing along with us. Remind them that when the store is built, it comes with a supply of healthy foods—fresh fruits, vegetables, meats, grains that have been inaccessible to them. Our prices will be competitive to the closest metro instead of hiking them up to take advantage of the food desert situation. We're coming in with community programs, working with local food banks and next-step programs, gardening and cooking classes. And we're bringing in *full-time jobs*, with competitive, livable wages — none of the part-time to avoid benefits bullshit," he added.

"You don't have to convince *me*."

"I know, just lining it all out. And once the people who will be helped by these things understand what's at stake, understand that people whose only goal is trouble are getting in the way of them having better options for a better life… they'll take care of it. Sure, we can hire security to make sure our people are okay up front, but when the community there sees that we aren't coming in to bully and subjugate, they're *not* going to stand for anybody causing them to lose out on that."

I blew out a sigh.

I knew Stanford was correct, but I was *still* irritated.

We could have easily devoted those resources to building a store in a neighborhood where I could hike up prices and make record profits, guilt free. But I wasn't going with that. I was following Stanford's lead on what would be good for people who looked like me, which was still important to this company.

It was *others* sabotaging shit that had me second-guessing it.

Others who seemed a little out of place in comparison to the residents of the area, per the surveillance footage that was being analyzed.

Probably some bored rich kids from nearby, with access to better stores than were currently available to the actual residents, with nothing better to do except fuck things up for somebody else.

It was *beyond* aggravating.

"Whatever you think is best, just do it," I said. "And keep me updated."

"As always." Stanford nodded. "Now, talk to me about something good. How does it feel to be married man now?"

"Man I thought you said talk to you about something good," I quipped back, even though I was talking just to talk. Since our return from Sugar Valley, for the most part Nalani and I had simply been staying out of the other's way.

She'd been in her space, and I'd been in mine, working on everything that had been neglected in order to facilitate our quickie wedding.

"Don't tell me you're already fucking it up." Stanford chuckled. "You've got a smart, beautiful wife who has too much on her plate to be needy and always be up under you. You're living the dream, young man, what's wrong?"

"Wrong?" I asked. "Nothing, not really. Just…newlywed growing pains, I guess."

Stanford shook his head. "Too soon for growing pains. You should still be in honeymoon mode. Whatever you're doing to get on that woman's nerves, stop it."

"Whose side are you on?"

"Hers." He laughed. "I'm going to go ahead and get started on our little PR campaign," he added, pulling up from his seat. "Like I said, I've got this under control. *You…* focus on your family."

While I appreciated the sentiment, that was much easier said than done. Still, I at least made an attempt, closing down all my tabs open with news articles about the vandalism at the build site.

I was going to go visit my wife at work.

———

THERE WAS ALWAYS something new to look at when you walked into *Nectar*, which I firmly believed was part of the appeal. Right up front, there was a display that changed every month, not necessarily tied to any nearby holidays or even the season.

Small booth spaces, highlighting different businesses and brands from around the store.

It had been updated since my last trip, with a business named *honey&hibiscus*. Even though the display was new to me, I'd seen the logo before—recognized it from a few products I'd noticed in Nalani's bathroom.

That realization tempted me to pop inside to pick up a gift. Women loved gifts, especially ones that were for "nothing," or even a surprise.

But… there was a line, and I didn't want to end up stuck in there, so I said I pulled out my phone instead, shooting a text over to Shiloh to look into it for me when she had time. I continued on my path, halfway hoping I'd simply run into her out and about in the store like I had before.

I had no such luck about the time I made it to the elevators.

So, I took it up to the administration floor, using my executive entry code to access the office suites. I knew exactly which one was hers, so I headed straight there, deciding along the way if I was going to knock first, or simply walk in, just to make a point.

The point being to get on her nerves.

It was an obvious choice.

Luckily for me, the door wasn't locked. I marched right inside, prompting her to look up from whatever on her screen had captured her attention.

An immediate frown passed over her face as she pulled an

earbud from one ear and stared at me for a tense moment before she spoke up.

"Whatever your reason is for bothering me at work, I don't have time for it," she said, then put her earbud back in.

"I think you should *make* time," I told her, strolling up to the desk. "It's important."

"Is it really?" she asked, with a raised eyebrow that practically dared me to lie… but I couldn't.

So instead of making something up, I hit her with, "I happen to think that us establishing our marital bond is one of the most vital things we can do."

"Oh whatever."

"I'm serious," I insisted, planting my hands on the hard surface on either side of her monitor, leaning over it. "Do you think I'm joking?"

She scoffed. "I think, exactly as I said at the top of this conversation, that I do not have time for this. I have performance reviews to go over, inventory reports to assess, supply chain issues to find solutions for, actual work, despite what you seem to think."

I frowned over her description of what was on her plate. "What's your official title here again?"

"Head of operations," she snapped. "Problem?"

"For me, no, just sounds like a heavy load."

"One I'm more than capable of handling."

"Which I don't doubt," I countered. "But most executive positions come with an assistant."

"I *have* an assistant."

"And are you delegating?"

"I am," she replied. "Everybody around here is doing their job, I assure you. And it would be great if I could get back to mine. If you want to talk, we can do it at home."

"Or… over lunch," I suggested, still pushing the issue.

"I was planning to eat at my desk."

"Change your plans then," I said. "And Nala… that's not a suggestion."

"Kiss my ass."

I smirked. "Now you know I gladly would," I told her, prompting rolled eyes. "It's lunch with your husband, not a fucking death sentence woman, damn."

"You see it your way, I see it mine."

"That's cold."

"Did you expect warmth when you took it upon yourself to interrupt my very busy day?" she asked, taking out her earbuds again to give me her full attention. Her eyes narrowed in genuine curiosity, waiting for my answer.

Actually… she had me there.

No, I *hadn't* expected her to be happy to see me. I'd expected exactly what I was getting — lots of attitude and annoyance over me showing up announced.

It was sexy.

I pushed away from the desk, walking around to her side of it as she watched, confused.

"What the hell are you doing?" she asked, as I removed my jacket and tie, and rolled up my sleeves.

"Cutting to the chase," I answered.

I grabbed the arm of her chair, swiveling it so she was facing me before I kneeled in front of her.

"Orion, *what is this*?" she asked again, a little more desperately this time, but I wasn't moved by her tone. I was focused on the fact that she was wearing a dress today, which made this a lot easier.

"Consider it a midday boost."

I pushed her legs open, granting myself access between

them. Her lack of argument spurred me on and I pulled her to the end of the chair. Once there, I buried my face against the seat of her panties for a deep inhale of her pussy, which was rapidly becoming one of my favorite smells.

"Is this really what you showed up here to do?" she breathed, hands clutching the arms of her chair as I pushed her panties aside, baring her to me.

I looked up, meeting her gaze as I pushed fingers into her. She was already wet, just from anticipation. "No," I admitted, shaking my head. "Just rising to the occasion."

I hooked her thighs over my shoulders and went straight to work devouring her pussy, allowing myself to get lost in what deserved a much more pleasant verbiage than "the task."

There wasn't a damn thing burdensome about the aroma, the heat, the sweet taste of her arousal on my tongue, the sounds of her desperately-toned-down moans, the sight of her eyes closed tight… a damn feast for all five senses. Her pussy clenched tight around my fingers as I dug in deeper, burying them to knuckles to reach that little spot that I knew drove her crazy.

"*Ah, shit!*" she screeched, then slapped a hand over her own mouth as I smiled against her clit.

Found it.

I stayed *right* there, not daring to let up as I sucked her clit hard against my tongue. Her ass bucked up from the chair, almost sending it rolling backward, but I kept my grip around her leg.

No reprieves here.

Not until her legs were vibrating, core pulled tight, that hand over her face practically suffocating her as I made her cum.

Hard.

Honestly, I was expecting that to be the end of the little in-office escapade, but she was still trying to catch her breath from her orgasm when she abruptly joined me on the floor, pushing me backward before she attacked my belt, my zipper, snatched my boxers down.

Aggressive as fuck.

I… had no complaints.

I went right along with every little action, moving away from the desk a bit to give her room to climb on top of me and sink right down on my dick. My hands went to her hips, and she immediately smacked them away, making it clear she wanted to be in control.

Again… no complaints here.

I was happy to just enjoy the feeling of her, tight and wet and hot as fuck around my dick. Her attempts to muffle herself earlier had smudged her lipstick, and what had been a perfectly layered silk press was tousled all over her head now, the two elements combining to make her look more than a little wild.

And the *sounds* coming from her, these quiet, growling moans as she pressed her hands to my chest for leverage to ride me harder, faster, take me deeper… *shit*.

I couldn't think of a better use of time.

I grabbed the back of her head, dragging her face down to mine.

There was no hesitation from her. She greedily granted me access to her mouth, accepting my tongue as I grabbed her ass, forcing her to stay where she was—impaled balls-deep on my dick. I didn't let up until she started squirming, bucking her hips to move against me again.

It prompted her to go harder.

I let her pull away from the kiss, but didn't break our gaze as she sat up again, riding me like she was trying her damndest to make me lose it. I couldn't help it, I rocked my hips to fuck her back, and next thing I knew, I was gritting my teeth to avoid making a sound that might have brought the whole floor to her door as I nutted.

Especially when she kept riding, prolonging that hypersensitive feeling until she got hers too.

Then she collapsed on top of me.

Reflexively, my hands went up, wrapping around her to hold her close to me as she panted.

"Looks like you had some time after all."

SEVENTEEN
NALANI

My lack of restraint where it came to my husband disgusted me.

Not fucking him outside the strictures of our contract was supposed to be the easiest thing in the world, and *yet*... all it took was the slightest provocation and I was wide open.

Wide open.

Greedily.

That was the best word to describe the feeling that came over me, really, at the mere thought of an Orion-induced orgasm in my near future.

Like now, I was supposed to be getting ready to leave the house. I had plenty to do today, between personal errands and my regular work *and* the board meeting today that would somewhat decide *Nectar's* fate.

My head was spinning.

And yet, when Orion had left his half-eaten steak breakfast to chase me down before I could get back to my room, I'd given *him* the attention that needed to be elsewhere.

It was hard not to, when his thick, shirtless body loomed over me, strong pecs and flat onyx nipples contrasting his deep skin, staring me right in the face.

He'd been working out.

I could smell it; not a musty smell, just that salty-sweat smell, mingling with whatever fragrance lingered from his last shower, generating this aroma that made me feel a little… sex-ragey.

I wanted to lick his nipples.

A wild, wild thought, that I didn't even have to articulate.

The way he smirked told me it was all over my face.

The only reason I didn't fuck him right there in the hall in front of the door was because Calli was in the house now.

Calli, and Ms. Wallace, and fucking *Breana*.

I had no desire to put on a show, so I just joined him in the shower.

A very, *very* hot one.

After which I was in a great mood — another annoyance — but one that was more tolerable, at least. My twist out turned out phenomenally, my schedule was falling into place, and after a quick email exchange with Soren, I'd gotten some assurance that the board meeting this afternoon was going to be well in our favor.

All of which should've clued me in that something was about to go wrong.

I was *not* expecting it to be car troubles.

I knew a lot about a lot, and exactly *none* of that knowledge extended to why the hell my paid-off Mercedes with a full tank of gas and a fresh oil change wouldn't start.

Fuck.

If I was still at my condo, this wouldn't be a big deal. I could call a car, I could take the metro. Hell, if I was feeling particularly perky, I could even *walk* to *Nectar* for the day. As it stood now though, Orion had me all the way out in Blackwood Hills. I didn't even know if a regular-ass car service would be allowed in the gate out here.

Ughhh!

I pressed the button to pop the hood, then climbed out of the car to go look at… I had no idea what. It would've been great if some particular area was at least smoking or *something* that could point me right to the problem.

Except… everything looked "normal".

With a sigh, I went back to the driver's side of the car to reach in, fishing my cell phone from my purse. I unlocked it, navigating to the search engine on my web browser to type in, *Why Mercedes won't start.*

The millions of results immediately told me I wasn't getting anywhere with *that*.

"Something wrong, Mrs. Sterling?"

The sound of Orion's voice startled the shit out of me, so much I actually screamed, dropping my phone. I watched, unable to do a thing about it as it fell, with a corner of the screen taking the most impact.

The worst possible fall, especially on the hard epoxy floor of the garage.

Cracks spread all across the screen before it landed, face up like it needed to make sure I saw just how badly it was destroyed.

Along with any last vestiges of the high from my orgasm earlier.

"Damn, I didn't mean to startle you," Orion said. I still hadn't turned, but he stepped around me, bending to pick up my shattered phone and handing it to me. "This is going to have to be replaced."

"No shit, Sherlock!" was off my lips before I could temper myself, pressing my mouth closed to take a deep breath. "I'm sorry," I said, even though there was clear amusement on Orion's face. "This day is going to hell really fast."

"I can see that." He nodded. "I heard your car, sounds like a starter issue?"

I shrugged. "I have no clue, and no time to figure it out. Will security let a car service past the gates?"

"Depends on the car service," he said. "But... there are cars here you can use, Nala." He chuckled. "Until we get a mechanic out to look at yours. Or we can just give you a ride, give you a chance to get a bit of work done on the way."

I blew out a sigh. "I think I'll take the ride. Maybe I can figure out how to get my cell replaced this morning."

"Not a problem." He nodded. "Leave your car keys – I'll get someone to look at it today."

"Thank you," I told him, not even grudgingly, I *actually* appreciated it. "You're saving me this morning. Guess I'm glad you hadn't already left."

"Even if I had." He shrugged, taking the keys from me to place in a lockbox on the garage wall. "I'm a call away and don't *ever* hesitate to dial it. You're my wife."

"Technically," I reminded him, earning a scowl.

"*Legally.*" He approached me again, looming over me in a way that made my breath catch in my throat. "And I believe at this point, our vows are a little too well-consummated for you to still be letting shit like that come out of your mouth."

"Anybody can have sex."

"Yes, but has *anybody* but me been in all three holes in your body *just this morning*?" He smirked.

"Do you *have* to be so crude?"

"Only when you're pretending you're not mine through

and through." He chuckled, then gestured at my car. "Grab your stuff. Let's go."

I hadn't noticed Henry before, but he was waiting at the passenger side of Orion's Range Rover, ready to open the door.

"We'll ride together in the back," Orion told him, and he immediately made that shift, opening the door for Orion to be the one helping me inside before climbing in himself.

The ride downtown was uneventful. Orion was busy on his laptop, and I had things to occupy myself too, mainly arranging delivery as soon as possible for a new phone, then tackling my overflowing email inbox.

"Let me know when you need to get home," Orion said as I was exiting the vehicle. "Even if I'm not available, I'll make sure you're taken care of."

I nodded. "Thanks again."

"You don't have to thank me. You're—"

"I'm your wife," I finished for him, rolling my eyes. "Damn, we get it, you're obsessed."

The smile he offered behind my words confirmed that he knew I meant them as a lighthearted jab, one he didn't challenge.

Instead, he just shook his head.

"I'll see you later."

I hated how… *warm* that interaction left me.

But, it was a much needed shift back to the energy the morning had started with. I was able to get a lot handled in advance of the afternoon board meeting and it only took a couple hours for the new phone delivery to arrive.

I rushed to the ground level to meet the courier, making sure the new phone was functional before I sent him on his way with a generous tip. With the device powered on, I was half-distracted making my way back to the elevator to return to my office. Being able to simply log in to the new phone and pull all my information from cloud storage made things very easy—a little too easy to get absorbed in, and not pay nearly enough attention to my surroundings.

"*Laaani.*"

I froze at the sound of that, taking my time to turn around and face the source of the voice.

EJ.

"What are you doing here?" I asked, tucking the phone into the pocket of my slacks and crossing my arms.

"Damn… you only been married what… a week or two? Already no love for EJ?"

"If you came here to start shit, no," I told him. "No love for EJ."

"That's fucked up, bae."

"*Not* your bae, haven't been that for a long time, so… please."

"Please… what?" he asked, stepping in much closer than I was comfortable with.

"Please go somewhere with the nonsense," I replied. I put up my hands, moving back to get some distance. "I'm busy and we both know you're not here with any good intentions, so…"

"Oh I'm here with the *best* intentions," he countered. "I was asked to keep an eye out for you."

I raised an eyebrow. "Asked by *who*?"

"Who do you think?"

"*I* think you and whoever asked you to 'keep an eye out for me' are both outside your lane."

EJ smirked. "Right… you probably think your little husband has you covered."

"There's nothing *little* about him," I snapped. "And yeah… I *do* think he has me covered."

"That's funny to me, 'cause… if you're so covered… what about *this*," he said, suddenly snatching me by the front of my blouse, dragging me against him. Before I could swing, he used his other hand to catch mine, holding me. "Where's your bitch ass husband *right now*?"

"You've got two seconds to get the fuck off me before I start screaming," I warned, and he immediately let me go. It was so sudden that I stumbled, but quickly caught myself instead of tumbling to the ground.

"Just showing you the vulnerabilities," he claimed, smirking as he backed up. "You're not as protected as you think."

"Are you offering to save me?" I asked, straightening my clothes. My wrists burned where he'd grabbed me, but I refused to let it show. "Get the fuck out of my store," I demanded. "And if I see you here again, trust me, you will regret stepping over this threshold."

He scoffed. "*Your* store? Not what I heard."

"You heard wrong and I will *not* tell you again. *Leave.*"

Instead of doing that, he just stood there, leering, daring me to do something about the fact that he wasn't removing himself.

So *I* moved, toward the security call button on the wall right above the elevator panel. Before I could press it, a new person rounded the corner, one I'd never been so relieved to see.

"EJ, what's up?" Soren asked, giving him a bit of side eye as he approached. He and EJ had never had an issue, but the tension was too thick for him to not feel it.

"What's up, lil bro?" EJ asked, extending a fist for Soren

to tap, which he did, but my brother's eyes were on me, seeking directions I didn't want to give.

"Punching in for the day, same old story," Soren answered, moving to stand next to me. "Everything good here?"

EJ nodded. "Peachy. Just... reminding your sister what home looks like, you know how it is."

"Nah, I don't know shit about that," Soren told him, shoulders squared as stepped in front of me a bit. "She's a married woman. I think she knows pretty well where home is."

"Oh shit." EJ chuckled. "I see you grew a couple balls over the years. Good for you, nigga."

"They ain't new, *nigga*," Soren countered, stepping forward. I couldn't grab his arm quick enough.

"This is not worth it," I hissed, smacking the security call button with my free hand. "*Leave. Now,*" I directed to EJ again.

He smirked between me and Soren, then bobbed his head. "I'll be seeing you motherfuckers around."

He was already gone by the time a security guard came rushing up, but I still gave his description, and directions to find him on camera and make sure he left *and* that he wasn't allowed back. The whole ordeal took time I really didn't have, but what *couldn't* happen was a security situation still brewing when the board meeting started.

Which was sooner than was convenient now.

"What was he *really* doing here?" Soren asked once we were finally alone. He'd followed me to my office instead of going straight to his.

"Being an asshole, as far as I can tell." I shrugged, trying to focus on my screen. "As usual."

Soren shook his head. "Nah, it was more than that. You know ol' boy has never been anything but trouble."

"Yes, I'm familiar."

"Are you going to talk to Orion about it?"

I raised an eyebrow, giving him my attention. "Why would I do that? I'm not trying to start a damn war."

"Okay but clearly he is," Soren insisted. "Antagonizing you here, of all places, knowing who you just got married to. He wants smoke, Nala. All of it."

"Yes, he does," I admitted, blowing out a sigh. "Which is even more reason to *not* give in to it. This is not even about me, I bet. He's just trying to flex, and get under Orion's skin, to get a reaction out of him. Even *more* reason not to say shit. We'll just… increase security for a while. Until whatever this is runs out."

"It doesn't just *run out* for dudes like that." Soren took the seat across from my desk. "Once it's a problem, it's *always* a problem. Until somebody puts an end to it."

"Okay then *I'm* putting an end to it." I shrugged. "As well as this whole line of conversation. We've got this meeting in less than thirty minutes and I need to make sure we're prepared."

"You sound… worried," Soren said, narrowing his eyes. "Why do you sound worried? We've got the votes, Nala. We'll be naming a new CEO in a week, and you're getting the deed and everything back, right?"

I nodded. "Right, but… we can't be cocky about this. It's been nothing but radio silence from Daddy and I do not have a good feeling about it. We don't know what he might pull in there."

"We don't know what he might *try* to pull," Soren corrected. "He doesn't know I've been digging into all the financials and shit around the property sale, and… he and Alan both will have some explaining to do if he tries to pull any bullshit."

"What are you talking about? You found something and didn't tell me?"

Soren shrugged. "I *just* found it this morning, after following a bunch of dead ends. He hid the shit well, made sure to cover his tracks. But… the way he claims the sale happened, *why* he claims it happened… it's not adding up. He was moving money into private accounts, shuffling investments, a bunch of shady shit to cover up the fact that the store was never *really* in distress like that. He didn't have to sell."

As Soren kept talking, rage built in my head, manifesting as a ringing in my ears.

He didn't have to sell.

Soren was explaining all about how he'd come to that conclusion, and how he could prove it if necessary, but I didn't even need the nitty gritty details.

I'd heard enough.

By the time we joined the rest of the board in the conference room for the meeting, I'd steeled myself. My father's entry to the room garnered no reaction from me, even though I could practically feel him staring a hole in my head, trying his best to draw my attention.

I refused.

When it was my turn to speak, I stuck to the facts. On paper, the store had been struggling, jeopardizing the entire company. We weren't built only on the businesses with storefront space. *Nectar* had its own brands, factories, warehouses, growing spaces, etc.

No, we weren't *Stellar Foods* by any means, but we were a force in our own right.

Had been, and could be again, with proper management.

Management we were *not* getting at my father's hand.

I provided facts and figures as evidence of all his poor decision making, being careful not to tread into anything that felt personal, at least until the very end. I revealed that irrespective of the way the *company* shares were split, or even anyone's official titles, *I* was the legal owner of the property now.

The land and the building.

I left out Orion's involvement, even though the big ass ring on my hand and my changed surname weren't secrets.

I ended my spiel with a plea to the board members to help me preserve not just the Joyce family legacy through this store, but also their own livelihoods – if *Nectar* failed, there went their pensions and salaries.

It was all quite compelling and not even *once* did I make eye contact with my father.

Which was a very likely added reason for him to stand up *seething*.

I kept my expression neutral as he ranted and raved through his justifications for remaining in place as CEO, taking a *lot* of credit for things that had gone forward either without his involvement or *despite* his involvement, with people working around him to actually succeed. The more he spoke, the clearer it was—to me at least—that he'd never had any business in the role in the first place.

He only had it because my mother passed.

Back then, it had seemed like a no-brainer.

I saw now that she'd likely shielded his reputation, loving him so much that she'd camouflaged the truth. He'd fumbled his way through his role as CEO because he wasn't the one with the head for business.

She was.

Luckily, everyone else saw it too.

Maybe they always had, but no one wanted to challenge it.

The vote wasn't unanimous, but it was certainly unambiguous.

William Stark was officially out as CEO of *Nectar* and Alan was out as CFO.

Alan was respectful, at least, but my father... he didn't take it well. Not that anyone expected him to anyway.

Soren and I cleared everyone out, assuring them that we'd reconvene to work through a new corporate structure. It took a bit, but after a while it was just the Stark family and my father took full advantage of the chance to sling a bit of unfiltered mud our way.

"After I spent my life taking care of you, you two little ungrateful motherfuckers should be *ashamed*," he ranted, but I shrugged.

"*You* should be grateful," I told him. "You're leaving this company without being sued or maybe even arrested for the fraud you committed that landed us where we are in the first place."

"You have no idea what you're talking about."

"Oh I know *exactly* what I'm talking about," I countered. "I'm talking about you lying, stashing money away so it looked like we were so broke you needed to make a little quick money to save the business. I'm talking about you and Alan cooking the books, hiding profits. You better *hope* that when I get a forensic accountant in here, we can clean up this mess without the fucking IRS knocking at the door. Because if they do, I'm pointing them *straight* at you."

He scoffed. "So you'd see me in jail?"

"If that's what it takes," I snapped. "You don't get to

pretend you've been slighted, especially when I don't hear you even trying to deny the claims." I shook my head. "I just want to know *why*. Clearly the money wasn't needed, so what was the reason for *any* of this? Why in the world would you risk losing the most important thing?"

My father's gaze narrowed, his face taking on a level of darkness I'd *never* in my life seen. "The most important thing? That's what you really think?"

"Yes." I nodded. "This business has been in the family for generation after generation. You should've wanted to pass it to your kids, so we can give it to ours, and so on. You *owed* us our birthright, Daddy. Why would you sabotage our legacy?"

"I don't owe you *shit*," he spat coldly, forcefully pushing his way out of his seat. "And this place could burn to the fucking ground and it wouldn't mean a damn thing to me."

"I can't believe I ever looked up to you. You're *insane*," I told him, shaking my head. "A disgrace."

"No, I *was* insane," he spat. "For playing dutiful husband to your whore mother; now *she* was a disgrace."

"What the fuck did you just say?" Soren asked, finally speaking up. He'd been lingering near the door, but approached our father now, fists clenched. "You don't have any right to speak on my mother."

"I have *every* right!" William snapped right back, nostrils flaring as he got in Soren's face. "That bitch lied for *decades*, letting me believe I finally had something of my own. And she didn't even tell the truth on her own, even when she was *dying* and I was fucking taking care of her. I had to force it out of her."

"What are you talking about?!" I asked, jumping up from my seat too. "What do you mean you *forced* something out of her? When she was sick?!"

William chuckled, looking back and forth between me and Soren. "Oh, *now* you need answers, huh? Well, I'm gonna take a cue from your mother. You can get your answers over my dead body."

With that, he stormed out of the room, leaving Soren and I both confused as hell.

EIGHTEEN
NALANI

"You can get your answers over my dead body."

What the fuck did that *mean*?

That question was still bouncing in my mind hours later, well after the excitement of the meeting had died down and it was time to get back to work.

There was still a business to be run, no matter who was at the helm.

Try as I might though, I couldn't seem to regain my focus, which made the knock at my office door, an hour before my designated quitting time, a welcome distraction.

"A courier dropped this off for you," my assistant said as she walked in, offering me a small, black satin box tied with stardust ribbon. She left the box on my desk with a smile and I eyed it suspiciously as she made her way back out, closing the door behind her.

This *reeked* of Orion Sterling.

I *really* didn't have patience for any of his antics right now.

Still, I reached for the box, noting the weight of it when I picked it up, too heavy for jewelry, despite the diminutive size. Before I opened it, I checked my phone, halfway expecting a prying message from my husband. He'd want my reaction to his "gift", no matter what it was.

But I didn't have any texts or missed calls. At least, not from him.

With my curiosity mounting past the point of my ability to resist, I pulled the top of the box open and my eyes went wide at the sight.

A key fob.

A *very* expensive-looking key fob, attached to a buttery soft leather strap monogrammed with a familiar constellation on one side and *Mrs. Sterling* on the other.

Immediate fucking eye roll.

But… curiosity wouldn't allow me to keep my seat.

A few moments later, I found myself outside of *Nectar*, standing in the parking lot. Studying the key fob, I found the button to sound the horn, a little scavenger hunt that led to me standing in front of a brand new, beautifully stark white BMW coupe.

I pressed the button again to make the horn go off.

My approach to the car was slow, like the damn thing was going to disappear if I touched it. It did not. When I unlocked the doors and opened the driver's side, I was immediately met with that leathery new car smell that made me do a deep inhale.

The interior was flawless.

Cognac on black merino leather seats, polished glass controls, a big display screen.

There wasn't a single thing I'd change.

A black envelope tucked against the console caught my

attention and I pulled it out, opening to find a note scrawled in what I quickly understood to be Orion's handwriting.

Knowing your penchant for independence, I thought you'd be comfortable with your own transportation, rather than needing to rely on someone. Your Mercedes is being serviced and should be ready within a week or two. Feel free to go back to it once the repairs are done, but in the meantime, please enjoy this gift. There is no debt, and it is solely in your name.

-Orion.

Shit.

Not a soul on earth could claim the man wasn't charming.

I slipped into the driver's seat and closed myself inside, loving the way it felt to just… *be* in a car like this. Not that luxury was completely foreign to me, but our wealth was modest and my mother had instilled a commitment to reasonable budgeting in me *and* Soren.

My Mercedes was cute *and* paid off, but it was mid-range.

There was no way *this* car cost less than twice the value of my old one.

Damn.

The *old one* already?

I shook my head and unlocked the doors so I could climb out. It was a nice gift—a *great* gift, even—but I couldn't afford to get too wrapped up in the kind of lifestyle Orion could offer, knowing that as far I was concerned, it was all temporary.

There was no "'til death do us part", it was "'til the contract says I can file for divorce".

I couldn't waver from that.

Back in my office, I was gracious enough to at least send Orion a text, thanking him—sincerely—for the car. When I didn't get an immediate response back, I shrugged it off, locking in mentally to get through the rest of my work day before I could head home.

I was in my condo before it struck me that it wasn't really *home* anymore.

I hadn't done anything with it yet, no subletting or selling had been on my mind.

Hadn't had the *chance* to be on my mind, honestly.

Between the wedding and work and getting settled into the new place, what I was going to do with this place hadn't even crossed my thoughts, but now that today's auto-piloted movements had brought me here... I *did* think about it.

I was keeping it.

And keeping up the bimonthly cleaning service that would help maintain an actually livable state for it, in case an occasion rose that I needed somewhere to go.

Just like with the car, I wasn't completely comfortable relying all the way on Orion, or any man, to be honest. Experience with past romantic interests had proven them to be fickle at best and volatile at worst. And unfortunately for me, even my *father* seemed to be deeply entrenched in the same "can't count on him" bucket.

The only man I knew on a personal level that I could implicitly trust was my damn brother.

Sad.

Instead of lingering, I did a quick perusal through the condo, making sure everything was as I remembered from the last time I was here. Satisfied that nothing weird was going on, I locked up and left, getting *back* into the car.

This time, I gave a little more focus to the road.

Just a little, though.

The drive out to Blackwood Hills was a beautiful one, but

I had too much on my mind to appreciate it. I was still lost as to what the hell my father meant with his words about my mother, a woman I'd only ever seen as elegant and classy, but still fun and full of life. Smart as hell, and *wise*—those were two different things—and notable, due to context... a dutiful wife.

Even when my father maybe didn't deserve that from her.

So to imply something different and give no evidence, was ridiculous.

Right in line with everything else he'd been doing lately.

By the time I pulled up to Orion's house, *my house*, I'd nearly convinced myself that William Stark was just spouting nonsense, that there was no merit to anything he said.

Nearly.

I couldn't shake the feeling that there was something to why he'd chosen to bring up such an accusation when he did, and what the hell it had to do with the topic at hand, which was preserving the store.

There *had* to be something to it.

Especially with Soren's revelation about money being hidden, which there was no explanation for outside of my father's greed.

It was all just fucking suspicious.

I made a mental note to fast track the hiring of a forensic accountant. The sooner we understood what was happening—and how much trouble we might be in—the better. I entered the house through the garage, intending to make my way straight to my room before I was interrupted.

By Henry.

"Mr. Sterling has requested your presence on the terrace for dinner."

I raised an eyebrow. "Requested? Why does that feel like that a very generous interpretation?"

Instead of answering, Henry simply smirked, gesturing toward the walkway that led out to the oversized second floor balcony.

"I don't even get to shower, change out of my work clothes?" I asked.

Henry shook his head. "He's been waiting for you since you left the store."

Oh.

Shit.

I didn't feel any need to rush, but I also didn't offer any further argument. I dumped my bag and everything else on a nearby side table, and headed down the hall, opening the door to step outside.

For a fireside dinner.

"It's a little cold for this, don't you think?" I asked.

Orion's back was turned, staring out at the trees that surrounded the property.

"The fire is more than sufficient temperature control. Come sit down."

Hm.

It occurred to me then that he never replied to my text from earlier and I was getting the feeling now that I'd done something to upset him.

As if this day needed a single shred more drama.

Dragging my feet was pointless. If we were about to go blow for blow—verbally—I'd much rather get the shit over with. I marched up to the table, kicked my shoes off, and picked up the bottle of wine I assumed was supposed to accent the meal. Without even pulling the cover off to see what it was, I pushed the plate away from me and brought my wine glass closer, pouring myself a generous serving as Orion watched intently.

I didn't say anything.

Just finished pouring, put the bottle down, and picked my wine glass up, taking a generous sip before I met his gaze.

He smirked. "Seems like you've had quite an eventful day."

"This one? No. It's just lasted approximately a hundred years and some change."

He chuckled. "I'm glad you're able to maintain a sense of humor about it."

"Sometimes it's the only thing you can do."

"Indeed."

When Orion picked up his drink, I noticed it wasn't a wine glass, or wine at all. The liquid was a dark amber, flashing gold in the occasional flicker of the firelight.

Probably bourbon.

"Dark liquor with dinner instead of wine?" I quipped. "Guess I'm not the only one who's had a long day. You trying to drink your way out of it?"

"Drinking as a relaxation tool," he replied. "So… I guess you're somewhat correct."

I nodded. "What's *your* problem?"

"*You* are my problem," was his immediate comeback, and I raised an eyebrow before a long sip from my glass.

"Well damn." I laughed. "What did *I* do? Is this about me going to my apartment first, instead of straight here? Because if so… this is incredibly dramatic," I told him.

"I *wish* it was that, Nalani," he said.

And something in the *way* he said it, something in his tone, made me feel a little… concerned.

"I heard you had an unpleasant visitor today," he spoke up, dropping the suspense as I scoffed.

"Yes, my father was upset about the way the vote went, which didn't surprise me, and *shouldn't* have surprised you either."

"*Not* your father," Orion said, swigging the rest of the bourbon down his throat before dropping the glass to the table with a loud clatter. "But we'll absolutely be coming back to him. I'm more concerned now with your retention skills, because what the *fuck* did I tell you was going to happen if I found out EJ was around you again?"

My mouth went dry.

Shit.

This day had been such a clusterfuck of drama I'd forgotten about his little pop-up.

"I *know* you're not pissed at me, as if I control that man," I replied, choosing indignation as my default. "I went to *work, and* he was there. Why are you confronting *me* about it?"

"*Only* because I can't find him. *Yet.* Otherwise, you'd be in the audience for quite a show right now," Orion said, leaning over the table. "But don't get it twisted, you're not innocent."

"So I was… what, supposed to *predict* that he was going to show up? I'm a lot of things, *dear husband*, but clairvoyant is not one of them."

"Nobody is asking your ass to predict the future, but that nigga ran up in *my* shit—yes, mine, because *you*, Nalani, *are mine*—snatching on you like he runs something and it never crossed your mind that might be something I needed to know about *from you*?"

My mouth dropped. "I… I was *busy*," I snapped. "And we had the board meeting coming up, which needed my focus. I couldn't let my whole day be threatened by something that wasn't even a big deal!"

"*Not a big deal?!*" he bellowed, making me flinch. My breath caught in my throat as he launched himself out of his seat, grabbing my arm to hold my wrist in front of my face.

The sight of the bruise I'd been too distracted to even notice made my eyes go wide.

"Not a big deal though… right?" Orion questioned, rage simmering behind his gaze as he dropped my arm.

"It doesn't even *hurt*," I tried to assure him as he stepped away, toward the fire. "And it's not like he fucking *beat me up* or something!"

"I've seen the video footage," he said, his tone scarily calm. "I saw exactly what he did and your attempts to minimize it are not making anything better."

I frowned. "How the hell did you see the video footage?"

"Soren."

My eyes narrowed. "*Soren* showed you our cameras?"

"Yes," he answered, turning to face me. "Because *he* understands that it's a big fucking deal and that there's zero room to let blatant disrespect ride. *He* understands that you are precious, even if you're too dense to get it yourself."

I scoffed. "*Wow.* Call me precious and stupid in the same damn sentence. I don't know if I'm impressed or insulted."

"I really don't give a shit, as long as you're *protected*, which is clearly up to me," Orion countered, shaking his head. "You can't move in the same way you moved before your last name was Sterling, do you understand that?"

"I am the exact same person I was before you called yourself doing me any favors."

"Which doesn't mean shit when your circumstances have so drastically changed," Orion replied, stalking toward me again. "You have a *billion-dollar-legacy* behind your name now, and whether or not you like it, shit is a little different now. The *optics* are different now."

"So is that what this is really about?" I huffed. "EJ running around acting an ass makes you look bad, and that's the real problem?"

His face pulled into an immediate frown. *"Hell yeah* it's a problem. *Nobody* gets to run around this city big and bold fucking with *anything* that belongs to me, *especially not my goddamn wife,"* he growled right in my face, crouching to get at eye level with me. "Yes, it makes me look bad, and I would be lying if I said that wasn't a factor. But more importantly," he added, grabbing me under the chin. "Soren said you were *scared.* And *my* wife doesn't have to be scared of *anybody."*

I swallowed.

Hard.

Wished I had something clever or disrespectful to say, but I couldn't find it.

Because he wasn't wrong.

I *was* scared.

Something I hadn't been able to recognize in the adrenaline of the moment, in the midst of so much shit swirling around me from all directions.

But clearly, it had been on my face.

Even with me immediately brushing past it in favor of focusing on the meeting, Soren had noticed and been stricken enough by it that he felt a need to reach out to Orion.

Faced with it now… I couldn't exactly deny it.

And I loathed that reality.

Before I could catch myself, I was blinking back tears, a shift Orion noticed immediately and his expression softened.

"Hey," he murmured, urging my face toward his. "Never

again. *Never* again," he repeated, against my lips this time, but he didn't kiss me. Instead, he pulled me into his arms.

"What did I tell you?" he asked, as all the emotions I'd suppressed from the day hit me at once—the frustration of the car issues, the fear of what EJ might do, the confusion and anger from the situation with my father.

I sucked in a breath as I accepted him embrace and gave up on trying to hold back my tears. "You were just a call away."

"Exactly. So what are you going to do next time anything happens?"

I closed my eyes, burying my face into his shoulder. "I'm going to call."

NINETEEN
ORION

V*ULNERABLE*.

Not a position I took to kindly.

I was not remotely a fan of anybody having one up on me in general, but *especially* not someone who wasn't well versed in the idea of boundaries. Or rather—someone who had no qualms about crossing them, despite being warned.

Reckless, volatile people.

Like EJ.

The nigga of my dreams to be honest.

I had every intention of falling and sleeping good as hell tonight to visions of knocking his motherfucking head in for putting his hands on Nalani. An opportunity he *never* should've had in the first place and most certainly was not going to get again.

Even more than that security footage had set me ablaze, Nalani's tough ass basically admitting that he'd had her afraid really shifted something in me. Her implication that my ego was the main reason for me to not put up with EJ's bullshit wasn't remotely the truth.

Not the *whole* truth, at least.

It wasn't my ego or reputation I was apprehensive about when I thought about what could happen to her once she'd left for work the next day, when she was out with her friends, running errands alone, all that.

I was concerned about *her*.

Not what might be said about *me*.

My status around this city was what it was, motherfuckers knew my name. Every once in a while somebody might try me or one of my brothers, but that wasn't something I carried with me from day to day, it wasn't triggering any anxieties over here.

This shit with Nala was… different.

A level of disquiet I'd never really had before, not even when Jess was my fiancée. Of course I'd made sure she was protected as well, but something about this felt unique, and I couldn't even chalk it up to feelings.

I was still learning and understanding Nalani. I'd loved Jess well before I put a ring on her finger. And those feelings had persisted past the time that we went our separate ways, because a lack of love didn't break us up.

Practicality did.

This time, I'd led with practicality and managed to make it down the aisle.

I didn't know what this other shit was.

But whatever it was, I wouldn't ignore it, *couldn't* ignore it, with the added layer of whatever the fuck William Stark was on. He was out of his kids' hair from a business standpoint, but that element of personal involvement couldn't be overlooked.

Not when he was being *so* reckless at the mouth.

It had taken some prodding, but Nalani shared *everything* that went down at the board meeting, including William's comments about her mother. His words were unsurprising to me. His son didn't look like him and I was privy to my father's side of their whole friendship story.

The idea of Larena Joyce having an affair was no revelation to me.

And it *shouldn't* have been to William, either. It had been well known among the friends that he wasn't faithful, so expecting fidelity from his wife was wild.

Especially once she realized any wealth or business acumen he walked into their marriage with was nothing more than a fairytale.

But I didn't tell her all that.

I didn't tell her *any* of that.

It didn't seem like the time *or* my place to connect those dots for her, but my mind was working through what my approach should be.

If nothing else was certain though, both William Stark and EJ would need to be dealt with.

In some way or another.

Which was the impetus of inviting Soren Stark to my house.

He was a good kid, barely thirty years old, but well-educated, not running around doing reckless shit, working in the family business. Most important to me, he was protective of his sister, and had the balls to stand up for her.

And the common sense to understand when he needed reinforcements.

Ones I would happily provide.

"So you're seriously telling me *nobody* knows where this

nigga is?" I asked, directing my question to Titan and Henry, to my left. For his own sanity, Ares wasn't at this meeting. He preferred keeping his hands a little cleaner, and I was glad to oblige.

Henry shook his head.

"We've got ears to the street though," Titan assured. "And if it comes down to it… he might be out of reach, but his people aren't. He's got lieutenants, soldiers… baby mamas, little cousins—"

"I'm not ready to go there yet," I told him. "That's an absolute last resort. I don't think he'll hide forever. He won't like word that he's pussy getting around. So let's make sure everybody hears it, real loud."

Titan nodded. "I'll convey the message to the right people. Should we hit up the Blacks?"

"*Hell no,*" I countered immediately, a sentiment echoed by Henry and Soren, who was seated opposite them. "Again, absolute last resort. We don't activate *those* motherfuckers for anything unless every other option is exhausted."

The Black family had been around since… hell, since before anybody remembered.

In a way that made the fine hairs on your arms stand up if you talked about it too long.

My family got along with theirs just fine, to the point where if I needed something discreetly handled, that was a call I could make, and it was good as done.

There was just… this *energy* that came with it. One I wasn't trying to get wrapped up in, as far as I could help it.

We had other means for now.

Favors we could call in, backs we could scratch… we could honestly end all the chatter and just make EJ disappear without it ever coming back on us.

Way too easy, though.

I wanted hands on him.

My hands.

"Soren, what's being done about security at the store?" I asked, and he sat forward in his chair a bit.

"We're contracted with *Five Star Security*, top notch. We're having them bring on ten additional people, some plain clothes, some uniformed. We'll have parking lot coverage, as well as more eyes on each floor, and on the cameras. In terms of tech, I got EJ and known associates flagged in our facial recognition system. If any of our cameras pick them up, a two-person team is on them immediately."

"Good." I nodded. "In addition to that, I need notification for my personal security on Nalani's comings and goings from the store. I'm comfortable that she's safe enough there, but outside of that—lunch with her friends, going to see your aunt, shopping, so forth... I don't have the same assurance."

"That's where I have to draw the line," Soren told me, meeting my gaze. "I know we have a common interest in keeping her safe, but I think she'd see that as a violation. I understand you doing what you've gotta do, I just can't help you with that one."

"Fair enough," I agreed. "I'll work it out with my team, with hopes that you don't feel a need to notify her...?"

"Notify her about what?" Soren asked, and I chuckled.

Good kid.

There wasn't much else to discuss after that.

Everybody had their tasks to see through and it had been a long day. I was ready to go to bed. We all shared our parting words, and while Titan and Soren were having a quick conversation, I took the opportunity to *really* observe him.

His laidback nature, his mannerisms, even his looks... he

reminded me of *somebody* I couldn't quite place. There wasn't a single doubt in *my* mind; that was not William Stark's son.

So whose was he?

Not my damn business.

What *was* my business was making my way back through the house, stopping by the room we'd designated for Calli when I noticed that her light was still on.

It was late as hell, well past midnight, so I gave a light rap on the door before stepping in.

"It is *way* past your bedtime, young lady," I teased, my gaze landing on where Calli and Ms. Wallace were over in the seating area, each with a cup of—likely spiked—tea in hand.

"What I done told you about trying to boss me around?" Calli fussed.

As soon as I sat down next to her on the settee, I could smell the bourbon in her tea, but damn if I was going to scold her about it. Not with… everything.

The need to start planning for hospice care had been brought up, which was some shit I was not remotely ready to think about, so I was ignoring it for now. Especially since her doctor said we had time.

Maybe not a lot, but time, nonetheless.

"Somebody has to be responsible around here," I said. "You need your rest."

"That's the same thing your wife was in here fussing about, about an hour ago. At least she brought tea."

"Oh so she was behind this?" I chuckled.

Ms. Wallace nodded. "And in her defense, we supplied our own liquor."

"Why am I not even a little surprised by that? Seriously though, what are you doing up? You all right?" I asked Calli.

"Oh just these old bones getting a little achy on me. Nothing outside the norm with all these pills and shit they got me on."

"Including one to help you sleep, right?" I asked.

"Why would I take a pill to help me sleep when a good finger or two of dark liquor ain't never steered me wrong?"

"Maybe not, but the interactions with the other medications…"

Thinking about that had me ready to backtrack on my earlier decision not to say anything about the alcohol. The last thing I needed happening tonight was a medical emergency because bourbon didn't exactly mix with one of her pills.

"We looked it all up, it's fine. Long as I just drink a little."

Eyebrow raised, I pulled the cup from Calli's hand against her protest and took a sip.

Hmmm.

It didn't taste like there was more than a splash of liquor in it.

"We're old biddies," Ms. Wallace explained. "Shaky hands. I spilled a bottle a bit, that's why it smells so strong."

"Okay," I said, handing the cup back. "I still need y'all to be real mindful and real careful though," I said. "And again, get some rest."

"Yes Papa," Calli told me in a dry tone before she reached out to grab me by the head. The movement wasn't as smooth as it used to be, but the love was there all the same as she pulled me into her to plant a kiss against my temple.

"You get on out of here let us grown women talk," she said when she released me.

"Y'all ain't talking about shit." I laughed as I stood.

"And whose business is that either way?" Calli countered, always with the snappy comebacks.

Once that stopped, that was when I'd really get worried.

In the meantime, I left her and Ms. Wallace to their tea and moved on, to my room. I looked past my door to Nalani's, no light on there. After the emotional chaos that the day had been, I didn't feel a need to disturb her rest.

I went into my room, where I was immediately struck by the feeling of something different. The energy was off. Well not off, just… different .

A quick glance around the room gave me an immediate answer on what had changed.

Instead of being in her own bed, Nalani had taken up residence in mine.

I glanced around again, searching for some evidence that I wasn't being set up.

Set up for what? Who knew?

But finding Nalani in my bed was an anomaly. I moved closer to where she lay, staying quiet so it wouldn't wake her. The lights were off, but the blinds were open, casting moonlight across her pretty ass face.

The covers on my bed were half on her and half off, showcasing soft-looking pajamas that clung to her curves, sexy without trying to be. I was just about to move on, to finally get in the shower, when her eyes popped open, keeping me frozen in place as she peered around, then met my gaze.

"What are you doing?" she asked, her tone thick with sleep as she stifled a yawn.

"Trying to figure out what you're doing," I tossed back, taking a seat at the end of the bed. "You do know where you are, right?"

"Yes, in my husband's bed," she replied, rolling her eyes. "You do so love when I emphasize that, right?"

I chuckled, going for the buttons on my shirt to start

taking it off. "Not when you do it in that tone and not in the comfy pajamas."

"What's wrong with my pajamas?" She sucked her teeth. "Not enough skin for you?"

"I'm glad you realize. At least take the shorts off."

"I will not," she declined. "I'm not in here for your pleasure anyway."

"Then why are you?" I asked, standing to take care of my belt and slacks. "And don't say it's because of the nice sheets. You've got the same ones."

"Because your stepmother was being weird. Asking me questions about why we had separate rooms, if I was taking care of you, yada yada ya," she huffed, sitting up to watch me undress. "If I wasn't in your bed, she would've been. At least, that's the impression I got."

I shook my head. "Nah, she damn well knows better. She's very familiar with the line around here. She won't cross it "

"You seem a lot surer about that than I am."

When I pulled my boxers down, her eyes went to my dick, and stayed there. "Is that why she's looney tunes? Were you dicking her down before I came along?"

I sighed. "We talked about this already, multiple times. I wasn't fucking anybody, and if I was, it wouldn't have been my father's widow."

"Then why the hell is she around?" Nalani asked. "She's young and beautiful, and probably got a decent allotment from your father's estate, right?"

"She did." I nodded. "Breanna is a millionaire; he was quite generous with her. But she feels like she should've gotten more."

"Were they married a long time?"

"Five or six years, something like that," I answered.

"She's hanging around to see what she can get from Calli or sucker one of us into getting with her," I said, laying it out. "I won't put a stop to it because I know she honestly does care for Calli, and I need somebody young and able-bodied around her to keep an eye on things. It makes up for the weird shit, to me."

Nalani nodded. "I guess I get that. But still."

"Still what?" I asked, moving back toward the bed, grabbing my discarded clothes on the way. "Feeling pressured by your competition?"

"Ew," she grunted. "Absolutely not. That lady can have you."

"That's what you say, but I see the way you look at me, woman."

"And how is that?"

"Like you're just counting down the seconds till you get to feel me inside you again."

She raised an eyebrow. "Get to? Wow. Just when I thought I'd hit the limits of your arrogance, I realize I've only scratched the surface."

"Confidence, baby. There's a difference."

"With you? Doubtful."

"Whatever makes you feel better." I chuckled. "I'm getting in the shower. Will you be here when I get out?"

She bit down on her lip, clearly considering it. "Do you want me to be here when you get back? I'm not fucking you tonight."

"That's fine."

"Don't say that."

"Why?"

"It makes me want to fuck you."

Shaking my head, I laughed. "This could be so much simpler if you just… let yourself do you what you felt."

"If I did that, I would've run you over weeks ago."

"Damn, it's like that?!"

"It was," she admitted with a shrug. "Now…"

"Now what?"

"Now I only want to run you over about half the time."

I grinned. "Okay. I'll take what I can get."

I turned to head to the shower, but before I could get all the way through the door, she spoke up again.

"Orion," she called.

"What's up?"

"Thank you for today," she said. "For everything."

I shook my head. "I've already told you; you don't have to thank me for any of that. And I've already told you why."

Instead of saying anything else, she simply nodded, and I moved on to take my shower. Through the time I was in there, I reflected a bit on the conversation just then, one of the first that was just… Cool.

Casual.

It was… kind of nice.

And when I left the bathroom, to find her still in my bed, peacefully sleeping again…that was even nicer.

TWENTY
NALANI

"You're wearing the earrings."

Instead of giving him the satisfaction of a response, I flaked another bite of honey-glazed salmon off with my fork, stabbing the piece to lift it to my mouth. *Then* I met Orion's gaze, my expression neutral as I chewed.

It wasn't until his eyes narrowed a bit, indicating I'd gotten just the tiniest shred of a rise out of him, that I smiled.

The win was small, infinitesimal, to be honest.

But every victory counted when I was fighting a losing battle.

Hell, at this point… I was sufficiently trounced.

I wasn't conceding though.

Never.

More than a month had passed since the wedding now, and I was—grudgingly—settling into my *Mrs. Sterling* title. The house he'd moved me into was home, I never spent a dime of my own money, and many of *Nectar's* big vendors were suddenly much more generous with their wholesale discounts.

Those were the easy things to accept.

The surface level stuff.

Changes I could happily take advantage of.

The other things, though, the *real* things… I was as disgusted by those as I had been about my willingness—*eagerness*—to welcome Orion's dick at any time.

Actually… maybe *more* disgusted.

I looked forward to sharing breakfasts with him in the morning, even got up early enough to join him in the gym sometimes.

Sickening.

His occasional, random text messages or flower deliveries at *Nectar* or tiny satin-wrapped boxes waiting on my pillow at home gave me butterflies.

Shameful.

And *worst* of all were these dinners he insisted I accompany him for; ultra-upscale places I had to get all dressed up for to get possibly stared at, maybe photographed, and *absolutely* hated on by women who'd unquestionably stab me to take my place… I *enjoyed* being on his arm.

Revolting.

I *hated* how deeply I'd accepted being Mrs. Sterling.

Diamond earrings and flawlessly cooked salmon shouldn't hold more weight than how this whole thing had come about and yet here I was sitting across from this man having a good time.

As usual.

"You're quiet tonight," Orion spoke up from across the small table. "What's going on?"

"Maybe I just don't want to talk to you."

He lifted an eyebrow. "Have I done something wrong?" he asked. "As I mentioned a moment ago, you're wearing the earrings I gave you today, so I'm assuming you like them."

"They're fine."

They were *fabulous*, actually, little white gold, half-butterflies encrusted with diamonds. I'd *squealed* when I opened the box and was immediately glad that I was alone in the room.

So later, I could pretend to be sufficiently unfazed by them.

"Okay."

Under the table, he reached for me, grabbing the hand I'd had resting in my lap. I took a deep breath, trying not to feel anything about his thumb skimming back and forth over my skin.

"Tell me what's going on."

Shit.

I hated *this* too; the way that my ability to keep my thoughts to myself had deteriorated to the point that all he had to do was touch me, and a solid six out of ten times, I was spilling whatever was on my mind.

This was one of those.

"I'm a little too comfortable," I admitted, pulling my hand from his. "I don't like it."

"Too comfortable with…?"

I rolled my eyes. "*You.*"

"*Me?!*" he whispered, a big grin spreading across his face in such a way that made it hard not to smile back.

Impossible, even.

"God you make me sick," I muttered, shaking my head as I turned away from him to look at literally *anything* else.

"That statement is in direct opposition to what you said

just a second ago," he teased, palming my calf under the table. "No harm in admitting you're really starting to fuck with me now."

"You're not embarrassed by that?" I asked, raising my foot to plant the toe of one of my sky-high heels between his legs. "We're good and married, and it took until now for me to even *start* the process of, as you put it, *really fucking with you*."

Orion shrugged, moving forward in his chair so that my foot was *actually* touching my target. "Most rich men's wives despise them, so I'm way ahead of the crowd."

"Seriously?"

"*Seriously*," he countered, his hand creeping up my thigh… coming to an abrupt stop when the shift in his expression told me he'd noticed someone.

It had to be someone he respected.

I pulled my leg from his grasp just as the *someone* reached the table. Orion stood to greet the man warmly, and experience—and social mores—had taught me that I should as well. Once they were finished, Orion turned to me, sending the man's attention in my direction.

"Stanford, this is my lovely wife, Nalani. Nalani, this is Stanford Reese," Orion said. "He's one of our regional managers at *Wholesome Foods*."

I extended my hand, offering a dip of my head to the familiar-looking older man. "Nice to formally meet you, Mr. Reese. You were at the wedding, right?"

"I was," he agreed, taking my hand. "And please, Stanford is just fine. Beautiful women can get away with *Stan*, though," he said, kissing the back of my hand. There was nothing *truly* flirtatious about it, but I grinned still. He was charming. And quite handsome, with his dynamic brown eyes, smooth dark skin and salt-and-pepper hair.

"Ay, break this shit up," Orion crowed, pretending to step between us as I laughed. "What are you even doing back in Blackwood already?"

Stanford frowned. "I'm on your schedule for tomorrow, updates on the new store expansion…"

"You're right." Orion cringed. "My apologies. Calli's had a lot of appointments this week, so I've been a bit distracted."

"Perfectly understandable. I'll be by the house to look in on her too if that's okay?"

"Of course, you're always welcome."

Stanford nodded, then diverted his attention back to me. "And maybe while I'm here this week, you and I can meet," he suggested. "I've been looking into *Nectar* and think the store would be well served by expansion."

My eyes went wide. "Seriously? I mean… it's something I was interested in, but it wasn't um… within my purview."

"As chief operating officer?" he asked, eyebrow raised. "I can't think of anything *more* within your purview."

Tell that to my damn daddy.

At least… before.

I'd brought the idea of more locations to him more than once, knowing that a place like *Nectar* would absolutely *thrive* on either coast or the right metro in the South.

We can't afford that.

It's too soon.

That's a risk we can't take.

Always a fucking excuse.

"What's on your agenda tomorrow?" Orion asked, pulling my attention back to the conversation at hand. "If we time it right, you can swing through on the tail end of our meeting, and we can talk through some preliminary plans. If you're open to it."

My mouth dropped open, but I quickly righted myself, not wanting to seem too eager.

Inside, I was *screaming*.

"I'm absolutely open to it, with the understanding of course that this would be heavily dependent on the viability of appropriate funds. With the recent changes in our corporate structure, and the findings from our forensic accountant, um... financing might be an issue. For a while."

God it hurt to admit that.

But I knew the transparency was needed, especially when having this conversation with men who got things done. It would break my heart to come up with all these grand plans for expansion, after wanting that exact thing for so long, only to find out they couldn't be executed.

"We can work out a cash infusion with no issue," Orion assured, shaking his head. "I could call twenty people right now who'd love to get into an investment like this. The money won't be a problem."

"I don't want to have to answer to twenty investors," was my immediate response, to which he smirked.

"You don't need twenty anyway, just one."

He raised an eyebrow with that statement, unnecessarily clueing me in to exactly who he was talking about—himself.

"We'll talk about it." I nodded, knowing better than to get into too much in front of his colleague.

And... honestly, not being sure if I'd accept or decline that offer.

The rest of dinner was uneventful. Stanford only stayed another few moments before excusing himself and Orion and I finished our meals and shared a dessert. Back at home, the house was quiet. Everyone had wound down already and retired to their rooms.

And now it was time for *my* choice.

I played this game with myself every night damn near, a "will I or won't I" back and forth over joining Orion in his bed. I knew without a doubt I probably *shouldn't*, and yet... it was always a difficult decision.

Our contracted "schedule" had long flown out the window.

"Goodnight," I told him at the top of the steps. His room was in one direction, mine in the other. His brow flexed, allowing a brief flash of confusion to cross his face before he nodded his acceptance.

He always accepted the answer.

Which shouldn't have been a turn on. It should be the bare minimum rules of engagement for adults, and yet...

"We'll talk about how much you need for the expansion over breakfast," he said, grabbing me at the waist to pull into him. I wasn't going to protest, but before I could've anyway, he dipped his head, bringing his lips to meet mine for a brief, sweet kiss.

"You're already talking about it as if it were a foregone conclusion," I said, lips still tingling a little, excited from the contact.

He shrugged as he let me go. "Isn't it?"

Was it?

That question knocked around in my mind for the rest of the night, into the morning. I had to drag myself out of the bed, forcing myself not to miss our somewhat-agreed-upon breakfast date.

Discussing the numbers with Orion was almost.

Whatever wariness I had over him getting

Nectar, I knew his ego was too big to let it fail while I was still his wife.

A fact it would be silly of me to not take advantage of while I could.

Any notion that Orion had simply lucked his way into a successful business due to nepotism was squashed as I listened to him speak. It was clear that he knew what he was talking about, knew this industry through and through. Not just that either. He was a visionary, honestly, playing off the things I said I wanted from *Nectar* to offer a plan that would see us not just expanding, but each location having its own energy and vibe.

In Blackwood, *Nectar* was a melting pot of different flavors and Black cultures while still having a baseline in the history of migration—Black American at its core, but warmly welcoming diasporic influence, reflective of the city itself.

In the south, we could dive deeper into the roots of Black American history, with a focus on "down home" flavors and vendors, making sure to incorporate the Caribbean and Creole cultures, with respect to the proximity the location could offer.

In the west, besides leaning into the stereotypical "Californian" diet, we could integrate the Afro-Indigenous and Afro-Latino influence prevalent there, with a location that took full advantage of beach access and ocean views, all that.

It... made me a little emotional to think about.

There would have to be a huge investment of time to bring any of it to light, but the *idea* of it was exciting. I couldn't even bring myself to play it cool. By the time breakfast was over, Orion was teasing the hell out of me because I couldn't keep a smile off my face.

There was zero point in pretending otherwise.

I was… *happy.*

"Do I *have* to have your security tail on me?" I whined on the way out of the house a little over an hour later. "I'm going straight to *Nectar*, my friends are stopping through for lunch in the food court, and then I'm coming right home. What do you think is going to happen?"

Orion shook his head, looking good as hell today in slacks and a nice sweater. "Not a chance. Your little friend has been in the wind way too long. It would be just my luck that today is the day."

I rolled my eyes over that "little friend" comment.

He was talking about EJ.

That scene he'd made in *Nectar* was weeks ago, which may as well be years ago to my mind. I was right back to not thinking about him.

Until I caught the occasional glimpse of the increased security.

A mood killer every time.

And fooling with Orion, there was no point arguing. He wasn't trying to hear it and it was easier to just let it ride.

So that was exactly what I did, simply ignoring them as I went about my day. Easy to do when I was up in my office, but much harder when I was out and about in the store.

Such as when Morgan and Alexis showed up for lunch.

We managed to snag a rarely-available, private table instead of the bench style seating—killing their opportunity to tease me about not using my "status" to simply mark one off as reserved. I was serious about our customers being a priority though, *except* where it came to waiting on our food. I *did* order that ahead, knowing Morgan and Alexis both would appreciate the efficiency of being able to eat while we talked and then get back to work.

Everybody was busy.

Not too busy to get on my ass though.

"You're *glowing,* Mrs. Sterling," Morgan taunted as she stabbed a forkful of salad. "Life as a billionaire's wife must be treating you well. What's happening with your face?" she asked, gesturing at me with her loaded fork. "A cheetah placenta facial or something? Why does your skin look so expensive?"

Shaking my head, I laughed. "Cheetah placenta? Where do you even come up with the shit? I'm using a new line from the spa that just opened on the first floor, *Face Card.* For the price point, that shit *better* work."

"I'm gonna need an exact list of whatever you're using," Alexis told me, wearing a dead serious expression.

Morgan nodded. "Make sure you forward it to me too."

"No need for all that." I shook my head. "I'll just send it to you. And I'll put it on Orion's credit card, like I did with mine," I added, sticking out my tongue as they laughed.

"*See*, with the rich bitch antics," Morgan insisted. "You're already acting up!"

"Am I acting up, or using *all* my contractually obligated perks while I have them?"

Alexis sucked her teeth. "*While you have them*? Please." She laughed. "Your ass isn't going anywhere. You messed around and started liking him and we all know where *that* leads."

"I don't *like him*," I argued, looking back and forth between her and Morgan, hoping to drop the unconvinced looks from their faces. "I tolerate him. There's a difference."

"How many times have you fucked him since you got married?" Morgan asked.

I scoffed. "Girl I don't know! I'm not keeping up with that."

"That's *exactly* the point." She laughed. "Six weeks ago you were lamenting having to submit to a biweekly poking, and now you're taking that dick so often *you can't even keep up*? Bitch who do you think you're fooling?"

"Myself, damn, can y'all let me live?!" I whisper-yelled, making them giggle again. "I don't know, I'm just…" I sighed. "My commitment to being disgusted at myself for *not* being disgusted by him is waning. He's wearing me down," I whined.

"Girl let that shit happen," Alexis insisted. "Seriously, *you're married to him*. It doesn't have to be miserable just because of how it started."

"But I can't let go of how it started," I countered. "It's just like… there at the back of my mind. And I'm *still* not really sure what he's getting out of this, which is nagging at me. What if I get too comfortable and *then* some bullshit comes out?"

"He's *getting* more pussy than he can keep up with and a beautiful wife," Morgan spoke up. "And even though he deeded the *Nectar* building and land back to you, he still benefits from that connection."

I tipped my head, nodding. "There might really be something to that. This afternoon I'm meeting with him and one of the *Wholesome Foods* regional managers to talk about expansion for *Nectar*."

Alexis perked up. "Expansion as in different locations?"

"Yep," I affirmed. "And guess who would be the main investor for an undertaking like that?"

"Mmmm." She nodded. "And I bet you're feeling iffy about it?"

"Hell yes," I answered. "I know I can bring on lawyers to make sure the terms aren't predatory, but *still*. I got married to make sure *Nectar* was solely in my hands. Having him—or anybody, really—invest feels like handing the reins over again, which is scary."

"Understandably," Morgan said. "But at the same time… the opportunity for expansion is pretty major."

My head bobbed. "It absolutely is, which makes this even harder. I don't feel just *one* way about it. Multiple locations has always been a dream of mine for this store, you know? I don't want to pass up the chance just because of some—unlikely—possibility that Orion just wants to screw me over."

"If it helps ease your mind at all, Orion is *very* careful with this kind of money," Alexis said. "Now, I can't say *too* much, but… knowing what I do about his personal portfolio, I don't think he would offer his investment lightly. He has to really believe in it. In… you."

I blew out a sigh.

I hated the way those words felt in my chest.

As much effort as I gave into managing my own feelings where it came to Orion, trying to keep them rooted in logic instead of letting my pussy lead the way, I was constantly ignoring and downplaying the vibes that came from *him*.

Did I think the man was in love with me?

Of course not.

But he was certainly all-in as my husband, as far as I could tell. The way he looked at me made me blush, the way he protected me made me feel invincible, and the words he sometimes spoke over me seemed deeply rooted in a level of respect I appreciated more than I could articulate.

And the way he *touched* me…

Chills.

This was *supposed* to feel like torture though.

"I'm pulling the subject change card," I said, shaking my head. "Conversation getting a little too real for me."

Alexis and Morgan looked at each other, then back to me, and nodded.

"Valid," Alexis said. "Let's talk about how I'm about to have to start my own firm because my boss ain't shit."

I frowned. "Anthony's ass *again*?"

"Yes, *him*." She blew out a sigh. "This new startup, *InnovaTech*. I'm the senior most junior partner at BWM, but they're giving the account to Isai Mason and his little crew instead. They're *children*."

"I thought you mentioned him being the same age as Soren when you complained about him before," Morgan asked.

"No, *younger* than Soren, who is a baby too. These guys are *newborns*."

"But... Lex... isn't personal wealth your thing? Startups are corporate finance..."

"Yes, but after I got us in at *Stellar Foods* because of my connection, I'd hoped the firm would see and appreciate that, and put me in on more corporate accounts. I *asked* for more corporate accounts."

Alexis went on with her complaints about the lack of respect she got at work, but I was only half tuned in. With the conversation still being about corporate investments, I couldn't help my mind drifting back to what she'd said earlier.

He has to really believe in you.

That statement shouldn't've have made such a big impact, but here we were.

So often—*too* often—I could trace the failings of my

romantic relationships straight to my ambition and lack of need on a financial level. I wanted someone I could build with; not a man so fragile he needed me to play a role of needing bills paid or whatever else.

I could take care of myself on that level.

The appeal of a partner was in having my emotional and physical needs met; two areas where far too many men were underdeveloped and showed no interest in improving.

Orion had money in droves and had sexual manipulation of my body down to a science. I wasn't *that* comfortable quite yet that I was laying out any emotional needs for this man.

And yet… he'd managed to find an itch to scratch.

The idea that he believed in my ability to successfully expand the store, and willingness to put resources behind it, was really doing something for me; exactly *what,* I couldn't pinpoint. It was little to do with the money, though it mattered to actually getting it done. I didn't want to feel indebted to him, but I wasn't afraid enough of failing to turn it down.

It was the other part, the part that didn't have anything to do with money, not really… *that* was scary.

If I was already losing my battle of keeping a wall up between us…

What kind of blow would him making an unspoken dream of mine come true deal?

TWENTY-ONE
NALANI

"Tell me something, Nala. You not running yourself raggedy trying to get skinny are you?"

It was a good thing I had a towel over my face, otherwise I would've given Calli a "girl what the fuck are you talking about" look that could've been interpreted as disrespectful.

And it would've been.

But I wasn't trying to give that energy to her.

So I took a moment to dry the sweat from my face before I turned to face her. I'd been passing by the entrance to the sun room on the way back to my own after a quick session on the stationary bike in the gym. She was sitting there alone, watching the wildlife in the trees now that the weather was getting a little warmer.

"Not even a little," I told her. "Just staying limber since your grandson has me out here in the suburbs instead of my place in the city."

"Good," she insisted. "Keep some meat on you. You're gonna need it when you start making babies, hear?"

My eyes went wide, and I forced a smile as I nodded. "Yes ma'am," I told her. "Nothing to worry about, okay?"

"You ain't gotta 'yes ma'am' me, baby." She cackled. "I'm just an old lady outside her business. I've gathered up enough years to do that, right?"

When I thought about it from that perspective, my smile shifted to a genuine one and I nodded again. "I think you're on to something," I agreed. "But… yeah. Like I said, just keeping the joints lubricated and the heart healthy, that's all."

"All I needed to hear."

It was all I planned to say. Though, *that* was a musing that would remain internal. I wasn't particularly interested in discussing the affairs of my uterus, *especially* not if it would be getting put to use soon.

Not that there was any discussion necessary, really.

Orion had been doing his damnedest to fill it and I was contractually obligated to let him.

That situation was going to be whatever it was going to be, without any outside input.

And yet, even with that thought in mind… I was surprised to find the telltale pink streaks of an impending period in my underwear when I stripped down to take my shower.

I wasn't *sad* about it necessarily. Pregnancy was a game of chance and Orion and I had only been having sex for a few weeks since the wedding. Those pink streaks were due *last* week, but with everything going on, there hadn't been room for me to panic.

Actually… I was *glad* to see them.

There was a little too much going on for a pregnancy right now.

Since that lunch meeting with Stanford Reese about

expanding the *Nectar* territory, my days had been exponentially busier and there were no signs of things slowing down.

In fact, thinking about it from that angle, I hoped it would work in my favor that our attempts at producing Orion's contractually obligated heir would take a little while.

We needed better timing.

In the shower, I let my mind run free, thinking through best case scenarios for this baby I'd agreed to before I knew just how bad things were going to get with my father. I lifted a hand toward the ceiling, scrubbing my armpit area as I processed it all.

Absently staring at the soap running down my skin.

Until my eyes focused on the *slightest* scar.

On my arm.

Where… my birth control implant was.

Fuck.

FUCK!

I dropped my arm *and* my cleansing net, covering the scar with my hand like someone was there to see it or like it would help anything if they were. Eyes wide, I glanced around the bathroom, looking for… nothing.

Anything.

FUCK.

I blew out a sigh, finding the wherewithal from somewhere to rinse the rest of the soap from my skin and leave the shower. In the mirror, I could see the panic in my eyes but quickly shook it off, searching the counter for my cell phone.

Shit. Shit. Shit.

Where — Oh.

Shit.

It was just under my towel.

I snatched the device up, quickly dialing my doctor's private emergency line after hunting down the number buried in my notes app.

I'd never had to use it before.

Her nurse answered after just a couple rings, immediately going into problem-solving mode after I frantically rattled off my problem the second time.

The first time, I was incoherent.

I hung up the call with an understanding that I was going straight to the office before work. Removing the tiny hormonal device was a quick outpatient procedure that ideally would only take a few minutes.

Still.

I was frazzled.

With how quick the proposal and wedding had happened, on top of everything else, setting up an appointment to remove the device that would prevent me from conceiving a child had simply fallen by the wayside. If things had progressed on a more reasonable timeline, it was the kind of thing I would've undoubtedly taken care of and my doctor would've wanted me on some sort of plan, starting vitamins, a special diet, something.

Shit.

This... wasn't good.

Shit.

I took as many deep breaths as it took to calm my racing heart, then hurriedly got dressed. I wasn't leaving the house nearly as polished as most days, but I was calling it a win that I got out of there at all without running into Orion.

The man sniffed out bullshit too easily.

At the office, true to what I'd been told, the removal took less than thirty minutes. Some imaging to find the exact location, which they marked, a shot to numb the area, a tiny incision, removal, then cleaning and bandaging. By the time I left, I felt about five hundred pounds lighter, but I still messaged Demetria to ask what I should do about my unintentional breach of contract.

Her advice was to not say a fucking thing, considering how early I'd corrected the issue. Even if it had been top of mind, it could've taken this long to get a regular removal appointment anyway. And the chances of me getting pregnant during the period between now and the wedding weren't a hundred percent.

So… no harm, no foul.

As long as I kept my damn mouth shut about it.

Which was *exactly* what I planned to do.

I breezed through the doors of *Nectar* precisely as I would any other day, stopping by the *Urban Grind* mini-shop for a double shot latte. The first thing I did at my computer was open my email, checking for anything urgent. I liked fixing problems at the *beginning* of the day.

Luckily for me, the only *problem* on my hands had been a personal one. There *was* a message of interest in my box though. The name Hailey Freeman in the "from" column pulled my attention, and I double-clicked the message to see what it was about.

Good morning Nalani,

We haven't had the opportunity to meet yet, but I'm a regular patron of Nectar*, in there a couple of times every week! You might be familiar with my family. I'm descended from the original owners of the Freeman's Bridal Shop, which provided your dress for your recent nuptials. Less known is the fact that my great, great grandmother—also Hailey*

Freeman—used to run a periodical for the town, back when it was still known as Sugar Leaf.

I know that introduction is a lot of "okay, get to point," but I promise I am!

I moved to Blackwood pretty recently and have found myself enamored with the history, especially knowing my ancestral connection; one we tangentially have in common. In looking through old pictures from the printing press days, I've found a lot of historical information related to Nectar that you might wish to look through and/or have in your possession.

I've been working closely with our local historian to parse all of these thing, and am also in the process of writing a book of essays that reflect the history of Blackwood and that connection to modern life. I'd love to speak with you about the project. I'm sure you have a lot of valuable insight into keeping the heart of family legacy alive while making sure the store remains relevant for the modern consumer.

Additionally, I have some pictures that would likely be of interest to you, or maybe your new husband? They're still in great condition. They've been taken through an extensive preservation process, but they have to be at least forty or fifty years old. They were donated to the museum project by the children of some people in the picture, but they heavily feature Nectar, your parents, the Sterlings (Daneitha and Caspian, Orion's parents) and some friends. I'll attach scans of them for you to see.

Clearly, I'm long winded. I like words, sorry!

In any case, please contact me at your convenience. Again, I'd love to speak to you about the store and any other historical context you could give me.

Thank you!

Hailey Freeman.

The message ended there but I kept scrolling, curious about the pictures she was referring to.

Pictures that immediately brought a smile to my face.

They were in color, but the grainy, muted colors synonymous with the time. So much of the store *hadn't* changed in layout because there was no need. My ancestors who built the store were *clearly* thinking beyond their time.

The biggest changes were signage and technology, which we'd integrated well. Everything still felt very organic and classic, without being old-fashioned. And of course, much different storefronts.

There was still a smile on my face as I came to the pictures where the people were the subjects, several of which were my mother. She was young in these, younger than I was now, and it was like looking into my *own* past self.

I looked *just* like her.

Besides my father, the other people weren't as familiar, but I could quickly pull Orion's parents out. He looked like his father *and* mother, a beautiful blend of the two.

It was wild to me that they'd all been friends, considering the way they'd always been spoken about to me.

But when I thought about it really... all the trash talking had come from my father.

Looking at him in pictures of him and the other men, I wondered what had gone wrong. In these pictures, they were all smiles, unloading boxes, taking a break to shoot dice, hands around each other's shoulders.

They seemed like *brothers*.

So what the hell happened?

When I clicked onto the last picture, my eyes went wide. There were three men in most of the pictures, Orion's father, my father, and a third man who was usually not facing the camera. In this one though, he was looking right at it.

Looking *just* like my little brother.

And I didn't have to wonder who he was. After the past week, his identity held *zero* mystery to me.

I was looking at Stanford Reese.

Seeing him now, much older than he was in the picture, it wasn't as obvious.

He was baby-faced here, clearly carrying fewer worries.

Stanford now was still handsome, but he was past graying, had facial hair, had lost some weight, and after a few conversations I knew he'd suffered some health problems a while back that had likely changed his appearance some.

But that was him.

In the picture, he had the very same face as Soren, who'd *never* looked like either of our parents really, but we already though it was just a result of the genetic lottery.

Seeing this image though… his looks seemed a lot less random.

And explained a *lot* of the energy we'd been getting from my father.

Maybe *this* was where his "whore" commentary was coming from?

That realization set off a million questions in my mind, starting with why Stanford hadn't mentioned knowing my mother? He'd talked about being close with Orion's father, but never introduced this other information.

And for that matter… why had my Aunt Lucy been so mum about this?

She was in a few of the pictures too, smiling right along with the rest of the group, despite my clear memory of her claiming the age gap had meant she wasn't in the same circle of friends as my mother. It could be coincidence, sure, but something about it felt... like something else.

What?

I had no way of being sure.

My computer pinged with a new set of emails coming through, reminding me that I couldn't fall down a rabbit hole with this stuff right now. I shot a quick message back to Hailey, checking her availability. If there were more pictures, I wanted to see them, and I needed to know everything she did about the generation of *Nectar* before me.

One way or another, I was going to get those answers.

I ARRIVED home to a quiet house.

Not that quiet was unusual around here, but it was a little eerie. I'd had dinner at my desk, so I didn't bother making my way to the dining room after my shower. I settled on the chaise in my room with my kindle and a glass of wine, intent on finding some peace after a stressful day.

Instead, I found myself thinking about Soren.

We'd spoken several times throughout the day, but I'd avoided the subject of Stanford Reese. It wasn't as if it were a natural topic of conversation.

Still, the couple of times I'd seen him person, I'd caught myself picking apart his features, comparing them to a man neither of us had ever met until recently.

At least... I didn't *think* Soren had met Stanford.

And I didn't dare ask, for fear of what it might bring up.

Even now, I tried to shake away the thoughts, but it was difficult to say the least.

Eventually, I put the kindle down and went to social

media, knowing the mindless scrolling would work better for my current attention span.

Until a knock at the door pulled me away.

I wasn't surprised to find Orion on the other side, peering curiously at me when I opened the door.

"Hey," he said, giving me a slow perusal with his eyes.

"Hey yourself," I said, meeting his gaze. "I'm on my period, so…"

A little smirk spread over his lips. "Damn, you think that's the only reason I'd come see you?"

"Only? No. Most likely…?"

He chuckled a little, shaking his head. "Believe it or not, that wasn't my motive. But I do have to say… your throat is still available, no? And your ass—"

"Okay, I was trying to wind down," I interrupted, shaking my head. "How can I help you?"

"That's what I was explaining."

"*Orion.*"

"Fine." He laughed, then sobered back to the serious expression he'd worn before. "I was coming to see if you were okay."

I raised an eyebrow. "Uhh… yeah. Why wouldn't I be okay?"

"You tell me." He shrugged. "You're the one who went to the doctor this morning."

Shit, I thought, eyes going wide before I could force my expression to remain neutral. Right before me, *his* face changed too, from concern to… *suspicion.*

Shit.

"Nala… let's not even play a game here," he warned, stepping past me into the room to close the door. "What the fuck is going on?"

"How do you even know about that?" I asked, stalling. I knew *exactly* how. The security detail I'd been too panicky this morning to think about. "That's private information."

"Pretty sure the rules are a little different between husband and wife and besides that... *like I said.* Let's not play games. Is there something I need to know about?"

"If there was, I'd let you know," I snapped, turning away to storm across the room.

Intending to storm across the room.

My decision to choose indignation as my shield backfired quickly. He grabbed my arm to turn me around, the same arm I'd gotten cut upon earlier that morning, triggering a wince.

Seeing my face made him drop his grip, but he knew something was up. Before I could stop him, he'd pulled up the arm of my robe, immediately zeroing in on the freshly changed bandage.

"Nala, *stop fucking playing with me,*" he growled. "What is this?!"

"First, you need to calm the hell down," I warned, snatching away from him. I took a few steps backwards, putting some distance between us. "You're already making it a bigger deal than what it really is."

"I don't think you get to decide that," he countered, nostrils flaring. "*Why* is your arm bandaged?"

"*Because,*" I countered. "I... had to have a little procedure this morning. A *tiny* procedure. It's silly to even call it a *procedure*, honestly."

"*Honestly,* I'm about to fucking snap if you don't give me a real answer, *real quick,*" he growled. "A procedure for *what?*"

"To have my birth control removed," I blurted, crossing my arms protectively around myself. "I... I had forgotten I had it. So I made it a priority, and it's out now, and... that's all."

For a long moment... he didn't say anything.

A tidbit I knew better than to take as a good sign.

He opened his mouth to speak, then must've thought better of whatever was about to come out, clamping a hand over his lips as he paced in a little back and forth.

And then, finally, in a terrifyingly calm tone, he spoke.

"I don't believe you."

My eyebrow shot up. "Excuse me?"

"*I don't believe you*," he repeated, stepping closer. "I *don't fucking believe you*."

"What is there not to believe?" I asked, tossing my hands up. "I told you, I forgot about the damn implant, my period started and reminded me, so I contacted my doctor to get it removed."

"Why wouldn't you just... tell me that?" he asked, shaking his head. "If it were an honest mistake, you could've just said that shit, no big deal. But the sneaking around, the secrecy... it makes me feel like you did this shit on purpose. Like you were intentionally putting it off."

My eyes narrowed. "By a month? What would've been the point?!"

"*You tell me!*" he bellowed, getting closer still. "But if it was just some oversight, you've had more than a month to correct the shit, *knowing* what we were trying to do. What's in the *fucking contract*."

"Now you want to bring up the contract?!" I huffed. "Orion, we've barely talked about it, and certainly haven't had a *real* discussion about planning a baby because when have we even had time?!"

"Oh, so you're trying to pin this on me?!"

"I'm not *pinning* anything on anybody, I'm just saying that it's not fair for you to react like this, when it hasn't even been a long time."

"How should I react, huh?" he asked, right in my face. "How *should* I respond to finding out you've been playing in my goddamn face?!"

"I *wasn't*," I insisted, not backing up. "It was a mistake!"

"Which you tried to sneak around about, instead of just fucking telling me?"

"Yes, because I was afraid you'd react *exactly* like this!"

"Because you know exactly how suspect it looks?!"

"Because I know exactly how much of a fucking narcissist you are. That you wouldn't accept somebody daring to overlook something that is not remotely a daily thought!"

"For *you*!" he spat. "Not a daily thought *for you*, but it is ever-present in the back of *my* mind, or is that not something you've considered?" he asked. "Probably not. It's funny that you can accuse *me* of narcissism like you aren't the one who's treating our contract like it's not a big deal because it's not important *to you*."

My mouth dropped open.

"I... I... *you haven't even mentioned it to me*!" I accused, shaking my head. "For you to now be claiming it's so important!"

He scoffed. "Nalani, it was a *clear* deal breaker in our contract and you agreed to it. We've been fucking raw, at every opportunity. I didn't think I *needed* to say it. And I was hoping that leaving it unspoken would make it less pressure on everybody, but I see you've taken that as an invitation to just do whatever you want."

"If I was doing whatever I wanted, I would still have the

implant in my arm," I told him. "Be glad I have a conscience about it."

Instantly, his whole energy shifted.

And *not* for better.

He simply gave me a nod and didn't say shit else before turning away and stalking out of the room.

Somehow… I did *not* feel like I'd "won."

TWENTY-TWO
ORION

My fingers tapped impatiently on a glass of bourbon that shouldn't even be in my hand.

Drinking on the clock—*especially* before noon—shouldn't have even been an option, and yet it was. Right at my desk.

I knew better.

But I was stewing.

I *hated* stewing.

For a few days now, I hadn't even been able to look Nalani in her face, too pissed off about the news she'd so cavalierly dropped in my lap.

I didn't believe for a second she'd simply "forgotten." The woman was too put-together for that. I'd seen what her calendars looked like, knew how organized she was.

And even if she *had* "forgotten"… the sneaking around was out of character.

And unnecessary.

So I didn't believe that shit.

"I thought we'd put a time limit on this," Shiloh said from the doorway, pulling me from my thoughts. When I looked up, she was tapping her watch. "I told you, at ten we were getting out of our feelings to get some shit done."

I blew out a sigh. "Shi… I appreciate your attempts to motivate, but I'm not in the mood."

"Glad I didn't ask that then," she said, stepping fully inside and crossing her arms. "My job is to keep you together, so that things around here keep running. You've been licking a superficial wound for like a week at this point and ignoring your schedule."

"Superficial? There's nothing superficial about the timeframe my wife and I agreed on. *Contractually.*"

"I'm not saying there is," Shiloh countered. "I'm saying that her delay in getting her birth control removed is *not* what you're turning it into."

I scoffed. "So you're telling me you believe she *forgot*? Please."

"Yes, actually." Shiloh shrugged. "The whole point of long-term birth control is *to forget it*," she argued. "To *not* have to think about it every day. Or ever, until you get the notification every couple of years that it's time to replace, but since you don't have to worry about that…"

"I'm well aware of how long-term birth control works," I griped. "That's not the point."

Shiloh nodded. "Right. The *point* is that, somewhere between you railroading her into a quickie wedding, having the wedding, and then coming back to deal with an accounting clusterfuck and corporate takeover, she should've remembered to have the birth control designed to be forgotten removed. 'Cause you wanted her to. Did I miss something?"

My nostrils flared as I blew out *another* sigh, this one

exponentially more exaggerated than before. "You've made it clear what side of this you're on. You can close my door on your way out."

"I'm not on anybody's *side*, Ri. I'm trying to get you to see *logic*. You know, that thing men seem to think they're the kings of?"

"My logic is perfectly sound. What makes you think it isn't?"

"Your hella emotional response to what happened," Shiloh answered, shrugging. "You're being a little irrational. Just a tad."

"Fuck off, Shi."

"I will *not*," she insisted. She dropped into the chair across from my desk. "Not until you snap out of this and give your wife some grace. She's probably *not* lying. And if she was… well… can you honestly blame her?"

I frowned. "Excuse me?"

Shiloh sucked her teeth. "Come on, Ri, think about it. You blew into her life like a damn typhoon, wrecking everything she understood about… hell, everything. You used your resources to needle your way into a position that mostly benefitted you and you *still* haven't told her the full truth about why. Only the most hurtful possible angle. From her point of view, you stole her mother's legacy, forced her to marry you to get it back, and now she's supposed to get pregnant, making herself *even more vulnerable*. To *you*, of all people. You should probably count your lucky stars if delaying the possibility of having your kid is all she plans to do to you."

"I haven't done shit her own damn father didn't make possible."

"And you think that absolves you?" she asked. "I mean, listen, I understand that the rules are different around here, that everybody has their motives, all that. But you can't put a woman in a desperate situation and then get mad when she makes desperate moves, which, again, is *not* what I think happened."

"I don't pay you for your opinions."

Shiloh lifted an eyebrow, a mischievous grin I was *not* in the fucking mood for spreading over her face. *"Don't you though?"* she asked, propping her hands on her chin as she leaned into my desk.

She really thought I was fucking playing.

"Listen, you've worked for me a long ass time. You're family, Shi, so I'm trying to be cool right now. I suggest you get the fuck out of my office, okay?"

"Oooh." She laughed, pushing up from her seat. "Okay, *Mr. Serious*. But think about what I said. You're being a jerk and you should really reconsider. Not everything is a personal slight against you."

"Shiloh."

"I'm *leaving,* grumpy ass," she huffed. "My bad for trying to give you some wise counsel."

"It's not wise counsel, it's bullshit and if you say another thing, you're fired."

She'd been turned toward the door, already on her way out, but she turned to glare at me. "You don't have to fire me, motherfucker. I'll see myself out."

"Good."

"*Good*!" she snapped, slamming the door behind her.

A moment later, she opened it again.

"I'll be back when you get the stick out of your ass and stop acting like a damn toddler."

She slammed the door again.

And I lifted that glass of bourbon to my lips.

This was *bullshit*.

She'd known Nalani all of two months—*barely*—but she was firmly on her side, not even giving my perspective a second thought.

And she wasn't alone in her favoritism. Of the few people I'd told about this situation, the select few that knew about the details of it, contract and all, *nobody* thought I was justified in feeling the way I did.

Which was fucked up.

Maybe I *was* wrong.

But it sure didn't feel like it.

Instead of Shiloh's morning interruption having the intended effect of getting me back to work, the opposite happened. I spent the next hour sulking even further over what I saw as a betrayal of our agreement and finishing my bourbon.

Was I being irrational?

I didn't see it.

To me, it was rational as *fuck* to feel blindsided, after I'd spent so much time, effort, money, trying to get this woman to understand that when I called her my wife, I meant that shit.

I was all in.

I was holding up every possible element of what I was supposed to be bringing to our arrangement, going above and beyond, honestly. As fucked up as the start of this relationship was, I didn't want our child conceived in misery. I wanted her *happy*.

As happy as I could possibly make her.

As much as it was in my power to do.

And her ass "forgot" she was on birth control?

Knowing that a baby within the first two years was one of my *few* stipulations?

That was fucked up to me.

And nobody would convince me otherwise.

My cell phone pinged with a message. A quick glance let me know it was from Henry. He was letting me know that after weeks in the wind, we'd finally picked up a scent for bitch ass EJ.

I swiped the text away.

With the shit Nalani had pulled on me, I didn't even care about that right now.

Actually, no.

I cared, cared about being played for a fucking fool. I was ready to burn this fucking city down over her, ready to start a damn war because some bitch that meant nothing to me before this had dared put his hands on her.

And she "forgot" she was on birth control.

Wild.

I tucked the need to respond to Henry at the back of my mind, ready to go back to what Shiloh had referred to yesterday —her first fucking strike—as my "he-motional crisis".

That was, until a new knock sounded at the door.

Before I could answer, it was already open, and I was fully prepared to curse Shi the fuck out before I put her back to work, We *both* knew she wasn't fired.

She wasn't the person who came in though.

It was Jess.

"Good afternoon, Mr. Sterling," she practically purred as she closed the door behind her. "Thought instead of meeting virtually, I'd just pop in. Haven't been seeing nearly enough of you now that you're a married man."

"With good reason," I replied. "Boundaries."

She smirked, slinking to the seat Shiloh had previously

occupied to settle in. "Let me guess whose idea that was, your lovely wife?"

"I'm not run by my wife or *any* woman," I said.

Words that felt hollow considering the way Nalani's ass had me twisted in knots right now.

It was a privilege Jess had never had, despite her attempts otherwise. And she should be well aware of exactly what I was talking about. It was a large part of the reason she and I were not together.

There were a lot of overlaps in personality between Jess and Nalani, which wasn't surprising to me. I *definitely* had a type.

I wanted a strong woman, not someone I could easily bowl over. I wanted someone with some fight to her.

The problem with Jess was her ass wasn't just feisty; she was *sly*.

Manipulative.

Some shit I absolutely *hated* as her partner. She was great at marketing, could spin any piece of news or data into exactly what she wanted to present, but didn't know when to turn that shit off.

Probably why this current issue with Nalani felt more than a little triggering for me.

It reminded me of a dynamic I thought I'd left far behind me.

"Just teasing," Jess said, her breasts practically spilling out of her top as she leaned forward. "But come on... even after we broke up, you and I have always been pretty close, right? We've *always* been good friends."

She wasn't wrong.

Even though Jess and I didn't work out as a couple, we'd

still been cool even after our breakup. I didn't see a reason not to be.

In fact, we'd still been intimate for a while after, until I put a stop to that too, knowing that discipline was necessary for what I wanted the next phase of my life to be.

A decision I was glad I had made when finding a wife and someone suitable to bear my children became less of a desire and more of a necessity.

It eliminated any messy crossover that would need to be explained to my wife and I *thought* Jess and I had something of an understanding.

When I was completely single, she'd never been pushy about it, never tried to put herself in the way. She was supportive.

But something about the news of my marriage to Nalani had her wilding.

Between her behavior at the cabin before the wedding and little flirtatious commentary and actions since then… she was pushing it.

Like today.

Usually, I would nip it in the bud, not wanting her to ever get comfortable disrespecting my wife.

Today… fuck it.

I was mad.

"You're right," I told her. "We *have* always been good friends, and that hasn't changed. You know what kind of man I am."

"Well yeah, *I* know," Jess mused. "I'm just starting to wonder if your wife does. We haven't seen you out at the cigar club lately, you haven't been… *around*, and in the mix like you usually are. You don't socialize anymore."

I scoffed. "I socialize plenty," I argued. "But let's not

forget the fact that I'm also running a billion-dollar business. There would be something wrong if I could hang out the same way I used to. I'm focused. And that was the case even before Nalani came along."

"Yeah, yeah," she agreed, putting on a flirtatious smile.

I could not and would not front. Jess was still an attractive woman and my brain—and body—remembered a lot about her. There was very little I could do about the fact that her current performance was causing a bit of commotion for my dick.

I shook my head.

"We should probably get to the real reason you showed up at my office, right?"

"You mean this alleged marketing meeting with just me and you?"

"Alleged?" I asked, eyebrow raised.

She smirked. "I mean… sure, we *could* talk a little about plans, but it would be much more productive with a team in place, right?"

So it was a setup.

And Shiloh hadn't caught it because it was originally supposed to be virtual.

There was that sly shit.

"I'll carry whatever we talk about back to my subordinates," she said. "*Or* we can schedule a different meeting, with the full team… and I could use *this* time… to remind you what you've been missing. You do miss me… right?"

I sat back, shaking my head as a little chuckle broke through my lips. "Jess… as enticing of an offer as that might be… I was serious about my vows."

She sighed. "Can't blame a girl for trying though… right?"

"I'm sure I could." I laughed. "But I won't this time."

"Right." She grinned. "But… in the interest of maintaining our friendship… maybe I should come by the house for dinner tonight or something? Unless of course, you think your wife would object?"

Ha.

I *knew* my wife would object.

Which was exactly why I nodded my agreement.

If Nalani wanted to play games, I was down with that and didn't mind getting under her skin in the exact spot I knew was already sore.

We *did* talk marketing, discussing plans for the next quarter for Jess to take back to her team. My spirits were high the rest of the day, making it much easier to get shit done, even without Shiloh there. She'd probably gone off to a spa for the day or something, but my schedule was already settled and I was more than capable of working through it on my own.

After hours, Jess met me in the parking lot, hopping in her car to follow me home, where I'd already given the chef a heads-up that we'd have a guest at dinner.

And Henry let me know that, for a change, Nalani was already home.

Perfect.

At some point on the way, Jess had lost a few more buttons. Her bra and ample cleavage were fully exposed in the now deep cut of her blouse. She offered a mischievous smirk as I held the door open for her and we headed straight to the dining room.

Ms. Wallace raised an eyebrow at me, passing on her way out as we stepped in. She looked at Jess, who'd placed herself on my arm, then back at me, shaking her head. "Calli is feeling a bit tired. She decided to have dinner in her room. I'm going to join her," she informed, then walked off, leaving no room for argument.

Good.

Calli's ability to handle too much excitement had been my only qualm about this stunt.

With her tucked away for the night, all bets were off.

"Go retrieve my wife from her room please," I told Henry. "I expect her at the table for dinner."

Henry's usual blasé expression hardened as he looked me in the eyes, giving a quick glance to where Jess had already moved to take a seat. "You sure about this?" he asked.

"I'm positive."

He let out a grunt and a quick nod, saying nothing else before he moved to gather Nalani for me.

"Why is everybody so uptight today?" Jess asked. "It's not like this is the first time I've come to dinner."

I didn't respond to that.

Jess wasn't dumb by any means, no matter how much she might fake it to get her way.

She knew *exactly* what was going on.

"Henry didn't mention that we had a guest."

Nalani's voice pulled my attention to the doorway. Her natural hair was out and wild, which I loved, but knew wasn't for my benefit. Her skin was glowing like she'd just finished her skin routine and she'd clearly already showered and changed into loungewear since coming home. I teased her about her comfort wear, but my body's reaction to her curves poured into the ultra-soft, clingy fabric of her matching set made me shift a little in my seat.

If I couldn't say shit else, she was… exquisite.

She wasn't looking at me, though.

She was looking at Jess, as Chef served dinner.

"Nalani, it's so lovely so see you," Jess gushed. "You look so… comfortable."

Nalani shrugged, making her way to the table, to the setting directly across from Jess. "How else should I look? This is my home."

"Oh. Well… of course," Jess said, taken aback. "I love that you've settled into the role."

"Role?" Nalani asked, smiling at her. The most beautiful, alarming smile I'd ever seen. "Surely we can leave the corporate speak at the office. I'm assuming that's where the two of you are coming from?"

Finally, she looked at me, expecting an answer.

I nodded.

"Yes, a marketing meeting that ran a bit long."

Nalani's eyes narrowed, and she nodded too. "Nice. I'm guessing the length meant it was productive?"

I met Chef's gaze, and he shook his head, excusing himself from the drama. I couldn't blame him. I was already regretting the shit I'd clearly started.

"*Very*," Jess chimed in, pulling attention to herself. She made an exaggerated point of wiping her mouth as she glanced at me. "I'm sure you know how Orion gets when he's locked in on… reaching a certain peak. Like a dog with a bone."

"Huh," Nalani said, looking at me, then back to her.

Then back to me.

Somehow, I knew exactly what was coming.

Just couldn't move fast enough to stop it.

In what seemed like the blink of an eye, Nalani was on her feet, reaching across the table. Jess couldn't get out of the way in time before Nalani had a handful of hair, dragging her across the dishes, spilling shit everywhere.

I watched in horror as Jess's hair came off. A wig, thank God, but from the way she was screaming, still painful. Nalani tossed the wig away, into a ruined dinner dish, then grabbed Jess around the neck to finish pulling her across the table before she let her drop to the floor, stepping back to pull her chair out of the way.

"Is this what you wanted?" she asked me as Jess scrambled up from the floor, backing in my direction. "You want me to act a fucking fool? Kill this bitch to make your point?"

"And what point would that be?!" Jess shrieked, looking around wildly for her hair.

"He knows."

They were both looking at me, but I refused to give the satisfaction of acknowledging her statement.

"*Orion!*" Jess whined. "What is she talking about?!"

"Why does it matter, bitch?" Nalani asked. "Regardless of what he and I have going on, the fact that you came into *my* home, implying shit about *my* husband in front of me, *your ass* is disrespectful. Be glad all I did was drag you across that goddamn table."

"*This* is what you married?!" Jess asked, turning to me again for answers. "This… barbarian?!"

"Girl get the fuck out of my house, before I *really* get active and give you what I think you deserve," Nalani said, still calm as fuck.

Scarily so.

"Go," I told Jess, who looked like she wanted to argue, but she started moving when Nalani did, clearly not fucking playing with her.

I… had definitely misjudged what this would look like.

"Do you feel good about yourself?" Nalani asked, from closer than before. "Giving me the silent treatment over a *mistake I immediately corrected,* and then bringing that bitch to this house. Getting in a little breach of contract of your own?"

"What are you talking about?"

"*Fidelity,* Ri," she said, her tone dry as she closed the last of the distance between us. "That's the game you wanna play? I delay getting pregnant, you use your trollop *head of marketing* to embarrass me? Is that it? Or have you been fucking and parading her around your office the whole time and I'm just the last idiot to know."

"*I don't cheat,*" I growled right back at her, right in her face. "I've told you that shit over and over."

She scoffed. "*You don't cheat,*" she repeated, sardonically. "You just let your ex-fiancée in our house with her tits out to make comments implying you've had your dick in her all afternoon to get under my skin?"

I didn't say shit.

Couldn't say shit.

'Cause that was exactly what happened.

When I didn't say anything—because I *couldn't* say anything—Nala smirked. "But *that* shit didn't work out like you thought it would, huh?"

"She might press charges."

"It would be three stories against one," Nalani immediately countered. "Or really just mine and yours against hers, 'cause you didn't see shit, did you Henry?"

We both looked to where Henry was standing in the doorway, stoic.

He shook his head.

"Damn, you too?!" I asked, then realized I'd had my eyes

off Nalani too long, since she was clearly feeling froggy and ready to jump.

She wasn't anywhere near me though.

She was back at the table, picking up her glass of wine which was miraculously still upright.

"If you want to play stupid fucking games with me, I can do that," she said, gulping down the wine. "But I'd prefer not to. I have more than enough shit to worry about. I'd prefer we at least pretend we can behave like actual adults and move forward. What's done is done, and that's it."

Before I could respond, a shout from somewhere in the house pulled my attention.

Henry and Nalani clearly heard it too because both of their eyes went wide. When it sounded again, we all took off in that direction.

The direction of Calli's room.

We were almost there when Ms. Wallace came rushing out, panicked, to look me in the face.

"Call 911!"

TWENTY-THREE
NALANI

"She's asking for *the lion queen*. Do either of you know who she's referring to?"

I looked up from my breakfast just long enough to glare at Orion for a few seconds before turning to the home health nurse in the doorway as I stood.

"*Nala*," I explained with a smile. "She's asking for me."

"Oh, that makes perfect sense," the woman nodded, relieved to have figured it out.

And I was relieved she was here.

We all were, especially after the other night.

Apparently, unexpected seizures were fairly common after a stroke, but none of us had… *expected* it. So watching Calli writhe on the ground, helpless until the real medical professionals showed up, had been one of the most heart-wrenching things I ever experienced.

Right up there with watching what terminal illness had done to my mother.

She was stable now, but it had been scary enough to render whatever else was happening insignificant.

Very likely the only reason Orion and I weren't at each other's throats.

I was *still* seething over his stunt with Jess. I couldn't say he'd pulled me out of character, but he'd certainly gotten me mad enough to drop any semblance of restraint. Was violence my default nature? Absolutely not.

I just never wanted to have to make the same point twice, and I needed *both* of them to understand me.

I was confident that they had.

Since that night, we hadn't said much to each other. We were waist deep in the dynamic I'd *expected* us to have when the marriage was first proposed. We lived in the same house, sure, but mostly steered clear of each other. There had been no texts, no random gifts, flowers, none of the things that, in their sudden absence, I realized I'd actually grown accustomed to.

I was fine with it though.

It cleared my head.

In fact, when I'd sat down to breakfast—after waiting until I was sure Orion was already done, so I could be alone—it was surprising to me when he came to the kitchen, making himself a cup of coffee and planting his ass at the end of the counter.

There was no reason for him to be in the same room as me.

I hoped he regretted that decision, hoped it burned him up that instead of asking for *him* first thing in the morning, she was asking for *me*.

Petty?

Sure.

But as I'd told myself at least a hundred times in the last few days... *fuck him.*

I followed Nurse Davis from the kitchen up to Calli's room, wondering what topic my girl had for me today. I'd grown quite fond of Calli. She reminded me of my own grandmother and great-aunts, all of whom were either back or *still* down south.

The room had been transformed. The regular bed was a hospital bed now, with monitors and all kinds of equipment readily available, despite the assurance that Calli's condition was stable. Everything had been made as homey as possible, but no chances were being taken, not again.

No one wanted to be realistic about how much longer we had with her. And if we wanted to extend that time as much as possible, immediate medical attention when something happened was a necessity. Orion was making sure not to repeat the same mistake.

"Well don't you look pretty this morning," I gushed as soon as I saw Calli sitting up in her bed, crochet needle and a skein of yarn in hand.

Calli grinned at me. "Nurse Davis isn't as bossy as Nancy," she explained, referring to Ms. Wallace. "She just greased my scalp for me, but let me braid my *own* hair. Nancy can't braid for shit, but wouldn't ever just let me do it myself."

I laughed. "She was just trying to help you. Trying to keep you from overexerting yourself."

"Her version of *help* was going to have me getting old even faster. Why you think I had that episode? Not enough use of my brain."

"I don't think it works like—never mind," I said, taking a

seat beside the bed. "You were asking for me. What can I do for you?"

She gave me a long look, then returned to her crocheting, what appeared to be a soft gray blanket. "I think you already know."

"Nuh-uh, I need you to make it plain for me."

She sighed, turning to look at me again. Despite everything—even the subtle cloudiness starting to take over—those eyes were still sharp, boring into me when she said, "You and my grandson. Y'all have got to stop all the fussing with each other."

"What fussing?" I asked, and she rolled her eyes.

"You think I couldn't hear all that commotion the other night, when he had that other heifer over here?"

My eyebrows went up. "Actually, no, I *didn't* think you could hear that," I admitted. "And I'm sorry you had to."

"I ain't hear nothing but that girl screaming about you attacking her. Ms. Wallace told me he brought her over here to get you riled up."

I sighed. "And I fell for the bait."

"You did. But you snatched the fishing rod out his hand too, beat him with it." She laughed. "I bet you he don't go fishing like *that* again."

I smirked. "So… you feel me then."

"I do." Calli nodded. "But now… whatever that was, let it be over. Life is too short for silliness to be getting in the way of anything."

"I know you mean well when you say that, but… you're a sharp lady. I don't believe much gets past you. And I think you know as well as I do, that there's nothing between me and your grandson for silliness to get in the way of," I admitted. "We have our agreement and that's all."

She shook her head. "I think *you* are too smart to believe that."

"I'm—"

"I told you," she interrupted, "the day you married him, that my Orion, much as I love that boy, was difficult."

I smiled, shaking my head. "I don't remember that."

"Well… I should've." She chuckled. "Because he is. So serious, and focused, and… more sensitive than he shows. More than he *can* show."

"Orion does whatever he wants to do."

"He gives the appearance of doing whatever he wants to do," Calli corrected, with a pointed look. "But he's always thinking about other people. It's not all about money and conquest with him, as much as I know it looks like it. He just wants to do right by the people he cares about. And their memories."

Was that why he bought my family's business from up under me?

I thought it, but didn't say it.

I just smiled.

"I can tell you love him, very much," was what I chose to allow out of my mouth. Even with everything that had happened, Calli's mind was still running very well. And even if it weren't, I wouldn't dare disrespect her.

Or hurt her feelings about her precious asshole grandson.

"I do, he means the world to me," she said. "His brothers too, but Orion… he's one in a million and even his brothers would say so. After his mother passed and then my Leo… he's held it together. Always. And he'll do that for you, too. If you let him."

Again, I swallowed my words.

Maybe before this latest bullshit I would've believed her,

but the way he'd overreacted to my honest mistake made me more inclined to simply brush it off.

"I hope I have someone in this world who believes in me as much as you believe in him," I said, grabbing her hand and lacing my fingers through hers. "It's honestly beautiful."

She gave me a sad smile. "I can see you think I'm just talking, but I'm telling you what I *know*," she insisted. "Be patient with him; he's having a hard time accepting what's next."

I raised an eyebrow. "And what's that?"

"That I don't have long."

"Don't talk like that," I immediately countered, and she immediately brushed me off.

"Ain't no point in pretending about what it is or what it isn't." She shrugged. "I'd hoped to see some great-grandbabies soon, but that's alright. I got to see one last wedding, one last beautiful bride," she told me, squeezing my fingers."

"Hey, you stop it," I scolded. "I just need you to hold on for me, okay?" I asked. "*I'm* not ready for you to go to glory, and I know Orion isn't. It would kill *him*. So you just… *stop it*," I repeated, squeezing her hand back. "Give us time. We'll make those babies for you. And you'll tell my mama about them for me. Right?"

She sighed, not exasperation, just… tiredness.

Deep, visceral exhaustion that took years and years and *years* to build.

I knew I was asking for too much.

But she nodded. "Make it quick," she whispered.

"I'll try my best."

Whew.

That was *not* the conversation I'd expected to have with her, not one I *wanted* to have either. Especially not ending it on a promise to essentially make amends with her rock-headed grandson.

I was a woman of my word though.

As such, I did *not* simply ignore Orion when I found him hovering outside, ready to pounce on me for any information about Calli's condition.

"What did she need to talk to you about?" he asked, blocking my progression down the hall.

"Making sure she gets enough mental stimulation. I'm sure you can speak to her nurse about it," I told him, keeping the bitchiness I *wanted* to give him out of my tone.

For Calli's sake.

"Why wouldn't she talk to me about that?" he questioned, stepping in front of me again as I tried to get around him.

"You'd have to ask her that yourself. Now could you please… I'm trying to get to work." I gestured for him to let me pass and after a moment he gave in, moving so I could step around him.

"I know you're lying," he said to my back, and I took a deep breath, choosing my words carefully before I chose to respond.

"I don't give enough fucks to *lie* to you," I said, not bothering to turn around. "As always, I've told you what falls into the realm of *your* business. Believe whatever the hell you want."

With that, I kept moving, stepping into my room to finish gathering my things for work so I could get out of there.

Before I said something ugly.

———

I took a deep, *deep* inhale of the pleasant aroma that hit me as soon as I walked into *Sweet Ambrosia*, soaking it all in. The satellite bakery at *Nectar* always smelled good too, but stepping into the real thing just seemed to hit a little different.

I smiled at the cashier and servers who greeted me, returning the niceties before I headed to the back, where I knew I'd find my aunt.

She had some explaining to do.

Any other time, she was more than accommodating for me, making sure our communication was open, a normal thing since we were close. Lately—or rather, since I told her about the email from Hailey Freeman and the accompanying pictures—she'd been hard to pin down.

Making it way past obvious that she was hiding something.

Why?

"Auntie," I sang, rapping my fist on the open doorway to her office.

She looked up from what she was doing, eyes wide as she looked around.

I shook my head as I stepped inside, closing the door behind me. "It's just me and you, sis," I told her. "Nowhere to run."

"What are you talking about, crazy girl?" she scoffed, standing to give me a hug. "Ain't nobody running from you."

"Could've fooled me," I countered, returning her embrace. "It seemed like I started asking tough questions and got ghosted. Something you've never, ever done to me before."

"Exactly, so why would I start now?"

I shrugged. "Again… you let *me* know," I told her. "Why are you so reticent to talk about those times? Everybody looked so happy, like good friends. *Especially* Mama and Stanford Reese."

There was a noticeable shift in energy at the mention of that name, and she took a step back, looking me in the face.

"I don't know what you want me to say, Nala."

I sighed. "I… want you to just be frank with me. I know she was your sister, but I really need to understand what the hell is going on," I explained. "A few weeks ago, William was ranting and raving, calling my mother a whore. Then last week, I see pictures of her with a man—Stanford Reese—who looks *just like* Soren." I clasped my hands together, pleading with her. "Please, Aunt Lucy, tell me what this is about."

She sighed, then took a seat back at her desk. "I… okay. Okay. Did you know there was a little while that me and your mother didn't really talk?"

I raised an eyebrow, 'cause this was something I most certainly didn't remember. "No, not at all," I answered, taking a seat too. "When?"

"I'd say… roughly around the time of those pictures."

I nodded. "Did you guys have some sort of falling out?"

She gave a dry chuckle. "That we did," she agreed, suddenly finding something very interesting about her hands.

"Okay…what was the falling out about?"

She blew out a sigh, taking a little breath before she answered the question. "It was about Stanford Reese," she admitted. "Let me be *very* clear. I won't claim to be proud of the things I did and I'm sure Larena wouldn't either. But… I was more in the wrong than she was. She knew Stanford first, liked him. Problem was… I liked him too once I met him. And he was closer to my age anyway."

My eyes narrowed. "So…are you telling me you took mama's boyfriend from her?"

Aunt Lucy shrugged. "*Boyfriend* is a generous way to put it," she said. "It was sort of wild times. She definitely had him first, and based on the things she told me... I decided to have him too. And I did."

"Oh you were..."

"A skeezer? Yes, maybe a bit," she conceded. "Or... a lot."

"So... did she fall out with Stanford too?"

She pushed out another of those dry chuckles. "Not the way she fell out with me. But she and Stan had their understanding. She and I... did not. So that wasn't surprising to me. She liked him beyond what their understanding was, but she didn't say that to him."

"But you knew?"

She nodded.

"Oh, *auntie*... that's dirty," I said, shaking my head and to her credit, my aunt did *not* try to claim otherwise.

"I never said I was proud of the way it went down. And if I wasn't working with a twenty-something's brain, it would *not* have gone down the way it did. But...I can't deny what happened. She and Stan were messing around, and me and Stan were messing around, and then she found out and she... stopped fooling with either of us. That was how she ended up with your father. Her feelings were hurt after the thing with Stan and William was right there, ready to swoop in, just waiting to be her knight in shining armor. And nobody could tell her anything, 'cause she was mad."

I nodded as little pieces of the story came together in my mind.

"But clearly you guys made up, because as long as I can remember... the two of you were best friends," I said.

"Oh yeah, we made it past that, after I apologized a *lot*,

and we were able to move forward."

"And what about her and Stanford?" I asked. "Because… Soren."

She dropped her gaze again, shaking her head. "I'm not sure what to tell you, Nala. Stan moved away and me and Larena didn't really talk about him, for a long time."

"Until…?"

"Until your brother came out looking just like him. She tried to pretend he didn't, that those features were William, but… she couldn't pretend with *me*. I think William knew too, but was too embarrassed or maybe just too prideful to admit it. Or make any accusations."

"Yeah, until now," I said, sitting forward. "He was holding that in, all these years, and he's clearly done with it now. Thinking about that kind of resentment… it's scary. Especially knowing that he was so heavily involved with her care at the end of her life. Knowing that he was selling things from up under her bit by bit just to spite her one last time. I'm pretty sure he only kept the business this long so he could steal from it."

"I *have* wondered," Aunt Lucy admitted. "He wouldn't really let me see or speak to her right at the end and I wondered if he was…"

"Wondered if he was *what*?" I prompted, when she didn't finish that statement.

She shook her head. "Wondered if he wasn't taking care of her like he should. I tried to insist on a nurse for her and he swore he had it under control. All her different medicines, all those instructions, and he just seemed… I don't know how he seemed. But something about it wasn't right. That wasn't anything I could prove though, and I certainly wasn't going to burden you kids with my suspicions."

"I wish you had," I murmured, letting my memories take me back to that time. "Because I always felt like something was off too. He insisted I wasn't needed at home, wanted Soren to stay at school... he was *so mad* when I left my job to settle back in Blackwood. But I wanted to be close to mama, knowing what she was going through. And then she was just... *gone.* And it felt *really* sudden."

"Which is how breast cancer works sometimes," Lucy said. "Especially the aggressive forms and with how weak she was after all those rounds of chemo. I'm not saying it didn't make me feel uneasy, I just don't want to jump to conclusions. I never liked William and don't care to defend him, but... implying that he had something to do with your mother's death? That's serious, Nala."

"It is," I admitted. "But... without clear answers, I have to take everything into consideration. Which reminds me of the other thing I was going to ask. I know he at least let you come and get some of mama's things after she passed. Did you happen to take any journals, her laptop, anything like that?"

"Just photo albums, mainly," she said. "And the family heirloom jewelry we went through together."

I nodded.

She'd brought my mother's jewelry box to me after the funeral and it had been quite cathartic to sort through it all. And she'd been generous with me, letting me take whatever I wanted.

And I'd seen the albums a dozen times already.

"Okay," I said. "I think I'm going to go over to the house, see if Daddy kept anything. If he hasn't destroyed it."

She sighed. "You don't really think he'd do that, do you?"

"The way he spoke about her the last time I saw him... I honestly don't put anything past him."

TWENTY-FOUR
NALANI

ONE OF THE perks of being in charge was taking as long of a lunch break as I wanted.

Did I have shit to do?

Yes.

I *always* had shit to do lately.

But after that conversation with my aunt, it felt much more pressing for now to make my way out to the home I'd grown up in. The one my parents shared, but was just my father's now.

My "father."

Whew.

It was wild to think about, but I really should've sought more clarity from Aunt Lucy about the timing of when my mother stopped fooling around with Stanford and *started* with William Stark. At this point, *Soren's* paternity wasn't really a question in my mind, but my own was a little more of a mystery.

Pulling up to the property was bittersweet. I hadn't been

here since my mother passed because honestly… it hurt. I'd helped her plant the roses out front and she built and stained her own custom shutters that flanked the front windows of the big brick house.

Home.

My journey from the car to the front door was slow, and out of respect, I didn't simply use the keys I still had to unlock it and walk in. I rang the bell a few times, waiting a while for an answer before I decided that maybe no one was home.

I had my keys in my hand when the door finally swung open.

William Stark had certainly seen better days.

His wrinkled, disheveled clothes and unkempt facial hair were a sharp contrast to the man I knew, who prided himself on a polished exterior.

"What the hell do *you* want?" he asked, spreading the smell of liquor in the air as he spoke.

I straightened my shoulders, meeting his gaze. "I want to come in… to have access to Mama's old office. Or… wherever she may have kept her personal things."

For a long moment, he just looked at me, then stepped back. "Good. Come get this shit before I burn it all up," he groused, gesturing at the stairs, where the office was. "Take it all. It won't be here when you come back."

Shit.

Clearly he wasn't even thinking about it until I brought it up and now I'd given him ideas.

No big deal, though.

Instead of indulging any conversation that was sure to go left with him in an inebriated state, I kept it pushing.

Not that I had much to say to him anyway, unless he was trying to offer some answers.

That was the only reason I didn't make a fuss about him following me up the stairs and standing at the doorway to the office as I poked around. I knew the only reason it wasn't covered in dust was because of the cleaning service that came to the house. Otherwise, the office was basically perfectly perservered, exactly as my mother had left it the last day she had the strength to cross the threshold.

It was a heavy sort of energy.

At first I took my time, just absorbing. In a lot of ways, it still felt like her, and if I concentrated hard enough, it *smelled* like her.

I wished there *wasn't* anybody home.

Because instead of leaving me be, my father decided it was prudent to just stand there, drink in hand, exuding a quiet agitation that made it all just… awkward.

I needed to get what I'd come for.

She'd always loved a good cube shelving moment, so I grabbed one from a shelf that was mostly empty. I took a few framed pictures, opening cabinet doors to look through until I landed on one that was of particular interest.

Her safe.

"Is there anything in this?" I asked, since he was standing there being nosy.

May as well be useful too.

He shrugged. "Hell if I know," he slurred. "Never knew the combination."

I frowned, then turned to the secured metal box, looking at the dial.

I knew the combination, assuming it was the same one my mother had told me on countless occasions when I was here with her in this office.

There was nothing *less* enticing to me than opening that

safe in front of him though, in case there *was* anything useful in it.

For now, I turned away from it, going to her desk.

His eyes never left me.

I kept ignoring him though, taking the framed photos from her desktop, and a few knickknacks here and there from her drawers. Relief hit me when the doorbell rang, but I was careful not to have any reaction to it other than looking at him when it rang again and he still hadn't moved from the threshold.

"Are you expecting someone?" I asked. "Do you want me to get that for you?"

Instead of answering, he just grunted something unintelligible before he moved on, presumably to get the door. Knowing I didn't have much time, I waited until I heard him descending the steps before I raced back to the safe, hurriedly dialing in the right combination.

My heart leapt into my throat when it opened.

No precious jewels, of course, but it did have her laptop and a few other electronics. There were a few file folders, which I took as well, and a key I recognized as one that unlocked the hidden drawer in her desk.

I took that too, burying everything except the key underneath the things already in my box before I closed the safe again, spun it back to the number it was on before I touched it, then went back to the desk.

I knew exactly where that hidden drawer was.

My hands were shaking as I went through the steps to access the keyhole, this whole *secret for just us girls* I'd had with my mother. Back then—when I was a child—there were letters in it that she would never let me see.

Those same letters were there now.

I didn't even bother looking at them, just snatched them up, putting everything back as it was just as I heard my father's footsteps drawing near again.

By the time he was back in the doorway, I had a stack of files on the desk, perusing through them as if they held anything of interest.

I knew they didn't, but it was perfect cover.

Still, my father was suspicious of *something*.

I could feel it with the way he was staring.

I switched to a new file box, ignoring him as best as I could, expecting it to be yet another one full of old reports from the store.

It wasn't.

It was… birth records.

Both official and non-official, cutesy milestone charts, things like that.

I tried not to have a reaction to those either. Just closed the box and put it with the things I wanted to take, but my father must've picked up on something in my expression. He practically sprinted across the room to take it.

"What is this?!" he demanded, shaking the box in front of me.

"Baby stuff," I answered. "Stuff you probably don't care about," I countered, taking it from him.

With effort.

He didn't want to let it go.

A sneer spread over his face as he relinquished it, shaking his head. "You're damn right. I don't give a fuck."

"That's fine," I told him, gathering the full box of belongings that was coming with me. It was heavier than anticipated and I prayed that it would hold as I moved to the door, ready to get the hell out of there. I damn near dashed down the stairs, stopping when I caught a whiff of... something.

I turned to my father. "Do you... have female company?" I asked, realizing I was catching a breeze of women's perfume.

"Not your damn business."

I raised an eyebrow. "You know what... you're right. Thank you for allowing me to get these things."

"You'd *better* be grateful," he huffed. "After the way you've treated me, I shouldn't do shit for you."

"Excuse me?" I said, then immediately thought better of entertaining an argument with him.

I had what I wanted.

It was best to just get the hell out of here.

"Never mind," I followed up, before he could reply. "I'm just gonna go."

"Don't fucking come back."

"I won't, don't worry," I called over my shoulder as I headed out the door. "You've made it perfectly clear you're not interested in being my father. I won't argue the point or force you."

"You wouldn't blame me for anything I've done if you knew the truth. You think your mother was some sort of saint?"

"I don't actually," I admitted, looking up from stowing the box in my front seat. "I think she was human, just like the rest of us. So if you have something to say... just say it, Daddy. What is all of this about?" I asked, stepping back to where he was hanging out of the door. "Is all of this because she hurt you? If it is... I understand you being angry with her, but... what did *I* do to deserve being treated like this?"

"You look like her," he spat. "Every time I see your face,

she's just... *right there*. And I have to remember the betrayal she wouldn't admit until I forced her to."

"Forced her how?" I asked. "On her death bed?"

"It was the only time she'd tell the fucking truth. Even with the evidence in her face."

"What evidence?"

"The test."

"A DNA test? For us? For me and Soren?" I questioned him and he shook his head.

"She already knew. We *all* knew. And I looked like a fucking fool for thirty-some-odd years pretending I didn't see it. Do you know what that does to a man?"

I swallowed. "I can imagine. Why didn't you just leave? Why didn't *she*?"

"I wouldn't let her," he growled, with such vitriol that I took a step back. "And me? Well... the business was hers. What the hell else was I supposed to do?"

Pushing out a deep breath, I shook my head again, half turning back to my car.

I only had the *slightest* bit of respect left for this man and it was disappearing fast.

"Did you kill her?" I asked, my last question.

I wasn't sure I could handle much more.

He glared at me, for long enough that I thought I knew the answer just from that.

But then he shook his head.

"I should've."

I... wished I hadn't asked.

Instead of saying a single word more, I just went back to my car.

My Mercedes, not the car Orion bought.

"Yeah, run off to the man who bought you. I tried to save

you from that shit, but it was just another thing you couldn't appreciate. I could've got the store back, protected you. I could've gotten you out of it. But did you listen? No. 'Cause you can't be bothered to, just like your mother," he screamed from the door, and honestly, that didn't bother me much.

"You're probably a whore just like her too!"

Okay.

He was clearly gone in the head.

"Run along home to the shitty house that bastard put you in and tell him I said *fuck you!* And that dead daddy of his too," he kept on, approaching my door as I closed it.

"I'm going to my place that *I* bought , but I'll give him the message," I quipped, then whipped out of his driveway, not knowing—or caring—if he heard me or not.

I didn't have the bandwidth for a *single shred* more nonsense.

Which was why, instead of bothering to go to *Nectar* at all, I did exactly as I'd said. I went back to my own damn apartment. It was quiet, and just the way I liked things, and didn't smell like Orion.

I ordered myself enough lunch to use the leftovers for dinner, then settled in with my laptop to tend to what I needed for the store.

And *then* I started going through the box from my mother.

The birth records file was on top, so I started with that, quickly realizing it wasn't just "birth records" for me and Soren. Those were there, along with footprint cards and other keepsake things, but there was a third, incomplete set.

Four incomplete sets, actually.

One from when I would've been two or three years old, and then another quite a bit later, before Soren.

Lost pregnancies.

Heartbreaks my mother had never spoken about or shared.

Just… shut away in a box full of other precious memories.

It was sad to think about. Even sadder when it occurred to me that she probably *would've* shared those stories with me, when the time was right, when I was ready to have babies of my own.

Like… now.

I couldn't bear to read all the details—the birth scans, the updates, the thoughts she'd jotted down journal-style on little cards.

I closed the box, ready to move on to the next things, the framed photos I'd used to hide the things she'd clearly intended to keep private from my father.

I set them all up, smiling at the images in them—mostly me, Soren, Lucy, other family members and friends.

None of my father.

Not that I'd taken with me.

The next thing in the pile were the letters, but before I could dig into them, my phone started ringing. I pulled myself up to grab it from my purse, rolling my eyes when I saw the name on the screen.

Still, I answered.

"Beloved husband," I answered keeping none of the annoyance out of my tone. "How can I help you?"

"Funny," Orion said. "Where are you?"

"I would wager a disgusting amount of money that you already know the precise answer to that question."

"And yet I asked, so how about we cut the bullshit and you tell me?"

I shook my head. "Oh… are we still on this *Nalani is a liar* fantasy of yours?"

"Until I'm convinced otherwise."

"Or... I could just hang up the fucking phone. As a matter of fact I think that's the option I'm going to take, because... kiss my ass," I told him, already pulling the phone away from my ear.

I could hear him squawking about something, but that didn't keep me from pressing the button to end the call.

Exactly one minute later, my phone rang again.

"*Beloved husband*!" I gushed, repeating my sarcastic greeting in hopes it would get under his skin.

"This is childish," he growled into the phone and I laughed.

"Yes, it is. And you started it."

"I beg to differ."

"Beg as much as you want," I countered. "And the facts will still be what they are. I was trying to be cool for Calli's sake, but I see you can't come to the same conclusion. Until you're ready to stop being an asshole, I'm going to give you back your exact energy."

He scoffed. "Grow the fuck up."

"*You first*," I replied, pulling the phone from my ear again to end the call.

This time when his name popped up again I didn't bother answering.

Who had the damn time?

I put my phone on do not disturb, then moved back to what had previously held my attention, the stack of letters in the box from my mother's office. The envelopes clearly hadn't been through the mail, not traditionally at least. The only thing on them was my mother's name, right in the middle, written in neat, beautiful cursive.

I didn't recognize the handwriting.

The letters inside were done in the same lovely script, but I didn't read the words.

It felt like an invasion of privacy, especially when the letters were signed *S.R.,* which I could easily deduce as Stanford Reese.

They were love letters.

Which made me wonder if my aunt's version of events was quite accurate.

Maybe it was *her* truth, but not *the* truth.

There were no dates on the letters that might clue me in to a timeline, but I'd seen glimpses of them as a child.

The pregnancies she lost… was Stanford the father?

Had they reconnected over *her* grief or was the grief theirs to share?

Curiosity had me practically *itching* to just read the letters to get answers, but I couldn't bring myself to do so, out of respect. At the very least, I would contact Stanford first— maybe under the pretense of talking business, maybe not— and give *him* the opportunity to define his relationship with my mother.

And explain his absence as Soren's father.

Assuming he even knew.

But he had to know, right?

He was still alive and well, and working with *Wholesome Foods*. No one who wrote a stack of letters when email existed was just going to happily ignore the one who got away, even if the only feelings that still remained were spite.

As a matter of fact… *had he shown up to the funeral?*

I closed my eyes, letting my mind go back to that time, a little over ten years ago. I'd been too absorbed with my family and my own grief to pay too much attention to the crowd, but when I forced myself to pull up the memories... *Calli was there.*

Caspian Sterling was there.

And... yes.

So was Stanford.

Another memory hit me then, how utterly agitated my father had been that day. His mood could easily be explained by the fact that we were returning the—supposed—love of his life to the earth. But knowing what I did now, it was more likely frustration that the unresolved love of *her* life had dared to show up.

It also eliminated any chances Stanford *didn't* know about Soren.

He *had* to.

Right?

A loud pounding at the door made me roll my eyes, and I immediately put away the letters. There was no point in bothering to get up to answer it. Orion came stalking into the room like a damn panther a few moments later.

"I see you broke yourself in just fine again," I said, not bothering to look up from what I was doing, plugging in my mother's laptop, and searching my desk for a charger that might fit the old tablet.

"Why are you playing with me?"

I did look up then, meeting his gaze. "Nobody is playing with you. I'm just trying to live my life, fulfill this contract, and then handle all future contact with you through a well-trained mediator."

"So the contract *does* matter to you then?"

"Oh *God*," I huffed, sitting back and crossing my arms. "Why are you *so* hung up on this absolute bullshit? Why is it so hard for you to believe I just made an honest mistake because I'm an honest person? I'm not some shark in the water, business tycoon looking for ways to fuck people over. *I made a mistake.* And immediately fixed it. Because I'm not what you're trying to make me out to be, which at this point, I'm starting to think is just to make yourself feel better."

He scoffed. "Feel better about *what*?"

"About your *purposeful* breach," I snapped back. "Our fidelity clause is very clear, in case you didn't know."

"I didn't fuck her!"

"Maybe not, but you certainly conducted yourself in a manner that gave her the impression she could insert herself between us," I explained. "And in case you didn't read it, or maybe just forgot, *that* is a breach of our contract too. You don't get to use women against me to piss me off, make me jealous, hurt my feelings, whatever the fuck you were trying to do."

"Which I only did because of what *you* did."

I let out a dry laugh. "Because of what you *convinced yourself* I did, because of whatever insecurity *you* have going on. I know you only did that shit to get back at me. It's the only reason I didn't immediately just call my lawyer."

His nostrils flared as he pushed out a sigh.

"Fine. So you got your lick, and I got mine, can we move forward from the bullshit?"

"There was no lick from me," I corrected. "But you know what... *whatever*. It's even. Sure. What next?"

"What's next is you bringing your ass home."

I shook my head. "No can do," I told him. "I need space and I'm taking it. If you don't like it... do whatever you feel like you have to."

I shifted attention back to my task at hand—my mother's devices—ignoring my "husband".

Trying to.

There was a noticeable lift in tension when he turned away and stalked back out of my apartment without saying another word.

Leaving me to wonder exactly what would be our next "round".

TWENTY-FIVE
ORION

This motherfucker...

I frowned at the photos enlarged on my screen, scrolling through one by one. I just needed to see it for myself, to confirm what the people I paid for such things had already assured me of.

Eric Jarvis—*EJ*—at my fucking construction site, causing a mess.

So *that* was where he'd been.

As of now, his absence around Blackwood was the only thing that made sense.

Sure, he and his little gang-affiliated buddies were deep in number and organized enough that petty crime wasn't really their usual thing. But corporate sabotage?

That was some other shit.

And traveling for it, at that... this didn't feel like simply trying to get back at me for what happened on Christmas. And it didn't affect Nalani at all, so there was no reason to believe it was targeted at her.

What it *really* felt like was... William Stark. He was familiar with EJ because of his connection with Nalani and this kind of petty shit had his name all over it.

But again, for fucking *what*?

Nothing, really, was going to keep the construction from moving forward, and William didn't have the power or capital —especially now that his kids had scrubbed him from *Nectar* —to go to battle with me.

If these were his last desperate attempts to just get under my skin and annoy me, he was doing a pretty good job of it.

But really, it was probably more frustrating for Stanford than it was for me. He was the one at the helm of the expansion efforts and it was his territory. In the grand scheme of things, I was just the man who wrote the checks and expected people to report back.

On a day to day basis, the shit was mildly annoying to me, when put into real perspective.

Stanford was the one with the real frustration.

Which made an even stronger case for William to be at the crux of it. I knew in passing that he and Stanford didn't really get along, but Stanford *never* brought the man up. The closest he'd come to it was mentioning Nalani and his interest in potential expansion efforts for *Nectar*.

As with most of William's beef, it seemed to be one-sided.

In any case, I couldn't let my thoughts linger there. I had better things to tend to. I let my security team know to keep me in the loop on his movements and then shut my laptop down, heading to go check on Calli before I left.

Running the risk of getting cursed out, but I had to take it.

When I entered the room, the nurse had Calli up out of bed, helping her walk to the window, a *great* sign. I'd hated seeing her confined to monitors and shit, so I was glad the recovery from the seizure had been relatively quick.

And glad that the new medication cocktail they had her on seemed to be getting a good immune response.

"Good morning," I called as I approached, prompting both women to look in my direction.

"I thought I told your ass not to show your face in here until your wife was back on the premises?" Calli asked, and the nurse looked away, hiding her smirk as she helped Calli take a seat at the chaise by the window.

"You forgot this was *my* house?" I asked, taking a seat next to her. "You're always trying to tell me what to do."

"*Somebody* has to," she quipped. "Since you're hellbent on stirring up drama."

I frowned. "*I* am?"

"Yes, *you*," she countered. "You're the one brought that heifer into your wife's house, right?"

"But she—"

"I don't care about none of that." Calli waved me off. "Whatever was between you and her, *you* brought somebody else into it, and got that young lady hurt. She doing alright?"

"Jess? She's fine." I shrugged. "A little banged up, but that's all."

"Then she got lucky; the lion queen has some decorum. I would've pulled my pistol out."

"No you wouldn't." I laughed, until… the look on her face told me that wasn't meant to be funny. "You… *wouldn't*, right?"

"I *have*," she corrected me. "Your granddaddy tried to play one of those games with me *one* good time, thought making me jealous would tighten up my attitude. I put an extra hole in both of their asses and would do it again too."

"Calli... you're serious?" I asked her.

"As a stroke." She winked at me. "Why you think your granddaddy had that limp? I gave him that," she said proudly. "And it's not to say I *didn't* need to tighten my attitude up. I was a hellion, and he wasn't wrong for thinking it. But there's a way to go about things and *that* wasn't the way. You get what I'm saying to you?"

I grunted an affirmative answer, then turned to look out the window too.

At this point, it didn't even matter who was right.

This rift had gone on longer than it should and felt as if it had undone all the progress we'd made toward being an *actual* couple.

Not just strangers who fucked.

We were enjoying each other and then... she went to the doctor.

I thought something was wrong with her.

I hadn't *immediately* jumped to the worst conclusion.

But then she was all sneaky and cagey about it, not wanting to just tell me what was going on, and it felt like... like I'd imagined us growing closer.

Like she couldn't trust me and like I *definitely* shouldn't be trusting her.

And in a way... she was right.

She *couldn't* trust me, not the with the way I'd reacted to something she insisted was a mistake. And when I really thought about it rationally... probably was.

It was just hard to accept.

Why?

I... wasn't even sure.

Calli reached for my hand, giving it a light squeeze.

"Pride is gonna cause you to lose the very thing you

thought was important, baby," she said, giving me an encouraging smile. "Let go of whatever is holding you back and apologize to your wife so you can move forward. I don't know how much longer I've got and that one ain't giving you any babies on bad terms."

I shook my head, turning my hand over to return her squeeze. "Two months ago you were telling me you planned to be here a good while longer. Why you talking like this now?"

"Reality is setting in." She laughed. "And when it's my time to go, I'm going."

I knew that, obviously.

It still wasn't something I wanted to hear, though.

Calli's mortality had been staring me in the face a while, but with her seeming to take on a rapid decline in the past year… things felt so much more urgent.

More important.

Too important to let stubbornness continue making a mess of things.

I stuck around with Calli a bit longer before I had to head out for the day to tend to things at the office. Shiloh's ass was especially smug since hearing about what happened, but was somehow finding the strength to not rub anything in my face.

She *did* show up at my door with a big ass grin when I sent her a message asking her to get a flower delivery over to my wife.

"Is this your way of making amendssss?" she said, hanging in the doorway. "Cause, it's a cute start, but I'm telling you… plane tickets. Reservations. At minimum? *Jewelry*," she added. "Or maybe shoes. Nalani dresses her ass off, so shoes would definitely hit a great note. I *just* saw the absolute cutest pair of—"

"Just the flowers for now," I interrupted, putting my hand up. "I don't disagree with you, but... I need a soft opening here. The situation is delicate."

To say the least.

Since the day she'd insisted on needing a bit of space, she still hadn't been back home, and it was coming up on four days.

I was *not* a fan.

I also knew better than to push the issue too hard with a woman like Nalani.

Shiloh didn't argue, she just gave me a nod and stepped out to make the order.

But she came back shortly after, wearing a frown.

"Uh... the security team is saying Nalani missed a checkpoint."

I sat up straighter, my face instantly dropping into a scowl. "How the fuck does that happen without a notification?" I asked.

"Apparently it *just* happened."

Checkpoints were something my contracted security team had used for a while. Everybody had their normal routines and anything that fell outside was considered a missed checkpoint. Nalani had been against the idea of more hands-on security, so I didn't have a dedicated guard on her.

Trying to be respectful of her wishes.

Now though, finding out that she'd left the office for lunch and then never come back, and nobody had eyes on her, I made the decision right there that I wouldn't be making *that* mistake again.

Instead of panicking though, I pulled up my cell to utilize my private tracking methods, the standard GPS tags that let me know where her car and cell phone were.

Both were at her apartment.

"We're panicking over nothing," I let everybody know. "She just went home."

Whether she was simply working there for the rest of the day or not feeling well, I had no clue. Still, I had Shiloh get the flowers delivered to *my* office, and once they arrived, I took the rest of the day to myself.

I would be the one to deliver them.

Did I know how she might react to that?

Of course not.

I just couldn't shake the compulsion.

There was no need for me to break in anymore. I had a keycard that accessed her door. As polite as it would've been to knock first, I opted against it, gesturing for Henry to wait in the hall in case she wasn't dressed when I entered.

Or in case she decided to throw something at my head.

I knew something was off as soon as I walked in.

Nalani *always* had music of some type playing when she was in her zone, not loud, just ever-present. The apartment was eerily quiet now though.

Except... *what the hell is that?*

Somewhere, someone had dropped something, causing a loud crash. I put the vase of flowers down, sticking the keycard in my pocket as I crept around the counter in the kitchen area of the condo, intending to move down the hall.

I promptly almost tripped over something on the floor.

Something being... someone.

Nalani.

Panic spiked in my chest at the sight of her sprawled on the floor, still dressed for work. I dropped to my knees, looking her over, trying to see what was wrong. There was a knot on her head, swollen and bloody, and when I moved my hands to her neck to check for a pulse, the bruising there, like she'd been choked, made bile rise to my throat.

And then I heard another loud thump.

I shot a text to Henry to come and tend to Nala, then I made a quick decision about my plan. I *always* carried protection when I was out and about and this time was no different. I pulled it from its concealed holster as I moved back to my feet, searching for the source of the sound.

I found it in her bedroom.

EJ was there, snatching drawers from the dresser and dumping them out. From the state of the room, he was clearly looking for something. I must've made a sound, something to draw his attention in my direction, because he looked back at me and smirked.

"Go on and take your shot, pretty boy," he said. "Better not miss though."

I wouldn't miss.

But I didn't shoot.

I grinned.

I tucked the gun back into the holster.

And then I barreled at him.

There was nothing on my mind but murder, and if I had the chance to see it through, I'd be damned if it was gonna be *quick*.

EJ wasn't a small guy though or weak. He took the impact of me coming at him and then recovered quick, hands up, ready and willing to go toe to toe with me.

I wouldn't have it any other way.

Adrenaline rushed through me as EJ and I traded blows back and forth, but he wasn't matching me in pure fucking rage. With every swing of my fists, I thought about Nalani being here with him alone, scared, wondering if somebody was coming for her or not.

Knowing him… he'd probably taunted her with his hands around her neck, getting off on the abuse.

Abuse I was more than willing to give right back to him.

Not just for this time, but for the other time he'd run up on her in *Nectar*, and then a little more, just on principle since I'd warned his ass to stay away from her.

At some point… he stopped fighting back.

It wasn't until then that I realized I had an audience. Henry was in the doorway, with a now-conscious Nalani scooped into his arms.

Both were wide-eyed.

I glanced at my blood-covered hands, then straightened up. I couldn't look at that knot on her head, so I looked at Henry. "Call Shiloh and have her arrange for a doctor to meet you at the house," I told him. "Make sure she's taken care of."

"And what about…"

The crime scene.

What about the crime scene?

I shook my head. "I'll worry about that," I told him. "You just… get her home."

I HESITATED at the door to Nalani's room.

The trip to bring the flowers was going to be the first time we'd spoken to each other beyond a few cursory words in several days and *this* was far from the way I'd expected any sort of reunion to happen.

I was cool now.

But I hadn't been before.

Aside from the obvious anger that he'd put his hands on her again, I needed answers from *everybody* on how the hell something like this had happened.

We were supposed to have eyes on him.

And eyes on *her*.

She was easier to keep up with. EJ had given security the slip, which wasn't that big of a surprise. There was no reason to have additional security in the building when she wasn't there, so that was when he took the opening to get inside.

He had to have already been there when she got home.

That was the part where the blank was drawn. There were answers only she could give.

Well... he *could* give them, but wouldn't be any time soon.

He needed time to recover.

Nalani though, I'd been assured was okay.

And waiting around was only prolonging the inevitable.

I went ahead and let my fist tap the door a couple of times, not waiting for a response before I stepped inside.

Nalani was upright in her bed.

A good sign.

"How are you feeling?" I asked, letting my eyes adjust to the low lighting she'd chosen as I moved toward the bed.

"I feel like I got choked and hit in the head," she answered, putting her phone down. "Other than that... I guess I'm alright."

Shit.

"I... I'm sorry this happened. If I could—"

"It's not really your fault," she interrupted. "I took some stuff from my mother's office that I'm pretty sure my father sent EJ to get back. It had nothing to do with you."

I sat down at the edge of the bed. "If we weren't at odds,

you would've been *here*. At home. Instead of at the apartment."

She rolled her eyes, tried to, at least, but ended up wincing at the pain the gesture must've caused. "So you want credit for me getting attacked?"

"Credit?" I chuckled. "Nah. But I'll definitely take the blame. You were supposed to be protected, and you weren't, because of my fuckup. I dropped the ball. Which is *absolutely* my fault."

"Fine then." She reached out to touch my hand, running light fingers over my bandaged knuckles. "I would say I'd hate to see the other guy, but…"

"I'm sorry about that, too."

"Sorry that you beat him down?"

"Sorry that you had to see it."

Her fingers stopped, leaving her hand resting on top of mine. "After the things he said to me with his hands around my neck… I'm not."

I closed my eyes, trying not to read more than I should into those words. Still, I turned my hand over, clasping her fingers. "Nalani… tell me the truth. Did he…"

"No," she whispered. "I can't say that he wouldn't have, but he um… he hit me, first. I came to the apartment to change my shoes," she said, letting out a dry chuckle. "And um… he came charging out of my bedroom, and just hit me, before I knew what was happening. I kinda blacked out for a second, and when I opened my eyes again, his hands were around my throat. Demanding that I tell him where '*it*' was."

"It?" I asked. "What was he referring to?"

She shrugged. "I still don't know, honestly. I took her computer, a tablet, a keepsake box, and some letters. He was um… he was choking me too hard for it to be an effective interrogation tactic, but I don't… I don't think he knew that."

Fuck.

I released my hold on her hand so I could move closer, examining the angry purple bruising around her neck. I fought back the heat building in my chest all over again, knowing this wasn't the time or place for it. Instead, I took my wife's face in my hands.

"I'm sorry," I told her again, and she shook me off, pushing my hands away.

"Why do you keep saying that?"

"Because I am," I explained. "And I wish I'd shown up sooner. That you'd never even had a reason to go there. That I hadn't *given* you a reason to go there."

She shrugged. "Whatever. It is what it is."

"It's not," I countered. "I'm… sorry for my overreaction, about the birth control thing. I…" I pushed out a heavy sigh, shaking my head. "I know you weren't lying about that. I just… I couldn't… *fuck*," I whispered, not knowing what to say. When a few moments had passed without me finding a good way to articulate my thoughts, I decided to shift direction. "You know um… you know Calli probably doesn't have much more time… right?"

She frowned at me, but nodded. "I do. But she might surprise us."

"I hope so," I agreed. "But I… I realized several months back that I had to be realistic. For the longest time, she seemed… ageless. And then it started hitting her all at once. All of a sudden. And I realized I was running out of time to fulfill this promise I'd made her, when I was still basically a kid myself."

"What was the promise?"

"To prove her wrong." I chuckled. "I was such a serious young man, especially after my mother passed. She would always say, *you know what attracts more flies than honey? Shit! And boy your lil mean ass is full of it!*"

Nalani's mouth dropped open, then she smiled. "That definitely sounds like Calli."

"Classic," I agreed. "But she would say that because we'd go to these functions, and people would try to push their daughters on me, and I was never interested. I just wanted to build, and conquer, and be the best in the business. Better than my father, better than anybody. But they were always trying to… temper me. Get me to see the value in having a family and a legacy. I wasn't trying to hear it."

"Okay, but… how do you go from that to a marriage contract requiring your wife to give you an heir within the first two years?"

I chuckled, but… it wasn't really funny.

Not anymore.

"One day, I got so sick of Calli chastising me, that I told her, 'I'm gonna have the prettiest wife and babies out of everybody. You'll see'." I laughed. "And she said, 'Boy… I'd like to see that before I die'. And then she laughed her ass off, 'cause she knew better than to take me seriously. But she'd remind me of it every now and then, and as I got older… it stopped seeming so ridiculous. And as *she* got older, and my father passed, and she and my brothers were all I had left… if felt… *serious.*"

Nalani blinked.

Then blinked again.

"Orion… are you seriously telling me that all this, this contract, buying the *Nectar* building, everything… was to fulfill a promise to your grandmother?" she asked, eyes narrowed.

"Uh... yes and no," I admitted. "Buying the building was just dumb luck. I came across the opportunity and took it, knowing my father would appreciate the *fuck you* to William. But it wasn't until I realized that I didn't have much time to see my vow to Calli through that I realized... the potential."

Nalani nodded. "I... wow. That definitely explains a lot," she said. "Including why you reacted the way you did about the birth control, and then... got mad all over again, it seemed, when she had the seizure. You got the marriage part out of the way, but... you're afraid your children won't meet Calli."

My eyebrows went up.

Damn.

She'd pinpointed the exact problem before I could even articulate it to myself fully.

"Again," I told her, "I'm sorry. For blowing up at you about it and for bringing Jess into it."

Nalani smirked. "How is her hairline doing?"

"That's mean."

"Fuck her." She laughed, then winced again from the pain. "Oh, *shit*," she muttered. "I guess that's what I get for laughing, huh?" she said, lowering herself from the upright position she'd been in to lay down.

"I don't know about all that, but... you probably need to rest."

"And you don't?" she asked. "Have you seen yourself in a mirror?"

I chuckled.

I had, actually.

After showering EJ's blood off me, I'd definitely caught a

glimpse of myself. He'd gotten more than a few good shots in, so I was a bit black and blue myself.

Trophies.

"What happened to him?" she asked, and I met her gaze.

Decided to tell the truth.

"I called some people I trust, and they took him somewhere he won't be causing any trouble."

She blinked.

"Is that code for him being dead?"

"He's not dead. Do you want him to be?"

She considered it, then shook her head. "I don't feel comfortable giving you my blessing to have somebody killed. But… I like that you offered," she admitted, bringing a smirk to my face.

"I've already explained that to you, Nala… anything for my wife."

"Anything… including your trust?" she asked, after a moment, and I pushed out a sigh.

"Yes. That too," I told her, bending to press a kiss to the side of her head that wasn't bandaged. "Get some rest, okay?"

She nodded, but then extended her hand toward me. "Will you stay?"

"You want me to?" I asked, eyebrow raised.

"Duh. Why else would I ask?"

"You and this damn mouth," I muttered, shaking my head. But…

I stayed.

TWENTY-SIX
NALANI

"I'M VERY, *very* much not a fan of this shit," Morgan fussed, fidgeting with my hair to make sure the lingering bruise on my head was covered. "You're a billionaire's wife; this isn't cute."

"You're right. Next time I get attacked I'll try not to lead with my head," I quipped, grinning as she took a step back to admire her handiwork.

She and Alexis had come by the house to hang out, a plan that got spun into us going out for dinner. I thought I'd done a fine job of getting myself together, but Morgan clearly disagreed. In her words, she was trying to *make sure I didn't look like a victim.*

Which would undoubtedly turn heads.

Which I definitely didn't need.

"I know you're not trying to be funny," she responded, propping a hand on her hip. "Cause I'm dead serious. You can let that husband of yours know that *this* is unacceptable. We thought we were putting you in good hands. Matter of fact, where is his ass? *I'll* tell him."

"It's not his fault," I countered, and this time it was Alexis who stepped forward, eyebrow raised.

"Oh we're defending him now?" she said. "You must really be in love."

My eyes went wide.

As hell.

"Um... *I'm* the one with the head injury here," I said. "I should be saying the crazy shit, not you." I took a quick glance at myself in the mirror, adjusting my collar a bit to make sure that any signs of my lingering bruise were covered.

"It's not that crazy. He's your *husband*."

"I've literally known this man for like four months. Has it even *been* four months? More like three," I reminded them both.

"Bitch it's definitely been at least four months, can you not?" Morgan laughed.

"Can *y'all* not, is the better question."

"Ooooh, she sensitive about it," Morgan quipped, and I pushed out a sigh.

"Not sensitive I just don't think it's accurate to say I'm *in love* with that man."

"*That man*," Alexis grumbled. "*You mean your husband.*"

"Or even realistic," I continued as if I hadn't heard her. "Like... are we forgetting that I had to drag a bitch across my dining room table behind this man, not even two weeks ago?"

"Oh I *do* remember." Alexis laughed. "And to be honest, that's making it even harder for you to beat the *in love* allegations, babe. I mean... unless you're trying to convince me that you drag bitches about men you don't even want? 'Cause that's definitely not the Nala *I* know."

Morgan scoffed. "The dragging part? 'Cause finding out she did that was literally what made the most sense about this whole situation since it started." She giggled and Alexis joined her.

"Yes we know our good sis is with the shits, but *I'm* talking about this fictional narrative that she'd do said dragging over a man she doesn't care about."

"It was about the *disrespect*," I huffed. "Was I supposed to just let that ride? Honestly I should've gone upside *his* head too."

"Don't front Nala," Morgan said. "We all know you're unfazed until you're not. And then you're very fucking fazed. You cannot convince me that you did that shit and don't care about this man. 'Cause if you didn't care, you would've just laughed in that lady's face for trying to play in yours."

"Mmmmhmm," Alexis agreed. "And I keep coming back to, *why* do you think there's something wrong with you caring about this man?"

"Because with everything that's gone on, I should still be thinking about what I can slip into this nigga's pie so I can widow myself," I answered with a shrug.

"Oh please," Morgan huffed. "Just face it, sis, you've accepted the reality of your situation, and we've had this conversation before," she reminded me. "There is nothing wrong with making the best of it. Including…falling in love with his ass a little bit."

Alexis raised her hand, doing a pinching motion with her fingers, and I shook my head.

"Stop," I insisted.

I didn't even like the *sound* of that shit.

I was tolerating him fine, now that we'd gotten past the whole birth control thing, but *in love*?

With Orion Sterling?

Ew.

"Dinner is what the plan was, not whatever this is," I spoke up, shaking off the weird feeling this whole conversation was giving me. I didn't give them a chance for rebuttal. I headed for the door and they were quick to follow behind me.

Our progress was quickly impeded by someone coming up the stairs.

Orion.

His eyes went wide at the sight of us, not because he was surprised they were here, I'd told him they were coming. My immediate assumption was that he wasn't expecting me to be dressed for leaving the house—which I hadn't, in the week that passed since the attack.

"Hey, Lex," he greeted Alexis first, and she gave him a nod.

"Hey, Ri."

"Morgan," he said and as usual she was doing too much.

"Heeey, Mr. Sterling," she sang, making him chuckle.

And then, finally, he really looked at me, giving me a head-to-toe examination that made me want to melt into a puddle.

"Looks like you ladies were planning to head out?" he asked, and I nodded.

"Just dinner." I shrugged. "At 81st and Clarke."

Not that I needed permission.

I was trying to offer him some security.

He pushed out a sigh, shoving hands into his pockets. "I'm afraid I have to discourage you from that," he said. "I mean… if you insist, I'll make sure you have proper protection, but I'd rather you didn't. EJ is under control, but regrettably, I don't know who he might have working for him or who be coming to ask questions on his behalf. And unfortunately... that same caveat applies to your father."

Shit.

No matter how badly I wanted to argue... he wasn't wrong.

And honestly, I'd considered the same thing.

I'd just been hoping no one else would bring it up.

Hoped I was simply overthinking it, and that maybe even through sheer luck, everything would be perfectly fine—no weird run-ins, especially knowing that security would be following me, and that I'd be with my homegirls.

...Not that being followed by security had prevented the other attack.

Which was probably the same thing on Orion's mind.

"If it's any consolation, I can run back downstairs and have the chef whip up enough dinner for everybody," he offered. "So you'll be well fed either way. Ladies... please help me convince my wife that caution is the way to go?" he asked, appealing to my friends, even though it was unnecessary.

They were the ones who needed convincing, not me.

"No wait time and top shelf liquor I *know* you've got somewhere in this house?" Morgan asked. "Lex, you're on designated driving."

"*Hey*," Alexis fussed, following her down the stairs, past Orion. "Not if I get a shot in me first, bitch!"

"Sorry to ruin your fun," Orion said, pulling my attention back to him.

I shrugged. "It's fine, but I do eventually have to leave the house again, you know?"

"Another unfortunate truth I have to reckon with." He

nodded, climbing a few more stairs to get closer to me. "Give me another week. I'll have this all sorted."

I raised an eyebrow. "What about my father?"

"He's included. And anybody else who makes you feel unsafe. You want to give me a list?"

"I don't think that's necessary." I laughed.

"If that changes, let me know."

I nodded. "I will."

For a moment, he just stared at me, and then, "Can I be honest with you?"

"Please do."

He smirked. "I wasn't lying about my reasons for discouraging you against going out, but…"

"But what?"

"A further reason for my hesitation is that… I'd prefer you not look as good as you do right now without me on your arm."

My mouth dropped open a little, but I quickly recovered. "Are you telling me how I can and can't dress?" I asked, gesturing at the—admittedly sexy—form-fitting orange dress I'd chosen to wear out with my friends.

"Not at all, you should be admired," he answered. "I'd just like everybody to know who you belong to while they're looking."

Challenge that, bitch.

I should.

I *really* should.

Instead, I couldn't get over my internal squeal over those words, couldn't fight off that little giddy feeling fast enough before he'd already turned to go back down the stairs, and the moment had passed.

Shit.

By the time I'd gathered myself mentally, he was already halfway to the kitchen, presumably to speak to Chef. I took a slightly different path, landing in the dining room with Alexis and Morgan. They'd already located the bar and quickly mixed a cocktail for me too as I joined them.

"Uhh... wait a damn minute. Lex, *where* is your engagement ring?" I asked, noticing the absence of the mega-watt rock her man had put on her finger not that long ago. She'd been in no hurry to move forward with the planning of a wedding, but this was the first time I'd seen her without it since the night he put it on.

"Oh!" she exclaimed, looking at her empty hand like I'd just given her breaking news. "I must've left it in my jewelry tray on my way out earlier."

I looked at Morgan, and she looked at me, mirroring my skepticism.

"Don't do that," Alexis begged, slumping onto a bar stool. "It doesn't mean anything."

"Would Dale agree that it doesn't mean anything?" Morgan asked. The same exact question on my mind as I took the seat beside Alexis.

"Yeah... did you really *forget* or is it more like a *forget him*?" I prompted, leaning in.

She sighed.

She *sighed*.

What was with the heavy sighs?!

"I don't know." She shrugged. "He's been weird. But work has been crazy, and he doesn't like how busy I am. He tried to *pay me* to quit. As if I'd ever!"

My eyes went wide.

As much as plenty of women might—rightfully and understandably—dream of being "retired" from work, Alexis wasn't built like that; it was a trait all three of us had in common.

We'd been blessed to find our passions and as such *loved* our careers.

Trying to make her give it up verged on kinda disrespectful.

"So you were gonna go out looking good, no ring, show your ass a bit, to get back at him?" Morgan asked, but Alexis shook her head.

"No, it wasn't like that. It's *not* like that. I'm just… wondering now if he's a good fit. Especially seeing you and Ri together."

My eyes went *even wider*.

"Me?" I questioned. "And *Orion?* You remember that he blackmailed me—wait… bullied me? Forced me? Shook me down? Whatever he did, damn, the point is, I didn't even *want* to marry his ass. I should *not* be your relationship goals, friend."

She rolled her eyes. "You say that, but the way he looks at you? Protects you? Supports you? *Fucks you*," she teased, leaning in to nudge my shoulder. "I'm just saying… there's a lot to admire."

"And a lot to fucking pity, are you crazy?" I countered as she laughed. "Morgan, you understand where I'm coming from, right? You've dealt with this damn family."

She shrugged. "My only opp was their snooty bitch mother and she dead."

"*Morgan*," I gasped, but her only response was another shrug as she sipped her drink.

"What? I didn't kill her!"

"It's mean!"

"And so was *she*," Morgan insisted. "You never met her,

so you don't understand. I was a damn kid, Nala, and that lady was *nasty* to me. And Ares listened to her, so… I don't know what you want *me* to say. Fuck them."

"Yeah, exactly, *fuck them*," Titan called from the entryway, *clearly* only catching the very last part of her statement.

My eyes remained wide as fuck as he sauntered in, followed shortly by Ares himself, an appearance that caused Morgan to knock back the rest of her drink and reach for the bottle of liquor again, not bothering with a mixer.

"Uh… hey," I said to the guys. "I didn't know y'all were coming through."

"Yeppp," Titan said, extending his arms to hug me, which I of course obliged. "Ri hit us up this afternoon."

Whew.

So their presence had nothing to do with Alexis and Morgan being here, a fact I was trying desperately to communicate with my eyes.

Alexis was cool either way, greeting Titan as a friend who immediately said something to her in a low tone that made her start laughing.

Morgan, on the other hand…

She wasn't feeling it.

"Morgan," Ares greeted her, after he'd given me a quick hug too. "We didn't get a chance to speak at the wedding, b—"

"Oh, we had a chance," she interrupted. "I just didn't want to fucking talk to you."

His eyebrows went up. "I… understood." He nodded. "I was just going to say I was glad to see you looking well after all these years."

"I *do* look good as fuck, don't I?" she challenged.

"*Oh God,*" I muttered, covering my face with my hands.

I just needed a second, and then I was going to let Orion know that we'd changed our minds, we'd eat in my room, or on the porch, hell, anywhere but here.

But he was already at the doorway, insisting we take our seats for dinner to be served.

"*Behave*," I hissed at Morgan, who rolled her eyes at me, but didn't say anything else.

To her credit, she *did* behave.

As long as Ares was quiet.

Or rather, as long as he left her alone instead of trying to make even the politest conversation with her. Titan found it amusing and kept trying to draw it out until Alexis and Orion teamed up to make him behave.

So... there were a few moments where it was a little tense.

Overall?

It was fine.

The food was great, and mostly the conversation was too, and afterwards, Alexis did indeed end up being the designated driver tasked with getting Morgan safely home. Ares and Titan left when they did and Titan took it upon himself to make sure Lex got home safely too.

Then... it was just me and Orion.

Me and my *husband*, as my friends so loved to point out.

"How are you feeling?" he asked, walking me up the stairs to my room. Not that I needed the help, but he insisted.

"I feel... fine, I guess?" I answered, shrugging. "Are you asking if I had a good time with you and your brothers?"

A little grin played at the corners of his lips. "Maybe?"

"Oh please." I laughed. "This isn't the first dinner I've had with y'all. I always enjoy your family. Most of them," I corrected. "Where has Bree been lurking?"

"A question I hope to have an answer to soon." He

nodded. "But I had to ask because this was—however impromptu—our first social gathering since I uh…"

"Lost your goddamn mind?"

That grin turned into a full-blown smile as he chuckled. "Uh… something like that," he said. "I prefer to think of it as… growing pains?"

"Uh-huh," I replied. "Whatever makes you feel better."

"There's only one thing that would make me feel better."

I tipped my head to the side. "And what's that?"

"Come to my bed like you used to."

Those words made a breath catch in my throat, and I looked away, buying time to respond.

He was the one who hadn't touched *me* since then.

Of course I was pissed at him at first, so trying to fuck me would *not* have gotten him any kind of desirable result.

After that, though.

After that terrifying encounter with EJ, after getting poked and prodded by a doctor and making sure there was no concussion and all the shit I'd found out from my father and about my mother and just… *everything*… I'd craved his touch.

He'd been *present* for sure, had honored my wishes to join me in my bed, all that.

But he wasn't… hungry for me.

Not like he'd been before.

He'd been gentle with me.

Which I'd needed, and appreciated.

But that just wasn't the vibe our relationship, if we could call it that, had been built on.

We had chemistry when we had nothing else, and it felt like it was just… *gone.*

"Hey, no pressure, if you're not—"

"It's not that," I told him, shaking my head. "It's just been a little awkward. And I didn't think…"

"You didn't think… *what*?" he asked. "That I wanted you? Nala… there has never been a point in a time where that was the case. Where it was even a question," he added. "The question is… can I have you?"

I scoffed. "Well, our contract—"

"*Fuck the contract*," he growled, moving in closer to me, looking me in the face. When I backed up, into the wall, he moved in again, essentially trapping me there as he met my gaze. "I'm telling you… beyond what's on the paper, that I want *you*. I want to know you, and… *have you*, Nalani. I…" He pushed out a sigh, looking away for a moment like he was choosing his words. "I want this to be… *real*. Tell me if that's something we can work toward. Something we can do?"

I… didn't even think about it really.

Bafflingly.

The "yes" was off my lips in a damn near immediate answer and his lips were on my lips in a damn near immediate response.

And I kissed him back, *eagerly*.

Probably *too* eagerly, but whatever.

I was into whatever came next. Him picking me up like it was nothing to carry me through his door, stripping me out of the dress he'd complimented, and the lingerie underneath.

His mouth between my legs, devouring my pussy like it was his favorite dish.

The anticipation as he stripped down while I caught my breath.

The fullness of him buried in me to the hilt.

His gentle hands, lips on my bruised neck.

The filthy affirmations in my ears as he fucked me until his words were replaced with static.

The pain and pleasure of the final plunge of his hips as he emptied his dick in me.

Every damn moment.

Plus… whatever came after that.

TWENTY-SEVEN
ORION

From the outside, *The Black Gallery* was quite innocuous.

Objectively beautiful in design, very clean, very modern. You walked in and were immediately met with stark white, accented with matte black, wood tones, broken up by the vivid colors from the art on display.

Great place to host an event.

But then, for certain people, there was elevator access at the back.

And a button, near the top, that led *down*, past the basement with all the typical art gallery storage.

Down there was a room.

In that room... there was EJ.

EJ had definitely seen better days.

"You look awful, man," I told him, taking a seat in the chair I'd brought in with me. He was seated in another, in the middle of the room.

"*Fuck you*," he grumbled, his words much less muffled

than they'd been the last time I was here, when his mouth was still swollen and raw from our little tussle.

I chuckled, leaning back in my chair to get comfortable. "I'm a little disappointed in you, man. I'd hoped for a less predictable response."

EJ's head lifted, eyes narrowed. "What the fuck are you talking about?"

"I don't know." I shrugged. "It just seems… cliché. I'm clearly in the position of power here, and yet you still play tough. *Fuck you, fuck your questions, kiss my ass, I fucked your wife*—that's the script, right? Because you think you have nothing left to lose," I predicted. "You *think* that me killing you is the worst that could happen."

"Wrong," he grunted. "The worst that could happen is having to sit here and listen to your bitch ass."

I grinned. "Damn… you've lived a sheltered life if you think that," I told him. "You'll understand soon enough. In the meantime… I'm not going to hold you long. I just need to confirm a few things."

"I'm not answering shit for you," EJ spat. "You know my people are looking for me, right? It's over for you, and your little company, my instructions were clear. Even when I'm gone, you're not safe."

My eyebrows lifted. "That sounds pretty intimidating. Wow."

That must not've been the reaction he wanted. He planted his feet and tried to lunge, only to be snatched back again; his binds were connected to the floor, too. "Bitch ass boy," he growled, shaking his head. "You feel like a man?! Huh?! Untie me, let's really see what's up!"

"We've already done that; this is the result, remember?" I asked, gesturing at the way he was bound. "I wouldn't mind beating the shit out of you again. I just don't really have the time today and I messed up a perfectly good suit when we did this before. And... it would just be redundant. So we may as well just cut to the chase."

"I already told you I'm not answering shit, nigga."

"I heard that." I nodded. "But I don't think you have a true grasp of your situation. Do you know where you are? How long you've been here?"

"Why does it matter?!"

"Because, again... I don't think you understand the situation, but you need to. You're at *The Black Gallery*. You've been here a week."

All the pretense of toughness melted off his face, and he shook his head. "Nah. You didn't—"

"Oh, I did." I grinned. "Because see... I warned you. On Christmas day, remember?" I asked. "I made it clear that you were to stay away from my wife. And listen... I know you didn't know, but I still consider that strike one. 'Cause you were disrespectful."

"But these niggas aren't—"

"And then, there was strike two." I kept talking. "You put your hands on her, put a *bruise* on my wife. You told her I couldn't protect her. I told her she would never have to worry about that again. And then... strike three. You turned me into a *liar*, Eric."

"Orion, *man*—"

"Tell me flat out whose directives were so important that assaulting my wife was an acceptable action for you. Was it really William Stark?"

"Yes," he answered immediately, suddenly freed from his conviction to not tell me anything. "Nalani has her mother's computer, and he wants it."

"*Wow*," I droned. "So you're telling me that computer was important enough to die for?"

"No. Lani wasn't even supposed to be home."

"So you'd been following her?"

"Not me. The bitch was supposed to be keeping tabs on her."

I raised an eyebrow. "What bitch?"

"Your daddy's bitch," EJ answered, and for a moment I was confused. My father had been gone for *years*.

But he had a widow.

My eyes narrowed, and I sat forward in my chair. "Are you telling me Breanna is working with William?" I asked. "For what, and for how long?"

"I don't know." He shrugged, as much as he could. "Just looks like gold-digger shit to me. William has been fucking her for like a month—maybe two?"

I bit down on the inside of my lip, thinking back to the last time I'd seen Bree. I'd noted her absence, but hadn't thought too much of it until recently. And then Nalani asked about her, which highlighted it even more.

So this explained quite a bit.

"Thank you for sharing this with me," I said, snapping my attention back to EJ. "Anything else you'd like to add?"

"*Don't* leave me with these people, man," he begged. "Have you heard the shit folks say about them? Something is *off* about them."

I grinned. "Yes, there is, that's exactly why I brought you here."

"*Wait*!" he shouted as I stood. "I don't deserve this shit man. I can work for you! I can—"

"Nah," I shook my head. "You can't. Any chance of sympathy from me died when you decided to scare my wife.

And you know Nalani... she doesn't scare easily. So we *both* know you crossed a fucking line."

"But—"

"But nothing." I shook my head. "Because *that* killed my ability to sympathize with your situation. What you did in her apartment?" I blew out a low whistle. "Man... I don't give a fuck what happens to you now."

"My people will come after me!" he insisted desperately. "You'll never be safe. Your bitch will always be looking over her shoulder."

I shook my head. "No, actually. See, once I *handle* something... it's handled. Completely. You're neutralized, nigga. As good as gone and *nobody* is going to remember when it wasn't that way."

"*Just kill me*," he begged, as I reached the door. "Come *on*. You know this shit isn't right! They're fucking... cannibals or something. Freaky ass shit that nobody deserves."

I sighed, then turned the knob. "You're right, EJ. Nobody deserves to be handed over to the Blacks." I looked back at him and grinned. "Now I want you to guess exactly what you are to me?"

"Wait! Don—"

Whatever else he said got drowned out.

When I closed the door, Parris Black was standing in the hall.

I steeled myself immediately, refusing to flinch even though I was startled.

"You done?" he asked, nodding at the door.

"Yeah," I assured. "Do whatever. I don't want to have to worry about him *or* his people."

Parris grinned.

Creepy as fuck.

"Understood. All I needed was a reason; they're bad for the environment."

A flash of curiosity hit me, but I immediately shook it off. I didn't need to know what the hell that meant. "I've got another name for you too. Maybe two."

"I'm listening."

"William Stark. Breanna Sterling."

He raised an eyebrow. "Family?"

"She lost the opportunity to be considered that."

He nodded. "I'll talk to Elias about it."

"Thank you." I pushed out a deep sigh, knowing the next question I needed to ask, but desperately not wanting to.

"You don't owe us anything," Parris said, as if he'd read my mind. "Elias said to consider it a wedding gift. And he sends his apologies that he couldn't be in attendance."

I tried not to show the relief that sank my shoulders before I thanked Parris and got the fuck out of there. I could breathe easier in the public space.

EJ wasn't lying.

There was *absolutely* dark energy about the Blacks, but no denying that they got shit done.

Things I didn't need mine or my brothers' hands dirtied with.

There weren't many things that made me uneasy, but dealing with them was absolutely one, and I was glad it was over. Their invitation to my wedding had been a societal technicality only—one that Shiloh had the foresight to insist on.

So when I stopped at the jeweler on the way back to the office to pick something up for Nalani… I grabbed a little trinket for Shi too.

"*Oooh*," she gushed when she saw the gift-wrapped box.

"I'm not even going to ask what I'm being appreciated for since I already know I deserve it."

I shook my head, continuing into my office. "Don't ever try to claim you don't have an ego."

"Why would I lie like that?" she asked, following me. "Anyway, what do you want first?"

"Afternoon rundown," I told her, dropping into a seat.

"Cool. Jess and her team turned in their quarterly marketing focus; it's great. Very fresh. Should appeal well across age groups."

I nodded. "Good. No funny stuff with her, right?"

"No." Shi chuckled. "I think she's on the straight and narrow again. Getting snatched across—"

"*Shi.*"

"Okay my bad. But. I could've told you that shit was going to happen. Nothing about Nalani gives *play in my face* vibes."

"Which I'm quite clear on," I warned. "Now, *what else?*"

"Fine, but shouldn't you be in a better mood? Nalani likes you again now I thought."

"Damn it…"

"*Okay.*" She laughed. "Sorry. Okay. Uh… Stanford checked in earlier. There haven't been any more issues with construction and the new store is on track to be open by Q4."

"Good. Anything else?"

"Anything that's not gonna make you want to curse me out? No."

"Then, nothing else." I chuckled, shaking my head. "I need you to do something for me."

She rolled her eyes. "Don't you always?"

"You get well paid for it," I reminded her. "I need you to book a trip, just me and my wife. She likes the beach, so…

somewhere on a beach. Very private. As luxurious as humanly possible. No budget."

Shiloh grinned. "I love every single word that just came out of your mouth. When am I booking this for?"

"Get ahold of her calendar, work around anything important she has going on."

"Should I maybe… consult with her?" she suggested. "Instead of… you know… bulldozing? I mean I know that's your thing, but I don't think she likes that, so…"

"It's supposed to be a surprise."

"I'd bet she'd rather know you respected her time and autonomy than be surprised. I mean… remember how you sprung a whole wedding on her…"

…shit.

She had a point.

A good one.

"Fine," I said. "Pull together some dates that work on both calendars and I'll see what she wants to do. I don't have to give her all the details, just the rough plan."

Shiloh grinned. "Well look at that, he's learning! I love it," she said, slipping back out of the office before I could rebut her patronizing tone.

In all honesty, she'd probably just saved my ass from getting *back* on Nalani's bad side, so I was going to let her rock anyway.

By the time afternoon rolled around, Shi had gotten everything back to me, and armed with that information, I took a trip to *Nectar*. Today was Nalani's first day back at the office and I'd planned to pop up on her anyway.

Now, I was armed with vacation plans and a gift.

The odds of making her smile were leaning in my favor pretty well.

I found her at the wine bar—working, not drinking. I hung back for a bit, watching as she interacted with the manager and employees. Before everything else, *this* was one of the things I admired about her. She truly was good at what she did and I could see the respect in the eyes of the people she was talking to.

She was a leader.

Which had made it no surprise that the *Nectar* board offered her the position of CEO her father had held. She turned it down, but was filling the role until they found someone suitable.

Instead of accepting it just for the power, she'd stepped back, choosing to continue in the Operations Manager position she enjoyed.

It was smart.

It was the kind of wise decision that prevented the usual corporate burnout.

Not to mention, she was *beautiful.*

Again, the capability, intelligence, beauty… those were all things I'd already known about her.

Things I admired.

I pushed out a deep, private sigh, thinking about what could have possibly been between us if I'd simply pursued her in a normal manner, instead of bulldozing my way into her life.

And of course if there was no bad blood between our families.

Before I could approach her, she'd looked up, noticing me from across the bar.

Her eyes lit in recognition, and then, *ever-so-subtly,* she smiled at me, letting it linger for just a few seconds before she tucked it away, schooling her face back to neutral.

Not wanting me to know she was happy to see me.

Which... that was fine, for now.

I knew that was on me.

But it was also on me to change it.

Since she'd seen me now, there was no point in hanging back. I strode up to her as she said parting words to her employees, then took it upon myself to get all in her personal space.

"How can I help you, Mr. Sterling?" she asked, still maintaining that neutral expression as she tipped her head back a bit to meet my gaze. "You know it's still work hours, right?"

"I do." I nodded. "I just wanted to lay eyes on you myself. Make sure you were good."

"Why wouldn't I be?"

"Not the point." I laughed. "Like I said, just making sure."

She raised an eyebrow. "Mmhmm. It kinda feels like you know something I don't, but since I'm sure that will *always* be the case... fine. I'm good."

"Good. You got a minute to talk?"

"Aaand there it is." She nodded. "Is something wrong?"

"If there was, I would've fixed it before I ever brought it to you," I assured her. "I'm hoping you see it as something right."

The response I got at first was narrowed eyes, but then she nodded again, gesturing for me to follow her to a nearby table. It was quiet in here—since, as she said, it was still during most peoples' work day and wouldn't really start popping until later—so we had relative privacy.

"I'm taking you on vacation," I told her as soon as we were seated.

As Shiloh predicted, I definitely caught a prickle of irritation in her eyes, but she held it back. "Are you asking me or telling me?"

"A little of both," I explained. "A compromise."

"How so?"

"Well... we're going on the trip, full stop, not debatable," I said. "But... we'll plan around dates that work for you. I know you'll want to put certain things in place around here before we go."

She nodded, that little thread of frustration from a moment ago already gone. "I appreciate you not doing a wedding repeat on me." She laughed. "I won't pretend I couldn't use some time away—*not* hiding bruises from the world—but a real vacation. Where are we going?"

"That's confidential."

"You're kidding."

"Not at all," I countered. "My ability to surprise you with lavish things is one of my only tools in this relationship. I'm not giving it away any time soon."

She laughed. "It's not your only tool."

"What else do I have?"

"A massive dick. Skillful tongue." She winked and there wasn't shit I could do *but* grin about that.

"Glad to know my efforts in those areas are recognized."

"And appreciated," she added.

"So great sex and a bottomless wallet, those are my assets, huh?"

She bit down on her lip, keeping back another smile. "You've got a few more."

"I'm listening."

"I can't tell you, you're arrogant enough."

I shrugged. "Not my first time being accused of such a thing."

"*Really*?!" She fake gasped. "I would've never guessed."

"Uh-huh." I chuckled, pushing back my chair. "Shi is going to send you the possible dates for our trip. We'll go with whatever you want, but... the sooner the better."

"Okay, but wait," she insisted. "Before you leave... there's something I need to ask you. Something... less fun than your topic was."

Immediately, I pulled myself back up to the table. "What is it?"

"Stanford Reese," she said, leaning in a bit so she could lower her voice. "I... did you know he was Soren's father?"

My brow furrowed. "What?"

Even as the question left my lips, my brain went into overdrive processing the information, making me doubt myself.

Because... *did I* know that?

I suspected Soren wasn't William's but didn't know for certain. I'd just heard a whisper or two in passing and knew the two men didn't favor each other. Neither of which was evidence, just enough ammunition for a dig.

But if Soren *was* Stanford's son... it made a lot of shit make a lot of sense.

And when I pulled *those* two faces to my mind... the resemblance was wild.

Not enough that it was obvious to just anybody, but once my mind went there... it was obvious.

"I have a meeting with him about the *Nectar* expansion in a few days, and... I'm going to ask him," Nalani explained. "But I already know some things, know that he had a relationship with my mother, *before* my father did. And I know they were all friends, with your parents. The friend group fractured, but Stanford stayed close with your father. Is this something you ever heard mentioned?"

I shook my head. "Never," I assured her. "It didn't really cross my mind to think about, honestly, but... *shit*. It all fits. Actually... I remember speaking to Stan about purchasing the *Nectar* property, back when I caught wind of it being available. He's always been a 'take the high ground' type, so I expected him to tell me to leave it alone, to not continue a grudge like that. But he didn't, which I thought was... different. I offered him to come in on it with me, but he wouldn't do *that*. Said that if he went near it, William might catch on."

"Interesting." Nalani nodded. "Can you... not say anything to him about this before I do?"

I nodded. "Of course I can honor that. Do you want me there with you when you talk to him?"

"No." She shook her head. "I think I can handle it. I just have to know what's going on. For myself, and for Soren."

"Understandable," I agreed. "Does Soren know any of this yet?"

"I don't believe so. I mean, William hinted at it, but stopped short of telling us anything real. Just to be cruel. I'm not even sure he's *not* responsible for my mother's death," she admitted. "No, he didn't give her cancer, but... that's really all the credit I can give him. I don't remember him ever being outright *terrible* to Soren growing up, but he was also... distant. There was a relationship there because *we* made it so, you know?" she asked and I nodded. "I thought it was just how it was, but as more and more comes out, I realize that he is, and has always been, a narcissist. He's never cared about anyone but himself."

"And he's a safety concern," I reminded her. "For you, for your brother... he sent EJ to harass you."

She blew out a sigh. "Yeah. I was trying not to even get into *that* part, but... you're right. And the crazy thing is, as much as I would've told you I loved my father... even a year ago... I don't know him anymore. He's a stranger. And he made it that way."

Good.

That was exactly the sentiment I needed to hear to alleviate any guilt I might feel about putting the Blacks on his ass.

Sure, people were complicated.

I understood that.

What I *didn't* understand was a parent alienating their children in the way William had; parentage aside, he'd raised them.

There was a responsibility there.

And I had zero sympathy for men who usurped that.

"Well, enough about my daddy issues," Nalani said, trying to shake it off, but I could see the clear pain in her eyes. As much as she might want to, she didn't feel *nothing* for William.

He'd hurt her.

Badly.

Which was something I couldn't abide.

"No such thing," I told her, reaching across the table to grab her hand. "I've got nothing better to do than listening if you need to talk."

She gave me a little smile. "I appreciate that, but I'd much rather pour my energy back into work, so we can get into this trip. You said the sooner the better, right?"

"I did," I agreed, squeezing her hand. "Anything for my wife."

TWENTY-EIGHT
NALANI

I couldn't focus.

Well... I could, just on the wrong damn thing.

This meeting with Stanford Reese had already been on my calendar, but it wasn't supposed to be about heritage and secret affairs and all that.

It was *supposed* to be about expanding *Nectar's* territory.

If only that was what I wanted to think about, really.

I sat straight up at my computer when the expected knock sounded at the door—my assistant, letting me know Stanford was here. Instead of remaining in my seat, I hopped up, wanting to meet him at the door.

Knowing what I did now, I wasn't sure how I'd missed it when we first met.

He was Soren, in twenty or thirty years.

"Mrs. Sterling," he greeted me warmly, extending a hand. "Good to see you again."

"Likewise." I nodded, accepting his handshake. It felt *so* formal, knowing that he'd had such a deep relationship with my mother—who I looked just like, according to... everyone.

Was it bittersweet for him to see my face?

Did I remind him of her?

Was this awkward?

If so, he gave no indication, settling easily into the seat I offered to start his presentation. There was no doubt in my mind that he knew what he was talking about, that his ideas were top notch, but I couldn't get over his mannerisms, his passion for the topic, and again... that face.

So much like my brother.

There was no possibility William hadn't known.

Had he privately seethed for years, raising his former friend's child?

Had he known the truth and simply ignored it, trying to pretend?

"Mrs. Sterling, am I boring you?" he asked, snapping me out of my private musings. "If so, I apologize. I know I'm further into the weeds than this meeting calls for. I'm just galvanized by the possibilities of what we could do with *Nectar*."

I shook my head. "No sir, it's not that," I assured him. "Your presentation is engaging, and I love everything I've heard, it's just... I need to hear about your relationship with my mother."

Momentarily, his eyes went wide.

I watched his expression cycle from surprise to a worried sort of resolve as he closed the cover on his laptop.

Clearly, that part of the meeting was over.

"Your father told you?" he asked, and... *shit*.

Those words were an answer, a relief, and a disappointment all in one.

"So he is my father?" I countered, waiting for that response before I gave my own.

His reply was simple.

"Yes."

"You're sure?"

"Yes."

I nodded. "Okay. But... uh... no, he's not the one who told me. It was you and her, actually," I explained. "I found uh... letters, hidden in her office. And before that, pictures from someone doing an article about *Nectar*. Pictures of your group of friends. You look just like my little brother. Or... shit, I guess it's the other way around."

He sighed, leaning forward over the desk. "You read the letters?"

"No," I answered immediately. "They were private. Clearly. Out of respect for my mother, I wanted to let them remain that way, and I can give them to you, if you want them. But I need to understand what happened, if you can give me that. I know there was at least a fling, before my parents got married; Aunt Lucy confirmed it. But my parents ended up together and then you got involved again. How?"

He ran a hand over his face, quiet for a moment like he was considering his words before he spoke. "Yes, there was a fling," he confirmed. "And that was all I thought it was, at first—everybody doing their own thing. That what Larena said it was, after I expressed to her that I was... wanting more than that. I'm not proud of it, but that's how Lucy and I got involved. I was hurt and called myself taking it out on Larena by fooling with her sister."

"That's trash," I told him.

"Yes," he agreed. "It was. And again, I'm not proud, but that's what it was. When Larena found out, she was hurt—"

"Because she had feelings for you. She lied."

He nodded. "Yes. And Billy had always wanted her, but she never paid him any mind. Until then."

"She was vulnerable, and he took advantage of that."

"That's the way I saw it," he said. "And the way that she characterized it later, once we were back on good terms. She stopped speaking to Lucy and me, and the next thing anybody knew, she was marrying William. Not that long after… you came along."

My eyes went wide. "So… they got married because she was pregnant."

"He begged her to keep you, so she did," Stanford confirmed. "Billy swept her off her feet—her knight in shining armor, rescuing her from heartbreak. She didn't see the real him until they were married, but me and Cas… we knew what he really was."

"But you remained friends with him, enabled him."

"No." He shook his head. "We thought he'd grow up. Thought he'd see that the world wasn't against him, that *we* weren't against him. Whatever other bullshit aside, we were damn near a co-op, supporting each other, working the family businesses, leaning on the group. We thought he'd pick it up."

I scoffed. "He's too self-absorbed for that," I replied. "If you let him tell it, he's the reason *Nectar* is even here today, like it didn't come from *Joyce Grocery*. My mother's family."

"We didn't think it was as bad as it was," he insisted. "A few years passed, and they were basically shunned from the group, shunned *themselves* from the group. We'd been reaching out, showing up, and it was always ignored. Then… I got this letter. It was from Larena, but it was in another envelope, without her name on it. Different address and everything. But it was her. And she laid it all out, made it clear how bad she was hurting."

My eyes went wide. "When was this? Where was I?"

"You were there. You were... maybe six or seven years old? You were the only thing keeping her alive," he told me. "Her bright spot in the dark; that's what she called you. She told me about... pregnancy losses, and grief, how Billy had gotten himself wrapped all up in the business so she couldn't get him out, and gambling debts, and threats, and... so much that I'm sure you never saw."

I shook my head. "No, I didn't. She put up a good front for me, I guess."

"She never wanted you to worry. Never wanted you to feel the kind of stress she was carrying around. We started exchanging letters back and forth, and then... meeting."

"Having an affair," I amended.

He nodded. "Yes. Having an affair. When she got pregnant... she wasn't sure whose it was. But she expected to lose it. When she *didn't*... I knew whose it was. But she thought I was crazy for coming to that conclusion. For a while, we couldn't tell, but as he got older... we could see it. It was obvious Soren was ours."

"But you were both married," I interjected. "So of course you couldn't just run off and have a family together."

"I was divorced," he corrected. "I didn't remarry until after she passed. But where it came to Soren... I *wanted* to step in. But things with Billy were so... fucked up. He was volatile—unpredictable. She didn't know what he would do to you, to her, to the business, to me, if he found out. So... we never said anything. We let him believe Soren was his."

"But he *didn't* believe that."

"He did," Stanford argued. "For a long time. It wasn't

until he was a teenager, you were out of the house, and your mom had gotten sick the first time, that he put those pieces together. Probably because seeing Soren was like..."

"Seeing a ghost," I filled in with a sigh. "I think you're right though. That was when he started being... just... *different*. Growing up, he played the role of perfect father, perfect husband, at least where people could see. And to us kids. Looking back now, I know it was forced. But then he stopped forcing it," I mused. "He was never *abusive,* just... kinda cold? Like he wasn't our parent, more like... acquaintances. Just people he knew."

Damn.

That was... wild to say out loud.

Before all this, before the deep thinking I'd had to do trying to understand motivations and all that, I'd never thought my relationship with my father was... complicated.

He just was who he was.

I thought my mother's sickness had changed him, but he clearly still loved me, still loved Soren. I never thought much of Soren not looking like either of our parents, not looking like me, because... shit, genetics were complex. I just knew that was my brother, and I loved him.

That was it.

It was all so, *so* simple until I realized it was *never* simple.

It had always been a fucking mess, I just wasn't in on it.

"What can I do for you, Nalani?" Stanford asked, eyes begging... forgiveness?

But... he hadn't wronged *me*.

An argument could be made that he'd wronged Soren, but even that didn't feel quite accurate.

Of course... Soren might disagree.

"Tell me why you're being so transparent," I spoke up,

meeting his gaze. "My mother has been gone for years. William is no threat to her anymore. And yet... you never showed up. You never made yourself known."

He nodded. "Because he wasn't just a threat to her. He was a threat to you, to Soren, to what your mother wanted to leave for you. *Clearly*." He scoffed. "She asked me to promise, asked me to stay away. And I did... until you married Orion."

"Because he beat William at his little game," I explained. "Which I know you had some part in."

"I can't deny what's right in front of your face," he agreed. "I encouraged Orion to purchase the building, but *not* because I thought it would put you in a bind. Because I trusted it in the hands of someone I knew and respected more than a stranger. I had no idea he'd play it the way he did."

I sat back in my chair, just staring for a moment before I nodded. "I believe you."

"I'm glad," he countered. "Larena made me promise not to bring any of this to you. Not the land deal, but the affair and all of that. So I honored that. But she also made me promise that if either of you came to me for the truth... I would tell it. So that's what it is. And I'll answer any other questions you have. But I hope you'll still let me work with you on the expansion," he added. "It... it's important to me. It's something Larena always wanted for this place and it would be an honor to assist with seeing it through."

I nodded. "Yes, of course," I agreed. "I'm absolutely still open to all of that, but... there's things that have to be resolved first. Father or not, William is a wild card, and with everything he's done so far... he'll go nuclear if—*when*—he finds out we're working with you."

Stanford shook his head. "You let your husband and I figure that out. I promise you, Billy's sabotage days are over."

"I believe you," I said. "But that's not all. I… I'm going to need you to talk to Soren," I told him. "You have to explain everything—why you weren't there, all of it. With the things William has said, I think my brother is going to need that. And I can't be good with you unless he is."

Before Stanford could respond, a quick knock sounded at the door, followed quickly by its opening without waiting for an answer.

Only one person did that.

Shit.

I hopped up from my chair, eyes wide as the topic of conversation walked in, wearing a huge smile as he held up my mother's laptop. "Finally cracked it for you, sis," he said proudly, gesturing at it.

"Oh! That's amazing," I gushed, hurrying around the desk to take it from him. "Did you dig into it at all yet?"

"Nah, I brought it straight to you," he answered, eyes narrowing as let me pull the device to my hands. "My bad though. I didn't realize I was interrupting something."

"Just a meeting that's basically over." I shifted, trying to stay in front of him, but he easily gave me a gentle shove aside.

"Who are you?" he asked and a deep sigh pushed through me as I turned just in time to see Stanford turn.

As their eyes met, the air in the room immediately went thick.

"Stan Reese," Stanford answered, standing to shake Soren's hand.

Soren's hand was already out before he must've finally

made some connection, his brow dropping to a furrowed state as he looked into a face that drastically mirrored his.

Instead of saying anything to Stanford, he looked at *me*.

"Nala... what the fuck is this?"

What am I supposed to say?

This wasn't my mess, and I had no answer for it. I didn't know where to start.

Instead of leaving it to me though, Stanford clapped Soren on the shoulder, pulling the attention back to him.

"You've got an office here, right? You're Head of Tech, right?" he asked and Soren nodded.

"Uh... yeah."

"Okay. I think we need to talk," Stanford told him. "Let's leave your sister to her work and have our conversation there."

Soren glanced at me again, and I nodded, assuring him it was fine. It wasn't until then that he gave his own affirmative nod to Stanford and they headed off.

As much as I would've loved to be privy to their conversation... this was right.

I watched them leave and then, to distract myself from what might be happening with them, I dug into my mother's computer.

Instead of looking for anything that was necessarily about her private life, I decided to think like a man who was willing to accept harm to his daughter to get this device back into his hands.

What, exactly, would he not want to get out?

It occurred to me almost immediately that it was probably documents related to my mother's estate. Soren and I had gotten trusts worth good money, but the bulk of her estate, and the business more notably, had all gone to William.

It never felt quite right to me.

And I didn't have to dig very far to discover the truth.

The amendments to the will, the insurance, all of those documents, they stripped William of everything she could, putting the power in the hands of her children. Drafted just before she died, but not notarized or filed.

The last correspondence in her email was from her private lawyer, telling her that once she got everything in her hands, she could file it, and it would be done.

She never got the chance.

Because of William.

Did I *want* to believe that was the case?

Of course not.

And he'd all but denied it to my face.

But clearly the man was a liar and manipulator to a disgusting degree and so there was no reason to believe what left his mouth.

And *every* reason to believe the evidence in front of me.

Not only had he stolen our legacy, he'd tried to destroy it, to get back at our mother. I wanted to feel some degree of sympathy for him about the infidelity, but knowing that he'd manipulated the relationship, that he was this abusive narcissist, I just...*couldn't.*

It was too much to deal with.

And adding the thought that he'd possibly exacerbated her illness or maybe even outright killed her to get what he wanted... I just... *couldn't.*

And luckily, didn't have to.

A notification went off on my phone, letting me know it was time to move on from my desk, to head to a doctor's appointment. One Orion knew about, this time. I was due for bloodwork and a physical exam to test fertility, which we probably should have led with sooner, but... better late than never or something.

Orion had his own testing to do, but we'd opted against sharing the appointment, based on timing. It was refreshingly quick to get through. No hanging around in a waiting room, just straight back for everything, and we'd get test results later, once they'd done everything they needed to do.

Honestly... the distraction wasn't long enough.

When I got home, I immediately went looking for my husband, knowing *he* was good for a nice long while of wiping all the thoughts from my head.

Only... he wasn't home.

And Calli was resting.

And my friends were knee deep in work they couldn't break away from until later.

I'd just resolved myself to a glass of wine, my reading device, and my vibrator when the doorbell rang. Instead of moving quick to answer it, I used my app to pull up the cameras to see who it was.

I *did* rush to the door then.

It was my brother.

"Hey," I gushed, breathless from sprinting downstairs. I'd forgotten, somehow, that there was staff around the house.

Nobody expected *me* to answer the damn door.

"Hey," he replied, pulling me into our usual hug. "It's not a bad time or anything is it?"

I shook my head. "No, not at all. I wanted to talk to you, but... I don't know. I figured you probably needed time to process."

His reply to that was nonchalance, in the form of a shrug. "What is there to process?"

"Really, Soren?" I asked, gesturing to him to follow me to the nearby sitting room. "That's all you've got?"

"What more should I have?"

I sucked my teeth as I sat down. "After finding out who Stanford Reese is and who William Stark *isn't*… I would think a lot."

He sat down across from me, one hand pressed against his temple, eyes closed. "Honestly?" he said, without changing his position. "The shit doesn't even feel real. It's all just… wild."

"Yeah… it is."

"William is a bitch."

"Yeah. He is."

"I know that's *your* dad and all, but…"

His head popped up, and he grinned at me as I shook my head. "Really, you've already got jokes about this?"

"Laugh to keep from crying," he explained. "You know how it is."

"Yeah." I sighed. "I do. Unfortunately. How did the conversation go? You okay?"

"I will be," he said. "It's crazy looking into ol' boy's face though. He wants to get together again before he leaves town. Have dinner. Get to know each other."

I nodded. "Are you going to do that?"

"I don't know yet," he admitted. "Like I said… it's wild. And it's not something I really want to have to deal with. I just… I have too many questions not to entertain it. Too much I need to understand."

"I get it," I agreed. "Can I tell you something?"

"Anything."

"I'm… kinda jealous," I confessed. "Knowing what I

know now… I wish William wasn't my father either. It would probably make everything hurt a little less."

Soren frowned. "Explain."

So… I did.

I told him everything I hadn't wanted to burden him with before and explained what I'd found on our mother's unlocked computer. Stanford had already filled in some details about William's interactions and relationship with our mother, but there were things even *he* didn't know.

By the time I finished revealing everything I could, Soren was steaming mad.

"I don't even feel bad that Orion put the Blacks on his ass anymore," he huffed, making my eyes go wide.

"Wait a minute, what?" I asked. "The Blacks… who is that? The only ones I know are from the art gallery… right? They live further up in the hills, by the lake…"

Soren was quiet for a moment before he answered. "They… the art gallery is the tip of that iceberg," he explained. "And it's best we don't dig. Just know that when you're on their bad side… you'll be looking over your shoulder forever. Too much to fuck with anybody."

"Okay… that's insane," I said. "And how would you know that Orion has these people looking for William?"

"Because we share a common interest."

"Which is…?"

"You, Nala. *Duh*." He shrugged, pulling himself up from his seat. "Even before I knew about Stanford, that man was dead to me, as soon as I knew he'd sent EJ after you. I went to the house, but he's MIA. And has been since then 'cause he fucking *knows*. None of us are playing around about you."

I shook my head. "Which I appreciate, but… don't like.

You're supposed to be my nerdy little brother, boy! Not... a shooter!"

"I'm *not* that." He laughed. "You're acting like I'm getting teardrops tatted on my face or something."

"That's what it feels like."

"Because you're bugging." He chuckled. "Listen... we can talk about this other shit more another time. I have a date I need to get to on time. I just wanted to check in with you."

"A date?" I asked, joining him in standing. "A date with *who*?"

"None of your business, *yet*," he quickly amended. "I'll let you know if it gets serious."

I sighed. "Okay," I agreed. "But... you're not mad at me for not telling you about the thing with Stanford sooner?"

"Nah," he denied. "I know you would've. Stanford told me how you confronted him about it in your meeting."

I nodded. "I needed to know for sure before I could figure out how to bring it to you."

"And you didn't have to do that at all. It worked out for the best."

"I think so too," I agreed, giving him another hug. "Now... go. Don't be late. I love you."

Chuckling, he squeezed me back, planting a kiss on top of my head. "I love you too."

TWENTY-NINE
ORION

"Ri hasn't taken you to the gun range yet?"

Every set of eyes at the table went wide over Calli's question, posed directly to Nalani, who looked at me with an accusing smirk.

"No ma'am," she easily tattled, turning her attention back to my girl. "Was that supposed to be one of my perks?!"

"Sure was," Calli answered. "It's one of the first things my husband did with me, one of the first things Cas did with Daneitha. Every person of every gender. In this family, we know how to shoot—even made sure my sweet Shiloh knows how to handle herself."

"Is that how you ended up shooting my granddaddy?" I asked, trying to put the spotlight back on *her*.

Bad move.

She looked me right in the face and nodded. "Sure is. Everybody talked about how it was a nice clean shot, through and through his ass. That man had a nice one too—good balance of fat and muscle tone—runs in the family now. Good strong hips too. That's from me, Nala, so you can direct your thanks—"

"*O-kay,*" I interrupted, chuckling over the road she was going down. "That's enough of that."

As glad as I was that what was supposed to be hospice care seemed to have taken a drastic turn, Calli's mouth still stressed me out.

"No, I'd like to hear the rest," Nalani said, at the same time Calli fussed, "Lil boy, I *know* you not trying to quiet me down."

I scrubbed a hand over my face, reaching for my wine glass as the current two most important women in my life went back and forth between scolding me and discussing if good stroke game could be passed down.

Not in those exact terms, obviously, but… still.

Since the dinner conversation was clearly going on without me, I took the liberty to check my phone when it buzzed in my pocket. Bold, considering the censuring look I'd given Nalani when her phone kept vibrating with calls.

Still, because *everyone* knew not to bother me during these specific hours, this was an indication there was some sort of emergency or some vital information that needed to be conveyed.

Definitely the latter.

Confirmation that the Blacks had caught up with Bree and William and had done what they did best.

Neutralized the threat.

I couldn't pretend I wasn't disappointed about Bree. She was a beautiful woman and could easily have hitched her wagon to another rich man, if that was what she wanted to do.

Clearly, was what she'd *decided* to do.

Just… the absolute wrong one.

It niggled at me to see if there was an opportunity to speak to her, to ask why, but... there was no point, really.

Why did it matter?

The fact was that she'd chosen someone with a clear ulterior motive, who was likely mining her for information against not just my company, but my wife.

Two things I didn't fuck around about.

I felt exactly nothing knowing that they'd caught up with William.

Well... not nothing. I was sympathetic to how Nalani might feel, once I shared the news with her. With everything that had occurred, I didn't think she'd be exactly heartbroken, but the man was still her father.

It wouldn't be *nothing* for her.

And I hated *that*.

Especially watching her laugh and converse with my people, clearly having a good time. This was the type of thing she deserved, not family secrets and lies and having to fight for what was hers.

"I'm sorry," she spoke up, when her phone started buzzing again, under the table. "Excuse me for a moment. I have no idea who this is, but they're very insistent on speaking to me. I'll be right back."

Shit.

Usually the Blacks did things quietly... how the hell was this news already getting to her?

I didn't bother stopping her from leaving the room to answer the call. It was probably better to not delay the inevitable. Instead, I dipped right back into conversation with Calli, Nurse Davis, and Ms. Wallace, looping in Chef when he came through to replace our finished dinner plates with dessert.

When Nalani came back to the table, she was noticeably subdued.

The prodding over her change in mood by the ladies at the table was diverted with a lie about something going wrong at *Nectar*. They bought it, but I didn't—couldn't—seeing the way her hands shook as she pushed aside her half-finished wine glass to gulp down water.

And she wouldn't make eye contact with me.

Shit.

She knew, and she was pissed.

After dinner, I helped Nurse Davis get Calli settled in her room before I moved on to face the emotional consequences of my decisions. I stood by getting the Blacks involved, so I wouldn't back down on that.

But... I guess I could find it in myself to apologize for not at least seeking her input.

William was *her* father after all.

I was surprised to not find Nalani in *her* room. She was in mine instead. She'd already showered and changed into a set of the super-soft pajamas she favored. I'd teased her about them too many times to count now, but I'd come to love them on her. She chose them when she was at peace and comfortable.

So... a good sign.

"Hey," I said, pulling her attention from where she was absorbed on her phone. "Everything okay?"

She bit down on her lip, suppressing a strange sort of smile. "Uh... that depends on... I don't know what it depends on. But I think everything is okay?"

I tipped my head to the side, frowning as I approached the bed where she was seated. "You... think?"

"Yeah. Uh... so, you know earlier, when my phone kept ringing?"

I nodded, taking a seat. "Yes. Who was it?"

"The doctor. Remember I went to do that bloodwork?"

That's not what I expected.

Still, I gave her another nod. "Yes. I went and left my specimens yesterday."

"Right." She laughed. "Um... you could've saved that trip."

"Oh..." My mouth went dry as the implications hit me. "Did your bloodwork raise some flags?"

"One *really* major one," she answered, shaking her head. "Um... I... am already pregnant," she explained. "*Very* pregnant, if that's a thing. I have to go in tomorrow for an exam and all of that, but they were calling like that because they wanted to make sure I wasn't doing anything that might be dangerous for the baby because I didn't know. Like... drinking wine."

I cupped a hand over my chin and mouth, trying desperately to truly process what she was saying. "Nala... what do you mean by *very* pregnant? It's only been what... three weeks, a month, something like that since you got the implant removed."

"Which means I had to already be pregnant when I got it removed. I asked about that though and apparently it could've been implantation bleeding or just... bleeding. It's not uncommon. But based on my hormone levels..." She sighed. "I've likely been pregnant since pretty close to our wedding night."

My eyes went wide. "*That long*? How the hell would you not know?!"

She shrugged. "Stress? Busyness? Emotional drudgery? *Super* mild symptoms?" She laughed. "I honestly have no idea, and I am... I'm as confused as you are. They have to make sure it's not like... ectopic or anything, and make sure everything is okay, considering... I was assaulted a few weeks ago, but... yeah. Congratulations."

Congratulations.

Congratulations?

That was the word that got me unstuck from what was happening in my head. I tamped down the excitement building in my chest to fully turn to her now, pulling her hands into mine. "How do *you* feel about this?" I asked, meeting her gaze.

She didn't look away, but I could tell she was suppressing a little smile when she shrugged. "I'm not sure," she said. "It's still... baffling. And kind of scary. I don't want to get ahead of myself. But... I'm... cautiously... excited?"

"So... *happy?*"

"Pump your brakes," she warned, laughing. "I didn't say that... yet. We don't even know if it's viable, which is a possibility, considering the pregnancy test I took before they removed the implant was negative. I haven't had any noticeable symptoms. Plus the attack. This could end up being... not a good situation."

"*Anything* could end up being not a good situation," I reminded her.

She nodded. "That's true. But still... I'm going to hang on to my watchful enthusiasm until we have more information."

"Understandable," I agreed.

She leaned in closer to me. "What about you? How do you feel?"

"Me?"

"Yeah, *you.*" She giggled. "Who else would I be talking to, *duh.*"

I chuckled, shaking my head. "I'm fucking around. I... shit. I feel... like everything I wanted is working out. I feel like you're gonna be having my baby and both of you are going to be perfectly healthy through the whole process. I feel amazing, Mrs. Sterling."

She rolled her eyes. "It's taking you a lot not to like... jump up and down, isn't it?"

"It *really* is," I admitted, laughing. "I'm trying to respect your misgivings. But after we get confirmation... I'm warning you now... a whole fucking celebration."

"As it should be." She nodded. "It's still just... *wow*," she said, falling back onto the pillows, propping a hand on her stomach.

There was no noticeable difference yet, but I still didn't hold myself back from moving with her, resting my head right next to her hand.

"You're going to run my damn nerves in the ground through this whole thing, aren't you?" she asked.

I grinned. "You probably won't even notice a difference."

There was quiet for a moment between us—a good kind of quiet, not uncomfortable—but then I remembered *my* correspondence from earlier in the evening.

News I didn't want to overshadow what should be a joyous moment.

It only took me a few seconds of thought to decide it was better to tell her now, *before* we got the additional information tomorrow that would alter our sentiments around the positive test.

"I need to tell you something," I spoke up, turning so I was looking at her face.

Her brow furrowed. "What is it? Is something wrong?"

"That's subjective," I answered, sitting up. "I know Soren

already gave you the heads up that I had somebody put eyes out for your father and Bree."

She nodded. "Yeah. He told me. Did they find them?"

"They did. Do you… understand what that means?"

Her gaze shifted to the ceiling, staring for a moment before she pushed out a sigh. "I do."

"Okay… how do you… are you okay?"

"That's a loaded question," she answered, with a dry laugh. "Should any daughter be okay after hearing that her father was… killed? Tortured? Who knows?"

"It's fine to not be okay."

She laughed harder at that. "But… I *am* okay." She scoffed. "Which is… sad. Really, really sad."

"And not your fault," I assured her. "The grown folks made their decisions, good and bad. You don't owe William any certain level of feeling just because he conceived or even raised you. There's more that goes into it than that. Whatever you feel—or don't feel—about him… it seems a lot like it was *his* doing."

She sighed. "You're right, but… I think knowing that *I* might be having a child, I don't… I don't ever want this baby to become an adult who feels like I feel right now."

"So we make sure we don't cultivate that."

"I think we're already well on our way, considering *our* origin story," she countered. "Honestly… my parents had a better one. At least there was *some* emotion. Some passion."

"So there's no emotion here, Nala? No passion?" I asked. "You honestly believe that?"

She pulled herself upright and shook her head. "I don't," she admitted. "I think… that there's something here. I think we're getting to know each other, and working towards something, but this started with... a hostile takeover. Remember?" she huffed. "And we... we can't just skirt past that."

"I agree, but we also don't have to let that be the entirety of the story. I told you, Nala—fuck the contract. Was our process fucked up? Yes, it was. But that doesn't have to mean that we aren't real."

"So... you don't think we've set ourselves up to traumatize a future generation?"

I laughed. "I think it's *possible*, but I also think we're aware enough to *not* do it."

"Easy to say when your parents were in love."

"They weren't perfect though." I chuckled. "My mother was nasty as hell to the first girl Ares fell in love with. Just *mean* as fuck, 'cause she thought nobody was good enough for him—for any of us, actually. My father... his ass married a woman the same age as his damn kids and tried to get us to *really* see her ass as our stepmother. They had their weird shit too."

She nodded. "Okay... I guess that does make me feel slightly better."

"Good," I told her. "It should. Again... I'm not saying we'll be perfect, clearly not so far. But don't count us out. We've got room to grow. You're willing to grow with me, right?"

She smiled. "I am."

"Then... there's not shit that can stop us."

EPILOGUE - NALANI
ONE YEAR LATER

"You can turn your ass right around if that's the shit you're coming in here with!"

The sound of Calli fussing pulled me right out of the daze I'd been in as the baby peacefully nursed. He was zoned out, and so was I.

It had been a nice break from the house full of people—which I hoped would be over sooner than later—but now we were back to reality.

And somebody had decided to stress Calli out.

As if he'd noticed too, baby Leo detached himself from my nipple with his usual aggression, creating a *pop* sound that always made me smile. He grinned right back, milk dribbling from his mouth until I grabbed a nearby burping cloth to clean his chin.

The whole time, he didn't take his eyes off my face.

Not while I burped him, not while I changed him, making sure he was nice and fresh before I went back into the crowd.

The wrap I'd planned to wear him in, in hopes of avoiding entitled grabby hands, lay discarded to the side.

There had been no need for it with Calli around.

For a while, she'd stationed herself at the door, informing every woman that crossed the threshold, *"Keep your germs, your lips, and your hands to your damn self, you got me?"*

She knew what my preferred boundaries were and was enforcing them damn near more strictly than I was.

Between her and Orion, I hadn't experienced any of the horror stories of people's entitlement to a new baby I'd heard all about.

And I loved them for it.

I emerged from my personal, private break area with Leo in hand, tucked comfortably against my side—his preferred place at all times. The décor for his "welcome to the world" party was immaculately done, deep navies and silver and clouds and constellations, all very fitting to the "family" theme. It was beautiful, but not my focus at all. I followed the sound of Calli's voice. She was going back and forth with somebody I quickly discovered to be my Aunt Lucinda.

They both looked up as I approached and Lucy cut her eyes at Calli before turning to me with outstretched arms.

"There she is with *my baby*," she cooed at Leo, who gave her the blankest of blank looks before tucking himself closer to my body like he could feel the way that shit grated my nerves.

Did I appreciate that he had a room full of people who loved him?

Of course.

Did I appreciate *any* of those people, even playfully, doing the whole *my baby* thing like *I* wasn't the one who tore up to my ass pushing his big head out?

Absolutely not.

It wasn't cute *to me*.

Which was what mattered.

"You don't like to listen do you?" Calli snapped, moving fast on her cane to step in front of Lucy. "Your old ass ain't pushed out nothing but a turd and dust in the last three months, so what is the *my baby* shit about?"

My eyes went wide. "Calli, it's okay," I said, trying to soothe this trouble before it really got started.

"He's *my* grand-nephew," Lucy argued, propping a hand on her hip.

"Then let that be what you call him, and you let the mother *offer* for you to hold him, don't be demanding shit around here," Calli kept fussing. "You didn't like it when the mommas and aunties did that shit to you, so don't be around here thinking it's just your turn. We stopping that shit, just like I did with these boys' mama. Nobody did it to her and you're not gonna do it to this one? Y'all hear me?!"

She wasn't wrong.

And I *more* than appreciated that she'd brought that energy through pregnancy, delivery, and postpartum. She'd been my strongest ally, even more so than my childless friends, who were wonderful, but couldn't quite relate.

She'd even checked Orion a time or two hundred.

Still, I *could* use a little breather, so once that smoke had cleared a little, I *did* hand baby boy over to Lucy to dote on—*with* Calli, since the two women had grown to be friends since our families blended.

As soon as I was childfree, Alexis and Morgan led me to the bar for glittery blue champagne and to giggle about the "fight" that had just happened. I was on my second glass when they got quiet on me. And from the looks on their faces

—the same goofiness they always gave when this happened—I knew Orion had walked up.

"Can I borrow Leo's mother for a moment?" he asked, and as usual, they *never* took the route of telling his ass no.

Instead, they were all too eager to give me away, not that it was the worst thing.

His hands immediately wrapped around my waist, head dipping to plant a lingering kiss on my lips, publicity be damned.

"You doing okay?" he asked me quietly, and I sighed.

"I'm fine. I'll be glad when this is over, but I'm fine," I answered honestly.

"You want me to send everybody home? 'Cause we can clear it out right now if—"

"No." I laughed. "It's not that serious. Besides… there's only another hour left anyway, right?"

He glanced at his wrist and nodded. "Yes. And we don't have to wait around for everyone to leave. Our reservations at the Drake are finalized. We'll be in a suite there for a few days while the house gets put back in order."

"Good," I mused. The thought of being in a messy house after everyone left was honestly more stressful than the party itself.

Not that I'd lifted a finger for it.

Orion had made sure of that, prioritizing my rest and mental health over everything. Even the store had been functioning without me. Our new CEO—who had been in a corporate position at *Nectar* since my mother's reign and was perfect for the position—had been great.

Lately, I'd been using that word a lot.

But… it was accurate.

Which I was grateful for.

"Hey... make sure the staff leaves extra linens in the room for us," I told Orion, confusing him.

"You know they'll change things out every night, right?"

I nodded. "I do. But um... we might need the extras. If you catch my drift..."

At first he didn't.

But when he did, a smirk spread over his face and he dipped his head toward me again. "You sure about that, Mrs. Sterling? Have you been cleared by your doctor?"

"*Mmmhmm*," I answered with a lusty return grin that made him bite his lip and get even closer to me.

"Why you fuckin' with me like that in front of all these people?"

"'Cause you ain't gonna do shit in front of all these people," I teased, pushing up on my toes to kiss him.

Honestly... there was no way he was more ready than I was, after the longest twelve weeks of healing—because of his big head ass son—of my life.

If he asked me to duck off to the side with him real quick... I probably would.

Definitely would.

That looked like the very next thing on the way out of his mouth, but it was interrupted.

My head snapped around at the sound of familiar cries, my nipples immediately responding to my little boy's unhappiness.

I didn't have to search long though. The next thing I knew, Soren was approaching me, trying a soothing bounce motion to soothe his nephew, but Leo was *not* having it.

Before I could even move my hands to reach for him, Orion already had him, tucking him close. He was speaking to him—too quiet for anyone but Leo to hear—and whatever he was saying... baby boy went calm.

"Unless you want to get him, I've got him," he told me. "Enjoy the party, my love."

There was no sarcasm in that endearment anymore.

He meant that shit now.

And saying it with our son in his arms only made me want to fuck him more.

"Get a room, ugh," Soren teased as Orion walked away, joining his brothers across the room.

"It's that obvious?" I asked, laughing, and my brother nodded.

"And disgusting."

"Oh whatever!" I giggled, letting him lead me to the little buffet area for the snack I suddenly remembered I was supposed to have after a nursing session.

I was *starving*.

"This is wild, you know?" he asked, and I looked at him with curious eyes.

"What?"

"You and him," he answered. "And a baby. Who would've thought?"

"Yeah." I smiled, watching as Titan and Ares took turns playing peekaboo with Leo, still in Orion's arms. He was looking at them like they were nuts, not cracking even the slightest smirk, which made it even funnier. "Who would've thought?"

If you enjoyed this book, please consider leaving a review at your retailer of choice. It doesn't have to be long - just a line or two about why you enjoyed the book, or even a simple star rating can be very helpful for any author!

Want to stay connected? Text 'CCJRomance' to 74121 or sign up for my newsletter. I'll keep you looped into what I'm doing!

Check out CCJROMANCE.COM for first access to all my new releases, signed paperbacks, merch, and more!

I'm all over the social mediasphere - find me everywhere @beingmrsjones

For a full listing of titles by Christina C Jones, visit www.beingmrsjones.com/books

ABOUT THE AUTHOR

Christina C. Jones is a best-selling romance novelist and digital media creator. A timeless storyteller, she is lauded by readers for her ability to seamlessly weave the complexities of modern life into captivating tales of Black characters in nearly every romance subgenre. In addition to her full-time writing career, she co-founded Girl, Have You Read – a popular digital platform that amplifies Black romance authors and their stories. Christina has a passion for making beautiful things, and be found crafting, cooking, and designing and building a (literal) home with her husband in her spare time.